Antonina Irena Brzozowska was born and educated in the north-east of England. A former teacher, she has travelled extensively, especially throughout Poland, the Hawaiian Islands and Canada, from where she has gained a keen interest in the Polish, Hawaiian and Canadian cultures and traditions. She is an avid reader and enjoys writing, deriving material from her travelling experiences.

To all the children I have had the pleasure of teaching in various schools during my teaching career.

Thank you for the happy memories.

Antonina Irena Brzozowska

'KING' KAMEHAMEHA'S DILEMMAS

AUSTIN MACAULEY PUBLISHERS™

LONDON * CAMBRIDGE * NEW YORK * SHARJAH

A CIP catalogue record for this title is available from the British Library.

ISBN 9781398470972 (Paperback)
ISBN 9781398470989 (ePub e-book)

www.austinmacauley.com

First Published 2023
Austin Macauley Publishers Ltd®
1 Canada Square
Canary Wharf
London
E14 5AA

Table of Contents

Part One
'King' Kamehameha... on a Mission

A Special Address to My Loyal Subjects

A very special, sunny and cheerful, Aloha, to all of my subjects, especially to the little people, who are trudging back and forth, to and from, that dreaded place, I think, you call school. I know how you feel, my friends; I am residing in a high disciplined establishment myself, with Toni still firmly rooted at the helm; though, how she has not toppled off her self-imposed throne of authority I do not know, it certainly isn't for lack of trying on my part.

Anyway I hope you are all fighting fit, as happy as punch and being good as I… try to be. Since I last communicated with you, I have undertaken all sorts of simple and elaborate methods to show my Toni who the true boss of our castle really is; but, so far, she has not bowed down to me, neither has she willingly assigned to me the overall sovereignty of our fortress which, begrudgingly, we have to share until one of us wins the grand lottery and departs.

But, dare I say, there is a tiny glimmer of hope. Now, I would strongly advise you to sit down and hold on to your hats as I tell you this news. Toni is on a quest to find herself a hubby! All I can say is that she will need all the luck in the world and that the unfortunate specimen, when; or, rather if she ever manages to dig her claws into (claws being the operative word), will need nerves of pure steel; already he has my full sympathy.

If somehow, by some miraculous stroke of luck, Toni manages to harpoon an unfortunate male specimen, and that's a big 'if,' he will need to adhere to all of my strict rules, if he is considering a lengthy stay in my kingdom. These are my rules:

1. The candidate will have to provide me with a varied assortment of delicious doggie treats, each time he sets foot into my domain.
2. He will need to tickle my tummy for, at least, an hour after tea.
3. He will never even think of usurping my throne.
4. The guy will, at all times, walk five paces behind me and look jolly well pleased about it.

5. It is most essential that he is fun loving, loves spontaneous adventures and always sees the funny side of my mischievous behaviour.

6. He must never, ever think about, let alone discuss or use, the word, 'discipline.'

7. He has to persuade Toni that my rightful place is in the lounge, on her plush sofa and not in the kitchen, the servants' quarters.

8. At all times he must address me as King Kamehameha or Your Majesty. Never ever must he address me as Mayo, Mayonnaise or Kami-knickers; not if he wants to see the sun rise again.

9. He must adore my special friends, the butterflies; but he also has to have a soft spot for my mates the hedgehogs, the bumble bees and any type of birds, apart from the vultures, who I'm not that keen on.

10. This guy has to be good to my Toni, because I only have one Toni and she isn't such a bad 'old' soul.

If the candidate thinks he will conform to ALL of these regulations, he may have a slight chance with us. If he thinks he may fail in just one area, he needn't bother applying.

I am on an urgent mission of the utmost importance myself, folks. My mission is to secure myself a peaceful; but fun loving and sometimes a little mischievous life, without any opposition, or threat, to overthrow me as sovereign and, preferably, without a potential stepdad within a hundred-kilometre radius of my kingdom.

I am sure, my loyal subjects; that I have got you all on my side and, of course, I will let you all know how we get on.

For now, please wish me all the luck in the world.

Stay healthy! Stay safe! Stay happy! Have fun!

Your King,
Kamehameha x

Toni's Announcement

I know you may still be reeling from the shock of my news, regarding Toni's impending mission to find herself a hubby and you may be wondering what on earth has possessed a level-headed, super disciplined, independent female to completely lose her head and set off on this perilous quest, especially as she has got ME. Well, I'll tell you all about it; but, for goodness' sake, don't let her know that you know anything about it; between you and I; I don't think she wants the world to know. It all started off like this…

It all began about three weeks before Christmas. Toni was preparing to go out for the evening and I was eagerly looking forward to a blissful evening of undisturbed sleep when I happened to notice, out of the corner of one partially opened eye, as I lay sprawled out on my plush Hawaiian printed, extra-large cushion… a present given to me by Toni when her heart was full to the brim with remorse after she almost got rid of me one time… sorry, back to the present; I happened to notice that my mistress was not getting ready for her night out with her usual abundance of zest. In fact, I had noticed just lately that the usual sparkle had gone out of her eyes. She had not lost her appetite; so, I knew she was not going to pop her clogs any time soon; but something was not quite right; something was missing and, truthfully, I seriously wondered what it was. For it was one thing, and totally unacceptable in my point of view, to be rushing about our castle with an eye watering speed and determination, making sure that all of her rules were obeyed by Yours Truly; you know the rules I mean: spotlessly clean paws in the house and within a fifty-kilometre radius; walking obediently and sedately beside her on our leisurely strolls and so on; but it was another matter altogether to witness her moping about our kingdom like some lost soul. Yes, the sheen had definitely disappeared from her once sparkling eyes; not that we looked into each other's eyes for long; her constant chatting had ceased which, to be honest, was a blessed relief; her singing had stopped, thanks be to all the gods who prevailed here; the clothes had reverted back to the prim and proper variety. Something… something had changed. I couldn't quite put my paw on it but something was wrong and I wanted my 'old' Toni back, warts and all.

"Bye, Kamehameha." She mumbled as if she was setting off to the guillotine. The door closed and the sound of her heels clicking down the drive were the last sounds I heard before I swept my mistress, and her lack of sparkle, out of my mind and I allowed myself to drift into a bout of peaceful and welcome sleep.

Cautiously, Toni walked into the packed restaurant of jovial Christmas revellers. For long minutes she stood scanning the lively interior, her eyes wandering from one table of happy party goers to another until, finally, they rested on her set. No one noticed her as she stood and they clinked glasses, laughed and joked and while, ordinarily, she would have boldly strode over to her colleagues and blended in with the group, this evening she stood and stared, her guts writhing and twisting, her heart beating profusely, her feet itching to turn away in the opposite direction and run; for, for the first time in her career, she did not feel her friends and colleagues were a part of her and she did not feel a part of them. She was on her own; my Toni, sixty-four and counting, single and alone; in other words, an odd entity. Abruptly turning her back on the crowd her feet strode briskly towards the exit, as the jovial laughter echoed loudly in her ears.

"And where do you think you are going, Toni?" Her fast-beating heart stopped its frenzied pounding for a moment, as her startled eyes stared at Daniel Burley's twinkling eyes. "We're this way; come on, Toni." And, before she could stop him, he had yanked her arm and propelled her towards the crowd of people she knew so well.

Within seconds she was in the midst of them all, though a thousand kilometres apart, and while she chatted, laughed and drank with them all, she wished she was on her own small island, far away, where she could find her inner peace; for this night, as many others recently, she did not feel a part of the crowd; she felt inadequate, alone and lonely and, more to the point, she felt she had lost her equilibrium.

"Cheers Toni!"

The clinking of her glass forced her out of her reverie and she pinned on her best smile and said softly, "Cheers everyone," as her heart deflated once more; for, she did not want to be there. Her eyes passed from group to group of happy young revellers; to couples trying to snatch a kiss under the mistletoe; to colleagues pulling crackers whilst laughing hysterically; to young men attempting to catch the eye of a girl they've fancied for ages, and vice versa; to her best friend giving her boyfriend a kiss and back to a loud, and very jovial party, from another school. She closed her eyes tightly thankful she was sitting down; for, suddenly, she felt old, very old; an intruder in a young adults' world, which was becoming more alien to her by the second. The urge to run again invaded her mind. She did not belong. She had to get out. Now! Grabbing her bag and rising, she felt the soft touch of a hand on her arm and turned, focussing her eyes on Sally and forced a faint smile.

"What's up, Toni?"

Sally's innocent question made Toni involuntarily sit back down. "Nothing is up." She replied, because how could she possible explain to her best friend what was eating her up inside when she, herself, could not give an explanation? "Nothing is up," she repeated in a more convincing tone, as she tried to reassure her friend.

Her attempt went completely unheeded; like a dog with a bone Sally persevered with her quest. "I know something is wrong, Toni; you haven't been yourself for days; spill!"

"There is nothing to spill. I am just overtired, that's all. I think I need an early night." She attempted to rise once more.

"Oh, no you don't. You are going to tell your Aunt Sally what's on your mind, girl."

Reluctantly Toni sat back down again, a surge of boiling anger bubbling in the bowels of her being, threatening to spew out on her bossy friend.

Placing a drink in front of Toni, Sally focussed her questioning eyes on her friend. "Now, tell me what the matter is, Toni."

But Toni's eyes were focussed elsewhere, where they were glued on a happy couple, canoodling under a sprig of mistletoe. Sally's eyes followed that of her friend's and there she found her answer.

The evening was long and torturous as Toni clock-watched, continued to observe all and sundry enjoying themselves; while she felt utterly out of it, wishing she was at home enjoying a mug of hot chocolate with marshmallows and a big bar of chocolate at the ready. Thoughts of me drifted into her mind. She closed her eyes to all around her and envied my happy and blissful existence. An excited voice cut her reverie short. "I know exactly what you need, Toni; a man!" exclaimed an excited Sally. "And a man is exactly what I am going to get you."

Adamant remonstrations, a surge of disagreeing statements, swiftly followed by a profusion of full-fledged refusals did nothing to quell Sally's excitement and Toni, finally, resigned herself to the fact that, once her best friend had got something inside her head, nothing or no one in this world, or the next, would shift it. Sally was going to find her a man, whether she wanted a man or not and there was nothing she could do about it.

The click of the door stirred me out of my peaceful slumber and I, begrudgingly, raised one sleepy eye in the direction of my mistress, who seemed to have come back in better spirits. No doubt, she's been let loose on the 'pop', I mused as I closed my heavy eye, only to be subjected to her awful singing. She's definitely been on the 'pop', I concluded and wished she'd go up to her room, post-haste, and take her dreadful singing, if that's what you call it, with her. The statement she threw, as she haphazardly threw me a treat and clicked off the light, made my whole body freeze and both my eyes to snap open and widely stare like two saucers.

"I am going to get a man, Kamehameha!"

The 'Happy' Foursome with the 'Gooseberry' In the Middle

At that precise moment my mission began.

To say I was not impressed with this distasteful statement would be the understatement of the year. I was totally flabbergasted; but now that I have managed to cool off, I shall attempt to inform you, my dear subjects, what happened next.

Toni's ghastly singing did not cease. If anything, to my utter dismay, it increased in volume and vigour, leaving me to contemplate on whether I should abandon my castle forever and seek sanctuary elsewhere; somewhere far, far away; that distant island called Kauai would do; somewhere in the middle of the Pacific Ocean, where the possibility of hearing the echoes of Toni's tuneless screeching would be as remote as the island itself. Anyway, as I said, her horrible attempts at singing were the first indication that something had changed and the sudden spring in her steps, not to mention the endless hours she spent experimenting with her make-up and hairstyles, not that it did her much good, added to my inner convictions. Then came the rummaging through her wardrobes, which I noticed when I secretly ventured up to her opened bedroom door. Blouses, skirts and dresses were thrown haphazardly in every direction; one ghastly brown skirt landed on my head and was, indeed, a temporary cross I had to bear, as I peered over the garish heavy material at my mistress, as she tried desperately to struggle into a pair of trousers, which were about five sizes too small; though, I must say, her incredible techniques into squeezing into some items were most amusing and most certainly eye-watering. Would you believe, I witnessed her lying flat out on her bed, trying frantically to pull up a zip belonging to a pair of dashing blue silk trousers, only for the zip to snap and Toni to shout out a string of words I'd never heard in my life. I heard her sigh with heavy relief as she managed to, somehow, squeeze herself into a black cocktail dress and I had to close my eyes tightly to obliterate the scene; it was not a pretty sight. To this day I can still see the bulges and the whole affair happened months ago! All kinds of items, horrible and passable, flew out the wardrobe and cupboards. In the end she settled for a dark green velvet frock and that, in my opinion, still looked pretty odious. Anyway, I thought, it's her poor victim, not me, that would have to look at it all night and so that settled that matter.

Next came countless and lengthy conversations over the phone and, to my utter dismay, I happened to hear that the venue for the so-called date was changed. Toni had decided to cook herself. Now, at first, my heart was laden with heavy disappointment, and a certain amount of frustration, as I knew that my inner peace and balanced state of equilibrium would be shattered with the invasion of unwanted visitors; but, slowly, my ruffled mind began to change course at the thought of receiving delicious goodies because, let me tell you, when my Toni puts her mind to it, she is a first-class cook; the trouble is, she rarely puts her mind to it. Anyway, I was not going to abandon my mission before it commenced; but, at the same time, I was kind of thinking that this date thing could well be to my advantage, if I played my cards right.

The only dark blot on the horizon was the fact that, in order for me to be allowed to get my choppers around some mouth-watering delights, I would have to suffer this new guy venturing into my castle. And venture he must, I mused, if Toni has to have some sort of date and I my delights. You see, I know Toni's best friend is okay; in fact, Sally is a lot like my Auntie Anusia; she would do absolutely anything for me and, more importantly, she never fails to supply me with tasty treats on her visits; so, if all else fails, that won't. She has also taught her boyfriend well; but this new guy who was about to burst on the scene might be a different story altogether. Anyway, whoever this chap was, I would be on my guard. I would be on the lookout watching, scrutinizing intently his every move, especially where treats were concerned. One step wrong and I would make it my personal mission to banish him out of my kingdom… forever!

Disappointingly, the cooking smells were not much to my liking; some kind of cabbage mixture I think; however, the tasty bits of sausages, tossed over to me now and again, were very much to my liking, as were the freshly baked bits of chocolate sponge cake, I know I'm not supposed to have; but luckily Toni was in such a trance about this date of hers, dietary rules and regulations were temporarily abandoned. From my vantage point there were all kinds of tasty treats sitting on the worktops which, sadly, I could only muse about getting my paws on and pearly whites into: meaty items and chocolaty things of all shapes and sizes; crispy, swirly things and small buns with smooth white icing and cherries on the top… yum… yum! Finally, after a lot of toing and froing, nervous humming and seemingly endless preparations of one sort or another, which all made me feel quite dizzy and thankful I was not a human, the doorbell rang. The moment had come and, with it, the mysterious guy who was to be my Toni's date.

The first seconds went according to plan. Sally and her boyfriend, Derek, bestowed on me the expected treats, and a generous supply for days to come, and I allowed them to breeze into my castle. My curious eyes flitted to, and rested on, the stranger standing boldly before me. My shrewd eyes rose from his shiny black shoes, up his well creased trousers and well cut jacket, to his empty hands and there they rested. Not a treat in sight; not one solitary morsel or whiff of one. My puzzled eyes tarried there; but it was no use, even I could see that no treats were going to magically appear. The small-minded guy had not bothered to bring me one measly morsel of anything. My despondent lingering eyes narrowed a degree, still hoping against fast diminishing hope that, somewhere in his pockets, there would be something for me, anything would do; after all, beggars can't be choosers at this juncture a tasty marrowbone or a chocolate doggie treat, even a piece of any flavour cheese would be acceptable; but no, nothing appeared. The dastardly guy just stood and blatantly stared down at me as if I was an annoying fly and his lips, to my complete incredulity, dared to break out into a smirk, and what an ugly smirk it was, while I stood perfectly still and waited, in vain, for him to conjure up a treat.

Time told me this was not going to happen. With a deflated heart, and the sound of a rumbling tummy, I bitterly swallowed the juices that had gathered in hopeful expectation in my mouth, and stared unblinkingly at this abominable creature and wondered how he had the audacity to behave in such an unforgivable manner in the presence of royalty. After long seconds of torturous pondering on the matter, my disappointed eyes flitted to Toni and, instantly, my heart turned into a block of ice; for, would you believe, her eyes had come alive with a life and sparkle I had never seen before. My Toni had fallen in love, before my very eyes, with this fellow and there was nothing I could do about it. Slowly, I turned and walked away and curled up tightly in my den, knowing all too well how my friend, the hedgehog, feels on a bad day while all around happy chatter and laughter emitted from the joyous foursome. I uncurled myself a little and placed my sad, reflective head on to my paws and, as sure as day follows night, my fighting spirit returned. If they think this is the end of the matter, I silently and most determinedly resolved, they can jolly well think again. Several times I cast my inquisitive eyes in their direction but could see nothing, as Toni and her guests had moved further into the interior of the room and, as far as I could gather, were now seated at Toni's posh Italian dining table, wining and dining on delicious mouth-watering fare while I, King Kamehameha, was assigned to the servants' quarters, with just my meagre bowl of normal dry dog food and water on offer. I ask you, what kind of royal existence was this? Bountiful laughter was drifting through and Toni's high-pitched giggles were a sure sign she had had one sherry too many. I was not amused; not amused at all. But what was I to do? And then… I had a light bulb moment and it all became perfectly clear. I remembered, from past experiences, that one thing always broke Sally's heart and that was the sound of me whining or whimpering; or, both. These sounds, which I can miraculously switch on and off to my advantage, get her every time, like they do my Auntie Anusia. Don't ask me how or why; but they always work and so I quickly set the cogs of my super intelligent mind to arduous work and, never failing me, they soon came up with an excellent plan.

I decided to employ my whimpering and whining skills separately; my plan being that if one didn't quite come up to scratch, the other surely would. And so, I started slowly, quite quietly with the whining. I was quick to notice that no one rushed to my side from the inner sanctum. To be honest, I didn't think they would at this early stage of the proceedings, and so I adjusted my volume a little, then a little more, then a great deal more. Seeing no concerned figure bending over me, I decided that a good measure of serious whimpering would be a good thing at this point and, so, I kind of mixed the whining and greatly increased the whimpering volume with, to my inner delight, an immediate effect. I saw the pointed black stilettos at the foot of my downcast nose and I slowly raised my solemn eyes. There she was, my saviour and faithful friend, Sally; which is more than I can say for my mistress.

A deluge of hugs and kisses were bestowed on me; but, more importantly, lovely Sally encouraged me, not that I needed encouraging, to follow her into the inner sanctum, amidst a tumult of negative responses, including a most vigorous shaking of the head, from Toni whose disapproving eyes resembled two saucers as they followed my approach into the prohibited area; the area of light plush carpets and luxurious soft furnishings, where ninety-nine and a half per cent of kings would have free reign. But, to my sheer astonishment and utter delight,

Toni switched her eyes to her date and her objections remained silent, lest she should resemble that horrible gal with the spotty black and white dogs; you know the one I mean, don't you? My eyes switched to this date of Toni's too and what I saw I did not like at all; for, would you believe, he was blatantly staring down at me with sheer disgust, as one would look down at a despicable rattle snake. And he in my kingdom; my kingdom! Well, I was going to show him who the indisputable sovereign of this castle was. I carefully edged my cuddly body closer and parked myself in-between Toni and this scourge of a man, sat myself down and then sprawled out leisurely and made myself mighty comfortable. As I placed my victorious head on to my paws, I dozed off to the sounds of Sally cooing and Derek praising me to the highest heavens; I must say, Sally has got him well trained. Toni, by now, was telling her best friend off and my mistress's date was sneezing his head off. I had noticed earlier a sneeze, or two, coming from his cavernous mouth; though, I must admit, right from the start, I wasn't bothered if this specimen of a man was coming down with the plague. But now I had noticed that his sneezing had increased to such a level it was barely controllable. One swift glance at his glassy streaming eyes and red blotchy face, told me things were not going well for him. It serves him jolly well right, I concluded, as I eased myself into a blissful dream, my plan still securely locked in my intelligent head.

When I awoke, sometime later, there was no sight of Sally, or her beau, Derek. Toni had abandoned my side and I was looking out of the lounge window, as her date strolled briskly down the road, giving my Toni not one solitary backward glance, as he continued to sneeze profusely for England.

Needless to say, we never saw this selfish weakling again and my plan was still firmly locked in my head, ready and waiting for the next poor victim.

The Newspaper Man

After all of these years of virtually keeping herself to herself; making the whole world know that no man was good enough for her, although I happen to disagree and think my Toni, dear as she is to me, is not good enough for any man; anyway, after all this time of living her days as a devoted spinster, she has lost her head, her marbles; or, both. For at sixty-four, when most females, in their right minds, keep the man they have captured; or, if they haven't managed to secure one have abandoned their search, called it a day and settled for a nice pair of comfy slippers and a hot mug of cocoa, my Toni has decided to accelerate her mission and, I must admit, I am not amused. After the last experience with that greedy specimen with the sneezes, I thought she'd give up. But, no; on the contrary, her last experience has given her a flavour for a good challenge and, you know what my Toni is like when she gets a sniff of a good challenge. And, because her head has gone off orbit, so to speak, I now feel the need to press my paw on the accelerator pedal of my own mission; after all, any guy Toni manages to, somehow and by some miracle, get her clutches into is a potential stepdad to Yours Truly and that thought does not sit easy with me at all.

I swiftly allotted myself into the role of chief chaperone; in other words, the one who sifts the riff-raffs from the possibles; the decider of both our futures because, let's face it, I am the one with the mighty intelligence and, if Toni is left to her own devices, goodness only knows who we will end up with.

Anyway, as I had previously mentioned, Toni had well and truly got the man-bug and there was no stopping her in her endeavours, as she diligently scanned the lonely hearts page in the local rag for possible candidates. I half expected smoke to come out of her ears as she poured intently over each ad, examining each word as she desperately tried to see the man behind the glowing words. To be honest, I wasn't impressed at all; after all, who would advertise themselves in the local rag? Someone, I concluded, who no one else wanted.

I watched as she industriously cut out one extract, then another, then another and I wondered how many she was prepared to have a go with. This, I thought, was going to be hard work. I needed my beauty sleep and time to rest and refresh my super brain cells to their full and dazzling power. I left my mistress cutting out a fourth ad and soon I fell into an uneasy sleep where Suzi, she's my doggie cousin for those of you who don't know, ruled supremely in my dream; or, rather, nightmare. I woke up with a start and with a firm resolve of never falling into Toni's fatal trap of looking for a mate. And, lest I should lose my own head and think of succumbing, I have only to remember my past experiences with Suzi to bring me swiftly back to my full senses.

In total, six advertisements for six different males were propped up against the wall behind the mantelpiece. Six possible dates; six possible suitors; six possible dads! Heaven and Earth, please preserve me from such a fate! Anyway, there they were; six ghastly faces peering down on me; like unwilling soldiers waiting for Toni to make a second inspection and pick the chosen one and I can only ask all the gods, wherever they happen to reside, to leave their pedestals and swiftly come to the aid of this poor unfortunate. Within minutes, the unfortunate was chosen.

A few days later he turned up on our doorstep all spick and span, a bit like that sneezing fellow but with a bit more sense; or, so I mistakenly thought. This specimen turned up with bits of chocolate in his jacket pocket. So far; so good, I thought. However, I soon found out, the bits of chocolate were not intended for my tummy; but his, would you believe? And, as I obediently sat by his side in the kitchen, waiting with anticipated nervous expectation, he dipped his large hand into his pocket, snapped off a chunk, brought it up to his mouth and popped it in; not once asking Toni if she wanted some. Needless to say, I didn't get one measly look in either; both Toni and I were completely left out of the chocolate equation.

I could tell, to my sheer relief, that Toni was not impressed with Dan the man; incidentally, that was his real name. Personally I would have christened him Greedy Guts. I knew he was not up to her high standards for she scrutinized him with intense suspicion, when not clock watching until, finally, the chocolate bar and the evening came to an end.

"Will I be seeing you again, Toni?" He looked up hopefully at my mistress.

She smiled sweetly and shut our castle door firmly behind him.

Suffice it to say, I felt utterly relieved the next morning when, on the phone, I heard Toni relating to her best friend, Sally, "And, to top it all off, he stuffed the whole king-size chocolate bar down his gullet, without offering

Kamehameha or me a single bite. We were not amused. I will not be entertaining him again."

Hallelujah! I replied silently with sheer relief.

The Hawaiian

You may remember me telling you about my Toni's obsession with the Hawaiian Islands; hence my name which, if you don't know, hails from the royal descendants who were linked with the Islands. Her obsession with the Islands is still thriving healthily and when, one morning, she received a letter informing her that one of her Hawaiian friends, and her cousin, would be visiting us, Toni was beside herself with pure happiness and undiluted excitement. Out came all the Hawaiian phrase books she possessed, her Hawaiian print frocks, the CDs and anything remotely associated with the Islands. One item that came out delighted me immensely. It was her traditional Hawaiian recipe book; for, I am particularly partial to a spot of Haupia cake, which actually is a kind of a pudding cake; its coconut flavour drives me crazy and the texture of the cake, well, I can feel it melting in my mouth now. One bite positively sends me off into a delightful orbit. So, yes, I am greatly looking forward to the arrival of our Hawaiian friends and, more especially, to a generous helping of Haupia in the near future.

With the impending visit fast approaching Toni was pulling out all the stops; the house was spick and span; I was spick and span and smelling of jasmine and roses, having been sent off for a rigorous shampoo, clipping and full grooming session, and Toni was well rehearsed in Hawaiian phraseology. Everything was ready.

Toni was not ready for what she encountered when she opened the door. I saw her eyes open extra wide and almost pop out of their sockets, as they looked past her friend and rested on the Hawaiian hunk standing beside her. However, the effect the hunk was having on my mistress, was nothing compared to the effect he was later to have on me.

My first impression of the Hawaiians was one of admiration and approval; for, although they did not come bestowing gifts on me their compliments, admiring glances and hugs compensated, somewhat, and I was prepared to overlook their mistake.

My Toni was truly besotted by this Hawaiian hunk, named Akoni; though, I must admit, he was young enough to be her son, if not her grandson. Anyway, they all got on like the proverbial house on fire and, as I was never left out of the proceedings; but, rather in the midst of it all, I decided that these folks were okay and could stay for a while, with my royal approval.

On reflection, I wish I had not made such a hasty decision and never will I again because; let me tell you my dear subjects, what I soon heard shook me to the very core. Let me go back in time a little. This all happened on the third evening of our visitors' arrival, when the conversation diverted to the most important subject in the room: me. My ears automatically pricked up at the mere mention of my name. Well, that's nothing new, you may well say; but what they said is…

"Well, you know I was very much influenced by the life and rule of your Great King Kamehameha, when I chose my pooch's name," stated Toni.

All eyes darted to me as I feigned sleep and continued to listen intently; though, I fervently wish I hadn't.

"Yes, yes indeed. Kamehameha was a king to be marvelled," Akoni enthused.

Changing the course of the subject Toni asked. "Do you have many rough collies in Hawaii, Akoni?"

My ears sharply pricked up again. Where was this conversation heading? I wondered. And then it landed.

"No; but I am going to take this beauty back to the island with me," chuckled Akoni as he ruffled my fur with his broad hand. "After all, don't you think, with a royal name like Kamehameha, he belongs in Hawaii?"

"Yes… yes!"

I heard the three of them laughing heartily.

"That's it; I'm taking him." Akoni hugged me tightly as if he already owned me.

Now, my immediate mission was to save my skin; for Toni, I could see, was truly taken by this Hawaiian and any suggestion of his, no matter if it was said in jest or not, could so easily be set in stone. So shocked was I by the words I heard, I had not heard the light-heartedness with which they were intended to be taken. So, as I have mentioned, my job was to save my poor skin. In the future, Toni could do what she wanted regarding her potential suitors, as long as she didn't send me thousands of kilometres away, to an island I had never set my paws on; even though, through Toni's association of the place, I feel, I know the Islands inside out and back to front.

I mean to say, can you in your wildest dreams, imagine me ensconced on that far flung island called Kauai, in the scorching heat and in my thick, luxurious fur coat? Can you for one moment imagine me being ogled at by the natives who, incidentally, have never in their lives clapped eyes on such a fine specimen of a pooch and who will, undoubtedly, all want a piece of me for a souvenir? Can you imagine a bubbling, frothing cauldron and inside imagine I, King Kamehameha, sizzling away with a handful of sweet potatoes thrown in for good measure, for daring to bear the same name as the Great, and true, king of the Islands? Well, I could and the images were not at all pleasant. In fact, if the truth be known, they were far from being comforting images and actually were acutely alarming. Suddenly, I did not like this guy, Akoni. No longer did I welcome or appreciate his tight hugs and sunny smiles; for, now, I was aware that they were intended to lure me away without a fight on my side. Anyway, I decided; he can jolly well think again. But then an awful thought struck me. Where did Toni stand in this equation? She had certainly not been defending me; far from it. I strained my eyes to catch a glimpse of my betrayer. She was nowhere in sight. She was, I thought glumly, probably already packing my suitcase and checking my doggie passport. How could she? How could she just send me off to the other side of the world and not think twice about it? What kind of monster had I been living with? Suddenly I strode into my den, my sanctuary for the time being, and wallowed in my own misery and, let me tell you, there was a lot to wallow about. As I closed my weary eyes, I resigned myself to the fact, what will be will be.

My dreams; or, more accurately described, my nightmares took me to a dark and dismal place which kind of contradicted the light, sunny island of their setting where I was, once again, stuck in that dastardly cauldron, with only my ears and eyes visible to the world while, all around me, a motley gathering of excited witch doctors, sorcerers and wild looking natives, who didn't look at all friendly, danced crazily around my aching head as they chanted devilishly, hissed and spat into the pot making each strand of my fur stand rigidly on end, while my guts twisted, wrenched and writhed mercilessly and my super intelligent grey cells spun frenziedly out of control. Everything around me gathered speed and momentum the dancing, chanting, hissing, spitting, stomping, poking; faster and faster, louder and louder, spinning and whirling, faster and faster until everything became a blur and I closed my exhausted eyes and allowed my exhausted body to sink into the frothing, bubbling pot. My eyes snapped opened to witness a darker nightmare; for there, standing over me was Akoni and my Toni standing stoically by his side; two conspirators who had signed my death warrant. I don't know which image was worse; the frothy cauldron or the real sight of my betrayers gawping at me. To be honest, at that point, I wished the witch doctor had had his wicked way with me.

There they stood, like two eager vultures waiting to take the first generous bite of my carcass and, what's more, they had the audacity to smile at me. Well, I thought, three can play their game. No way was I going to be hauled across the world to be eaten, as a rare foreign delicacy, by a ravenous witch doctor and his cronies. No, if I was to meet my Maker, earlier than I had certainly intended, it would be on my terms. I began to furiously concoct a plan.

All sorts of delights breezed past my sensitive nose: alluring bits of sausage, tempting marrowbones, succulent pieces of roast chicken, morsels of tangy cheese which almost sent me into orbit; pieces of chocolate lay in my bowl, just waiting for me to indulge. Oh, how I was tempted! Time and time again, when Toni and her guests were well out of sight, I rose, cautiously approached my bowl, deeply sniffed the delights on offer, turned my back on them and sauntered dismally back into my den; for I had by now convinced myself that they were all laced with poison. Once I licked a juicy looking sausage. I licked it again, abandoning the thought of any deadly consequences, and, as I opened my mouth ready to surround the titbits with my eager gnashers, I heard footsteps in the hallway. With the speed of a leopard, I was back in my den feigning sleep and projecting an aura of misery, sadness and lost hope. It worked. Toni stood by my side; her Hawaiian friends stood by her side and the threesome conversed in low voices, shaking their heads as they looked down at me and there they stood, and I lay, which seemed to be for an eternity. Eventually I no longer pretended sleep as natural slumber, thankfully, took me for its own.

When I woke up the kitchen was deserted except for one figure, a mountain of ingredients on the kitchen table and the unmistakable aroma of coconut drifting lazily in the still air. I inhaled deeply savouring the delightful aroma, which was pure balm to my tortured soul. Coconut… coconut… I mused almost tasting the moistness, as saliva uncontrollably slithered out of my gaping mouth. Coconut…

"Coconut." I heard Akoni say encouragingly and, suddenly, its delightful taste felt like dry grit in my mouth, as my eyes opened wide, my heart pounded like the clappers and my hungry tummy rumbled furiously, as I stared wide-eyed at a slice of Haupia cake, held enticingly in my betrayer's hand willing me, urging me, tempting me, cajoling me, teasing and daring me to take a delicious bite. The dreadful saliva returned; I could feel it dribbling out of my mouth as it opened wide, ready to capture and savour the Haupia. I snapped my mouth shut, my eyes firmly fixed on my traitor before me. How did I know the Haupia wasn't laced with some exotic Hawaiian poison, to make the deliverance of me back to Akoni's native land easier? My steady wise eyes seemed to hypnotize the Hawaiian as we stared unblinkingly into the depths of each other's soul. For a split second my attention lapsed and I found my eyes switching to the tempting cake, still nestled seductively in Akoni's hand and then, as if through a faint mist, I heard the echo of his words. "Well, my dear friend, Kamehameha, if I can't take you to live with me on my beautiful island of Kauai then, I hope, I can at least offer you a slice of Haupia."

My heart leaped to the highest heavens and… fell. Was this some kind of an elaborate ploy in which to entice me to drop my guard, give into temptation and be hauled away? I looked at the cake and, I must admit, it looked mighty delicious; so delicious, in fact, that I didn't just look at it, I blatantly stared, fighting with all of my doggie strength for my willpower to prevail. It was no good. I could almost taste the kind of sweet and nutty flavour of the coconut. My eyes darted to Akoni and back to the Haupia… back to Akoni, only to turn back to the scrummy Haupia, as I continually asked myself the same question. Was it laced with poison? Would I pop my clogs if I took just one tiny bite? What I saw made my eyes widen like two flying saucers. To my utter amazement Akoni raised a piece of cake to his own lips, took a bite, swallowed and offered me the rest. I didn't wait to be asked twice. I devoured the lot and instantly made a new friend.

I decided there and then that my Toni could marry this Hawaiian chap; anyone, in my opinion, who could conjure up such a delicious cake had my royal permission to stay. However, I soon found out that Toni was no more interested in him as a mate, than I am in my cousin, Suzi. So, that was the end of that particular matter.

Well, actually it wasn't quite the end. As Akoni and Haukea were leaving Akoni bent down to my level and smiled saying, "The Haupia inside this tin is especially for you, my dear friend. And, every year on June the eleventh, King

Kamehameha Day, there will be a tin of Haupia sent especially for you, from our lovely island of Kauai."

And, with the taste of Haupia in my mouth, and a promise of delightful things to come, I lowered my happy head on to my paws and sank into a blissful sleep.

The 'Professor'

All I can say is that one teacher in the castle is enough for any king to cope with; two teachers in the same castle are totally and utterly unacceptable.

You may wonder how I happened to find myself in this appalling predicament; but here I was and, may I hasten to add, I was not happy about the whole thing; not happy in the slightest.

I had, my friends, mistakenly reached the conclusion that my mistress had exhausted all of her efforts, if not her inclination, to ever capture a man. But no; oh no, no, no, no like a true trouper; a determined musketeer in search of a desired prize, she carried on regardless in her futile quest; for, as I have told you previously, once Toni has set herself a challenge, there is no stopping her. And so, she marched solidly, and bravely, on, with more vigour than ever and, this time, we ended up with a schoolteacher, with his feet firmly tucked under our kitchen table.

I did not like this chap from the very first time I had clapped my suspicious eyes on him; you know how it is, don't you? You either like someone on first sight; or, you don't. And, needless to say at first glance, or even the hundredth, I didn't like the look of this peculiar looking fellow at all.

As you may well have guessed by now, this Roger dude did not come bearing gifts. So there you go; that's one stroke against him before we even get off the starting block.

Another stroke against him was the fact that he didn't even acknowledge me on his first, and only, visit. He just casually breezed in as if he owned the establishment and dared to look down on me from beneath his thick, dark rimmed glasses and, let me tell you, his intense glare made me shiver all over; for, it was one of total disapproval. And, lest I should consider my initial judgement of him to be wrong, he reinstated it firmly by turning his contemptuous eyes on Toni and stated, for the entire world to hear, "I hate dogs!"

Poor Toni; I noticed she didn't know where to look as her shocked eyes jumped hither and thither before, finally, they turned to me and softened, as I switched my eyes to this obnoxious trespasser, who had trampled into my kingdom and, let me tell you, I did not give him a look of love. To this day we would have been eyeballing each other, if Toni hadn't have stepped in to rescue us both from such a treacherous fate. However, the situation was far from satisfactory, as far as I was concerned; for the 'Professor,' which is what I shall call this dastardly fellow from now on; though, between you and I, a surge of other, less favourable names come to mind; anyway, let me get back to the point, the 'Professor' was ushered into the plush surroundings of our kingdom and I, as usual, was assigned to the servants' domain.

From where I lay my sensitive ears heard everything: Toni's high-pitched giggles; the 'Professor's' dull and monotone voice, yapping on about some highfalutin subject that I didn't think my Toni was interested in; though, at this point, I think she would feign anything to capture a man, any man including this ghastly specimen. And then, I heard the damning words once more. "I hate dogs." As if once wasn't enough. My heart froze. My eyes saw red, the deepest red imaginable and my intelligent grey cells were whirling crazily around my poor brain, trying desperately to formulate a watertight plan to show this despicable creature who the king of the castle really is and to make known to him, in no uncertain terms, that it was he who was the intruder; the uninvited interloper; or, at least, not invited by royal command; the unwelcome guest who had outstayed his visit. One thought after another crashed into my tired head and each scheme became more elaborate than the last. In the end, I settled for one that had already been buzzing in my mind from a previous torturous experience; a simple plan which, in my high opinion, promised an effective result.

In the meantime, I resigned myself to a very long evening and, unfortunately, I was not disappointed in my gloomy prediction. The agonizing hours trudged on laboriously. Toni breezed in and out of the kitchen, without a glance, or crumb of any kind, thrown in my direction and, on her return back to the lounge, the merciless talking and giggling for England resumed. I noticed that it was the obnoxious 'Professor' who was responsible for ninety-nine per cent of the gabbing and, I must admit, my heart pained; for, I know how much my Toni likes to chat and, this evening, she could not get a word in edgeways. Well, anyway, this torture went on and on until, at long last, the kitchen light flicked on and two pairs of shining shoes walked past my subdued nose.

That, my dear friends, was my cue. Like greased lightning I leaped out of my cosy bed and headed straight for the 'Professor's' feet; well, to be more precise, his ankles and then my plan came into delightful fruition. Let's say, I tickled his ankles with my pearly whites and the frenzied dance he simultaneously performed, as he jumped frantically from foot to foot, was of the highest calibre; one that, I feel, no witch doctor, no matter how proficient, could match. I must say, I was truly impressed at this spectacle as he jigged up and down, as if he had an excited army of ants in his pants; called me all the detestable names that came to his mind and gave me, when he had the chance, the most disdainful stares with his gleaming, angry eyes before he stated the most unforgivable statement, that has ever come out of the mouth of a human being. "This is the most awful dog in the whole wide world!" He yelled at the very top of his shrieking voice, while continuing to jump up and down as if he was dancing on burning coals. Now, I could have, maybe, slightly forgiven him if he had announced that I was the worst behaved pooch on my road; or, even in England, but in the world! The red mist descended on me once more; but, this time, with a vengeance and I did what any pooch, with a grain of intelligence in his head, would do. I stared at him with my smiling mouth, lulling him into a false sense of security, and then, I went straight for his socks and what a great time I had! The crazy dancing had resumed, as my pearly whites switched from one ghastly sock to the other ghastly sock; for, yes, like the 'Prof' himself, his socks were just as ghastly, a sort of greyish colour with bright red spider-like patterns. Yuk! Yuk!! Yuk!!! Anyway, enough of assessing his despicable foot attire which, undoubtedly, will take me a lifetime to forget. By now one shoe was off his large foot. So much the better, I thought. Now there was more of the ghastly foot to get my gnashers into. The second shoe flew off and hit Toni in the shin who, incidentally, stood there like some uncontrollable laughing hyena which, I don't think, impressed the 'Prof' at all, judging from the glaring look he threw her.

The fun ended abruptly when I accidentally nipped him harder than I should have done, shocking him into reaching out for the nearest item on the worktop, which happened to be a half-eaten bowl of strawberry trifle. That came down with a crash. There was more shuffling and scuttling about and, dare I say, I heard words which my delicate ears should never have heard and, more to the point; should never have been used in the presence of a king. Anyway, the whole affair ended when I was still happily creating delightful holes in the 'Professor's' horrible socks; he lost balance and slipped in a most ungainly manner on the slippery trifle, banging his head on the kitchen cupboard as he went down.

For a black moment I thought I'd killed the 'Professor.' My heart froze as horrendous images crashed mercilessly through my head: a stern looking judge… jail… my beautiful head in a noose… I closed my eyes and, in the unbearable silence and stillness, I awaited my fate.

When I finally opened my eyes Toni and the 'Prof' had disappeared, only the slushy trifle on the floor was evidence that it had not all been a dream.

It was sometime later, well into the early hours of the morning, that my ears and eyes perked up to the sound of the clicking door and a despondent, exhausted Toni walked in after, apparently, spending hours in casualty.

She didn't speak to me for a whole day. Needless to say, my tummy did not receive any treats. However, the upside of it all was that we never saw the 'Professor,' and his ghastly socks again.

The Dog Lover

Now, you may think that the dog lover would have been the perfect chap for my Toni and, more importantly for me; but you would be grossly mistaken. Yes, I must admit, I was mistaken too and it took me a good while to get over my incredulous misjudgement.

As you are well informed by now I didn't, and still don't, relish the prospect of any fellow stepping in as a potential stepfather; in fact I have always discouraged this type of outcome whenever I could; for, as you and I know, with that important status comes a lot of responsibility and with responsibility that detestable word, *discipline*, rears its ugly head. Now I don't know about you, my loyal subjects; but I am not a very keen fan of discipline; it kind of interferes, and gets in the way, of my carefree and often spontaneous, adventures and other plans I create for myself. This word, *discipline*, conjures up images of boredom, restriction and, simply put, a world of no fun at all. And so, my dear friends, I avoid it like the plague.

But with this chap, the one that Toni had named a dog lover, the image of a disciplinarian didn't seem to match his title. Dog lover, to me, summed up delightful images of glorious sunny days on the beach, where he threw sticks and I retrieved them; he threw them back and so on; images of him tickling my tummy for hours on end; bestowing on me bulging bags of treats; better still, him allowing me to share his meal of roast chicken, soaked with dollops of thick gravy; going for long, leisurely strolls. You get the picture. So, you can imagine my disappointment when all these wonderful images vanished into thin air and I was left with the infuriating man himself.

Let me warn you, young, elderly and anyone in-between never ever let yourselves be deceived by a gentle, friendly looking face. I let my guard down and it took me months to fully recover.

Again, I had mistakenly thought that Toni had abandoned this dating nonsense; after all, the signs told me that was the case. She had gone back to wearing her boring tweeds and comfortable flat shoes; her hair extensions had disappeared and she had gone back to sporting a tight bun; there was no trace of make-up; no nail extensions, thank the Lord. She had, mercifully, ceased her tuneless singing; or, screeching as I describe it. In other words, she was her old self again; though, for goodness' sake, don't tell her that I referred to her as being old. Anyway, she was back on form. All the boring rules and regulations were firmly reinstated, with definitely no room for manoeuvre on my part; the house was sparkling clean and gleaming from top to bottom and the shrubs and flowers all standing to attention in the garden, without one single blade of grass out of place. All that was left was Yours Truly and, so, she turned her full attention in my direction.

Believe me, at the first sign of this attention on me, I tell you truthfully that I would rather put up with any man, no matter how ghastly his socks. And, as I mused on what she was proposing to do with me, the fateful words came out of her mouth and my heart deflated, rapidly filling with dread at the thought of what was to come. And, sure enough, it came.

"We are going to a doggie behaviour class, Kamehameha." She announced with an extra amount of vim. Of course, you and I know, she meant that I would be the student attending the class; she would simply be the spectator of the gruelling proceedings.

I lowered my sad head and stared forlornly at the highly polished floor. Was it the episode with the 'Professor,' and his ghastly socks, that had determined my fate? I would have the obnoxious fellow back in a heartbeat, and be as good as I possibly could be, in exchange of the doggie behaviour classes; I would jump through a thousand hoops, and stand on my head and twiddle my toes, to avert these classes; I would go to the moon for moon rocks; the sun for sunbeams; anything for a swop of these excruciating tutorials. But no… no… no… I was going and that was the end of the matter.

Before attending this hideous programme of discipline, I was subjected to a severe grooming session; for, of course, it wouldn't do for me to turn up looking my casual self. Every single strand of my golden-white fur had to be in its rightful place, my nails clipped to perfection and, if that wasn't enough, I was told, in no uncertain terms, that if I wasn't on my best behaviour, my life wouldn't be worth living on our return home. Honestly, I don't know what got into my Toni. She never used to be so strict. Don't get me wrong, she's always been an ogre; but, sometimes, quite a nice ogre. Now, she was just an ogre and, the more I thought about it, the more I thought this was fallout from the 'Prof' episode. I guessed I should really have given her some leeway; after all, I did play a small part in landing that obnoxious fellow in A and E. Still, it was fun!

Anyway, all spruced up, she took a glance in the full-length mirror, not that there was much to look at except a stern mistress, who had lost her sense of fun, and who was out for full-scale revenge, with her faithful pooch standing obediently by her side and… ready for action!

Down the long road we walked together, the picture of perfect respectability for all to see. I heard the delightful sounds from a long way off; happy doggie sounds which were a joy to my ears. Maybe, I mused, this was not going to be such a bad place, after all. My steps quickened. Toni tightened the lead. My steps quickened further, as an echo of a command drifted in and out of my hearing lobes. My steps quickened. I pulled harder at the lead as the doggie sounds grew louder and nearer.

"Kamehameha; Stop!" Toni ordered a second time.

Are you for real? I asked myself, my feet urging and itching to go quicker… faster… quicker… In seconds we were both charging down the road at top speed and with a certain amount of fast panting, which certainly did not come from me. I dared to turn my head at this point and espied a red-faced Toni who didn't seem at all amused; quite frankly I didn't understand why. This was fun!

"Kamehameha! Stop this nonsense!!"

Not on your life! I headed straight towards the large open gates where, within, I spotted a variety of my furry friends. Big ones, small ones; black, white and brown pooches; curly and straight haired ones; long and short haired dogs all there under duress; but now, like me, determined to make the most of a bad situation and have a jolly good time. With their pooches, obediently by their sides, the owners were congregating in groups, pairs or stood on their own; all had a common purpose for being here and that was to instil some discipline into their beloved pooches; to make him or her a better living creature; or, a creature bearable to, at least, live with. We were all in the same boat, us pooches. We had not been very good; we had liked to have our fun and now we were paying the heavy price. But, now that we were here, who knows what could happen with the right mix of pooches, I mused thoughtfully. I could feel my fur bristle with sheer excitement as I took everything in the sights, smells, sounds… everything. What an adventure this was going to be!

Or, so I thought. The whole thing actually turned out to be a full-scale nightmare. But at this stage of the proceedings, while we were still pleasantly socializing, I was totally oblivious of what was to come; so, I prepared my mind, body and soul into having a jolly good time and to make lots of new doggie friends in the process.

Within ten minutes I felt utterly deflated and bored out of my skull. This was, I dismally concluded, going to be a school of pure discipline, after all. If any of you young ones are reading this, I can honestly say I identified with how you must feel sometimes in that place you call, school; for, I yearned to run free like the wind; well, maybe not as fast as the wind these days but you know what I mean; instead , I was forced to walk on a tight leash, with only dreams of running free, as my furry companions and I marched around the perimeter of a large field, feeling rightly sorry for ourselves while our owners, I was quick to notice, were stomping around looking as proud as punch. To say this rigmarole was boring would be to utter the understatement of the year; but, my friends, worse was to come. We were duly ordered to stand, sit, heel and all sorts of other boring commands and we had no other alternative but to obey, without the slightest hint of questioning; for, if we decided not to obey, for whatever reason, the tempting treats in our owner's hands swiftly retreated back into their pockets. What kind of justice is that, I ask you? Anyway, like all the other pooches I obeyed the ludicrous commands thrown at us and waited for my reward; the only solace I could lay claim to.

This torture seemed to drag on for hours when, in reality, it went on for twenty minutes or so. It was enough for me; an eternity with the witch doctor himself would probably be a more joyful scenario, I concluded, as we continued to walk using different paces; we ran, trotted and sat obediently on cue, to our owner's commands and delight, after which we were mercifully granted a five minute respite. It was during this time of brief rest, when the big people gossiped and compared notes and we pooches stood obediently by their side, that I saw my chance and made my break. I was free!

My big mistake was to cast a backward glance; for, the look Toni threw my way will stay with me until the day I pop my clogs. Furious, is not the word. Murderous, is more of a true description and the poor victim would, undoubtedly, be Yours Truly, King Kamehameha himself. I blinked hard before turning back, trying desperately to erase from my mind the red faced, teeth gnashing, furrowed browed mistress who, at this point, was psyching herself to make a run for me, one determined foot poised and ready for take-off, her grim face vowing silent revenge. She didn't get off the starting block; a firm hand, belonging to a chap I did not recognize, restraining her. This, I thought, was no time to assess the situation. Off I went, like a very swift breeze, straight into the carefully displayed row of colourful hoops, assigned for some dastardly purpose or other; through them I careered, like someone possessed; onwards and forwards I went with such stern resolve and iron determination that would put braver kings than I in the shade. I most certainly would have made that fellow Churchill proud; not to mention Napoleon. And, as for the Great King Kamehameha himself he must, by now, be considering me for a knighthood. In the midst of my musing, I suddenly came upon a makeshift bridge of some sort. For a second, or two, I did wonder whether the fragile looking structure would hold the weight of my cuddly body and wished I hadn't indulged in quite some many delicious treats; then, I thought no more; across it I ventured with the speed of a well-lived leopard the words, where there's a will there's a way, firmly planted in my head. I took another backward glance and my heart leaped at the amazing sight I beheld. There on my trail were ten, or more, dogs who had obviously seen sense and were now following my lead determined, like me, to have a fun time. On I went. On they went. Oh, happy days!

Through more hoops we went and across more bridges, my faithful fans hot on my heels, until I stood at the foot of a long and narrow tube of some sort. I must admit, I was rather dubious at the sight of this odd looking contraption; but, like a trouper, I ventured through and out the other side and into the fresh air, my loyal gang following me. On and on… on and on… what joy! What bliss! The last time I looked Toni, and her gang of followers, were on the point of crossing that flimsy looking bridge, their hands on their shaking heads as they vowed sweet revenge and the immediate withdrawal of all treats. No treats… I'll think about that threat in more detail later, I decided, when my adventure had come to an end. My feet came to the edge of a wood. Should I? Shouldn't I? Should I? Shouldn't I? Yes… yes… yes, I should! In I went, with the comforting sounds of excited barking and yapping behind me a joy to hear, as my faithful army continued to follow their king. On we all sauntered over broken branches, soft moss, cones, rough bits of broken twigs, coarse bracken and some very unfriendly branches with cruel spikes. Ouch! One dug deep into my skin. No time to sort it out now, I concluded as I strove onwards and forwards with the determination of a soldier of the highest ranking. As I strode bravely on, I decided that I loved these behaviour classes and, yes, in the future Toni could take me to as many of them as she wished; in fact, the more the better. As I mused on this delightful prospect I went on and on, until I came to an abrupt prickly stop. I could not move. Well, actually that's not strictly true; I could move if I was willing to endure ten thousand prickles, simultaneously, attacking me. I must admit, brave as I am, I didn't much care for that particular type of unnecessary torture. And so, I stood there, perfectly still like a solidified doggie statue, in the midst of some kind of horrible looking and most unfriendly bush and, let me tell you my friends, the witch doctor's bubbling roasting pot, I felt, would have been a far more preferable option. I closed my eyes; for, what else was there to do? I comforted myself into thinking that my loyal army of faithful followers would soon come to my rescue. For long agonizing minutes I stood there and I was rewarded; my heart leaped at the faint sounds of yapping and excited barking drawing nearer and nearer and nearer, until they stopped too and beheld the curious sight of their King before them. I stared. They stared. I stared more and quickly noticed that not one solitary pooch was coming to untangle me from my prison. I could not believe what my shocked eyes saw. A band of pooches which stood, stared, turned and scarpered, leaving me in the middle of my prickly surroundings and still wishing fervently that I was inside the witch doctor's pot instead, while my ears listened to the fading echoes of yapping and barking.

There I stood, alone with my sombre thoughts, for what felt like an eternity; vivid images of a dark, eerie night, an unfriendly fox and a multitude of ill-disposed birds pecking my intelligent head whirling menacingly around my fuzzy head. Then there was the horrendous image of having to stand still as a pin, for fear of a long, evil prickle lodging itself deep into my trembling, frightened body. And the thought of a whole night of hunger did not thrill me at all either, especially as I was already experiencing positive rumblings in my tummy and feeling a hollow space where a big piece of roast chicken should be happily residing. All in all, I was not experiencing a happy scenario. In fact, to put it bluntly, it was a very sad, excruciatingly unhappy and deeply disturbing picture. But what was there to do? I looked around, my hopeful ears listening carefully for any sounds of an impending rescue. None emerged. I was on my own; abandoned. I breathed a heavy sigh and resigned myself to my sad fate.

In the midst of my despair, and in one of the darkest hours of my life, my ears pricked. Was that the sound of humans I heard? Was it the sound of woodland; or, was it merely my overactive imagination? My heart beat like the clappers. Was it the sound of a pack of ravenous wolves? Laboriously, I attempted to move one paw. Agh! Ooh! Agh! I whined and yelped with excruciating pain as I managed to, somehow, park myself on top of an odious sharp needle of some sort and then… something like a tight knot decided to invade my leg. And, could I move it? No, I could not; not even a centimetre, that is, if I wanted to stay sane. Because, let me tell you, when I made the tiniest suggestion of a move, I saw stars and they weren't the ones in the sky. I was on the point of yelping out a forbidden word, I never dare even think of yelping in my Toni's presence, when I immediately abandoned the bold act, as my shocked eyes rested on a human approaching me. I closed my exhausted eyes. Was this a dream or nightmare; or, had I plunged into the depths of lunacy where I was now seeing things? Slowly I opened my eyes and the face I saw was not a kind face, promising me a lovely bowl of mouth-watering delights. The face I ogled was the sternest countenance I have ever seen and, let me tell you, the person I was staring at has certainly had her generous measure of stern moments. The colour of her face would match the shade of any ripe tomato and her eyes… I'd rather not explain those in any detail; suffice it to say, they were displaying a heavy quota of retribution; in other words, they were not nice and friendly looking. I was fast beginning to think that I would be better off ending my days in the middle of the ghastly prickly tangle than to go back to my castle to face a series of horrors, in the form of punishments. In the midst of my depressing musing, I switched my eyes to the tall guy standing by my Toni's side; the guy I had seen earlier and, before I could look away, because let me inform you my subjects he was not looking too cheerful either, I felt two large hands around my liberally prickled, somewhat bedraggled belly. Slowly I felt myself being hoisted up above the bush and securely cradled in this lanky fellow's arms; he turned and walked away from my former prison, with Toni hot on his heels. At that point, my friends, I thought it best not to start objecting in any way; but, to go willingly to where I was taken. After all, I surmised, this chap was kind of my saviour; he had probably saved me from the fox's gnashers or the wolf's pearly whites; not to mention the cruel spiked needles of the bush. So, I closed my eyes and allowed myself to be transported, in the sanctuary of this chap's strong arms; thankful that he existed and, I must admit, that with every step I was beginning to warm to this gentleman and secretly sending him warm glows of love until, finally, we reached the door of my kingdom.

Let this be a lesson to you all. Never ever allow a human, who has saved you from the grisly fate of an unfriendly bramble bush, on to your list of favourite people in the world. I did and never again!

After reaching my castle I thought that was the end of the matter. In fact, I foolishly assumed that Toni was so relieved that I had come out of my ordeal alive and, therefore, I was fully expecting royal status treatment. Instead, I got the cold eye, a bowl of boring dry dog food, some water and not the slightest hint of a solitary treat. No words of comfort; no doggie lecture took place. Toni marched upstairs to get her much needed beauty sleep and I was left in solitary confinement, to brood over my misdeeds and to dwell on my impending punishments which, I knew, they would surely come.

It was a long night. Not only could I not sleep, as haunting images of all those pooches deserting me in my hour of need, and Toni's angry face, kept flashing before my exhausted eyes; but also prickles, which had lodged deep into my now bedraggled fur coat, had no intention of leaving me anytime soon and tortured me mercilessly and, incidentally, I had noticed that Toni had not volunteered to take any out. I tried to extricate one or two and succeeded, leaving the rest for another day because as they say, tomorrow is a new day and, let's face it; it can't turn out much worse than my day in the bramble bush prison.

Well, how wrong was I on that score too. Between you and I; I must have been losing my touch. I was duly informed that the guy, who I appointed as my saviour, was actually going to take me in hand, whatever that meant, and give me private doggie behaviour tuition. So, if you think you have had hard lives, my little friends, just think what I had to look forward to. Needless to say with nightmares of one sort or another, a hoard of pesky prickles torturing me intermittently, and the grim prospect of being taken firmly in hand, I didn't sleep a wink.

Now, I think I have told you this before; I am not a great fan of discipline. In fact, I am no fan of it at all. Have lots of fun and think about the consequences later, is my personal motto and what an excellent motto, I feel, it is; however, this delightful maxim was not applicable where this lanky fellow, and his tutorials, were concerned.

My worst fears bore fruit. The man was a tyrant. And, if it wasn't for you, my faithful and devoted fans and subjects, I would have buried this ghastly memory deep… deep… deep into the recesses of my mind and never looked back. However, I feel, that you want to know what happened so, I guess, being an honourable king I shall have to be brave and relive the nightmare.

In the morning after the day of the bramble bush incident, there he stood on our doorstep, looking spick and span in a dazzling white shirt, neatly creased black trousers and a serious expression on his chops, looking very much the professor of discipline. His thin lips were set in a no-nonsense grin; his eyes were as cold as ice and made me shiver all over. I opened my mouth into a friendly doggie smile, hoping I could cast my usual magical charm on this specimen; soften him a little, so to speak; but, this tactic, I noticed very quickly, was a complete waste of time and energy on my part. He took one grim look at me, breezed straight past me and made himself quite comfortable at our kitchen table. I sauntered off to my den where I could see that Toni was quite taken with this chap; though, I was totally baffled as to why. The only plausible reason, I could possibly think of, was the fact that he was a member of the male population and, as I have told you many times before, if Toni managed by some sort of miracle to harpoon a specimen, then she certainly wasn't going to allow him to escape. Anyway, there he was sipping his black coffee projecting an air of strict authoritarianism, which I didn't like the look of one bit. Toni, I noticed, was nodding profusely at his every word, whilst casting me the occasional disparaging cursory glance. And, let me tell you guys, this egg could talk for England.

After about half an hour of this torture, which actually seemed more like ten hours, he cast his dark beady eyes on me and scrutinized me very carefully as one, perhaps, would examine a dead rat which was about to undergo a dissection; take my word, it was not a pleasant experience. At the end of his detailed silent assessment, he announced the dreaded words which made my heart, not to mention my other bits and bobs, freeze. "He needs to go on a diet; a strict diet and immediately."

Can you, in your wildest dreams, imagine how I felt at that particular moment in time? A king in his own castle, being told by a virtual stranger, that he would have to starve. What kind of masochist was this? I dared to raise my stunned eyes to him and desperately wished I hadn't bothered because, in so doing, I caught Toni in my line of vision and witnessed her nodding profusely in profound agreement with this tyrant. My heart sank to the deepest depths of despair.

And so, this chap, who I now know is called William, led me out into the garden, whilst I envisaged Toni swiftly removing delicious doggie treats and stuffing them into a big black bag, never to be seen again; pieces of succulent roast chicken and tasty slabs of pork pie and doggie chocolate, not to mention yummy strawberry or chocolate gateau, assigned to a past, glorious world called memory. I meekly followed this William fellow, feeling like a doggie going to his execution and, let me inform you, in no uncertain terms, my heart was not secretly sending him waves of love.

We spent what seemed like an eternity in the garden where I was ordered to stand and sit; run, trot and walk around a series of strange looking obstacles; catch a ball and all sorts of other horrible commands before I was eventually allowed back into my castle, where I witnessed Toni listening attentively to a thousand and one instructions and nodding her head in total agreement to each one.

The next day the fellow returned with an armful of books and strict instructions for Toni to read and digest and my heart saddened further; for, it was clear to see that she was falling into the role of a dedicated student with remarkable ease, zest and determination.

A few days later William arrived armed with a wad of posters and a set of videos, ordering Toni to watch each video intently and to display the posters around the house, lest she forget the rules.

By now, I kind of noticed that Toni was losing a little of her initial enthusiasm towards this chap, and his rules; or, perhaps, both. Her spirit, I saw, was flagging and hopefully, I willed, was her interest.

The treats, as I have already mentioned, had all disappeared and that meant Toni's treats too; for William insisted that Toni had to adhere to the strict dietary rules too. "If you are to understand your dog," he firmly stated, "then you need to understand yourself." This was a hard and heavy cross for Toni to bear for she, like I, loves her comfort food. I am sorry to admit that I derived a grain of comfort from this latest development; for, if Toni succumbed to temptation, there was a glimmer of hope for me.

Our mutual torture did not end swiftly. Remember, my Toni fancied this lunatic. Yes, I know she's insane too; but she dedicated herself to being a good disciple of his and, therefore, she was not ready to give up the gauntlet. To my utter dismay, she flung all her comfort grub away and brought in two big carrier bags of things I'd never seen before like skimmed milk, I think they call it, wholemeal bread, tins of some kind of oily fish, fruits and vegetables, wholegrain cereal and crisp-breads, which looked remarkably like small bits of bumpy cardboard, and low-fat spread. You may be more educated in these matters than I; so, please excuse my ignorance on this rare occasion. Not a solitary biscuit, piece of cake or slab of chocolate was in sight; so, I'm sure you can imagine how low I felt. If you can't, I'll tell you; my heart weighed heavy like a gigantic boulder. As for my Toni, she displayed a permanent pained grin, hummed some sad melancholy tune and stashed her healthy grub away into her cupboards. This, I thought to myself as I placed my gloomy head on to my soft paws, is not going to be a happy castle and one surreptitious glance at Toni's dismal countenance, solidly confirmed the matter.

William came and went. More books, videos, posters and two extra-large bags of reduced fat doggie food were brought in and, worst of all, I was forced to endure more doggie behaviour lessons, with many more fervently promised for the future.

By now I was losing the will to live and, judging by the look of Toni's visage, so was Toni. I noticed that her usual tight skirts were not so tight these days and her trousers were on the baggy side, even her grim face looked somewhat smaller. In the midst of my intense observations, I also noticed that she was not a happy bunny either; not a happy bunny at all and neither was I. And so we existed; two unhappy, disciplined creatures residing in a prison created by Mister William Fender. And, as for this particular despot, who knew whether he was happy, sad or neither; for, his grim, stern-set countenance never changed and revealed nothing.

The climax to our unhappy state of affairs reached its peak on my Toni's birthday. Her special day did not start off in a happy, cheerful way. Not only had Toni reached the grand old age of sixty-five which, I am told, is not a delight in itself; but, and more importantly, she had no delicious culinary delights to tuck her pearly whites into on her birthday bash; indeed, there was going to be no birthday bash, as my Toni, for the first time in her ancient life, had decided to cancel her birthday, and any bash that came with it. This, I thought, was no good; no good at all as I had been living in the faint hope that we would be granted a reprieve on her special day; that William would wave a temporary white flag of surrender and waive all the rules. But no… no… no; lest she be tempted to go back to her old ways, William was there to remind her that it was precisely at such times in the calendar year that all rules had to be tightened. This did not go down well with me, as all my dreams of treats rapidly evaporated before my eyes. As for Toni, I know, she was suffering in silence too. The only person who was carrying on as if all this was perfectly normal was this dastardly William fellow, who had no present, or future, plans of easing his foot off the discipline accelerator.

As far as I could gather, from the lengthy telephone conversations I heard, Toni had informed all her mates that all the birthday festivities were cancelled and, with these dour announcements and final confirmations, we prepared ourselves for a day of gloom and despondency.

To add fuel to the miserable fire the day of Toni's birthday heralded bright, sunny and cheerful, a complete contrast to our downcast spirits. As I have mentioned, Toni was sixty-five, not sixty-six so, I guess, that was a plus and there was, as yet, no sign of William, or his stupid rule books, on the horizon. Toni, bless her, was making the most of what promised to be a very excruciating, dull day by treating herself to a second bowl of wholegrain cereal and I, would you believe, was allowed a small slice of wholemeal toast with thinly spread honey. Delicious is not the word; for a few glorious moments I was in Heaven. The three loud knocks on the door made my heart rapidly plummet back down to Earth with a crash. It was him, the disciplinarian; Mister William Fender, the guy my Toni had lost her head over; but, had she lost her head? Anyway, there he was large as life and twice as ugly, standing there with a mighty mean look on his face, the kind of look I've seen in cowboy movies, where a certain character is planning on carrying out a certain treacherous deed; his stash of literature in his hand and, in his pompous head, thousands of ghastly rules whirling about, ready to be released on me. If anything, his irritating voice and unimpressive looks were even less pleasing to the ears and eyes than usual; the doggie exercises were more gruelling and the get up and go, as far as I was concerned, more hard going. I don't know about my mistress but I was willing to forgo seeing my next birthday, if it meant an immediate cessation to this nonsense; because, that's what I thought it was, pure undiluted rubbish. I mean, whoever heard of a pooch, of my royal status, being subjected to such uncouth treachery. In fact, if my poor head was not so mushed up with this nonsense, I would leave home; yes, I would abandon my luxurious castle, my kingdom and Toni; for, what other royal pooch, with a grain of sense in his head, would put up with this baloney? I am, my friends, beginning to seriously wonder whether I am losing my precious marbles!

I was brooding heavily on this last dismal scenario when, in the midst of plodding up and down the garden by Fender's side, I thought, I heard giggles. Yes… yes, you have heard me correctly; giggles. Yes… yes, they were, undoubtedly, coming nearer and nearer. My heart leaped and so did my paws. Up in the air and back down and away… far away I ran, my lead trailing on the stepping stones as I continued to dash at top speed, and breaking all records, to the source of the laughter. Abruptly I came to a stop, sat down and stretched out my paw as my happy eyes briefly rested on my Auntie Anusia, before they switched to something big, round, brown and scrumptious looking, while I felt saliva drooling out of my expectant mouth, and trickling down my face, in eager anticipation of what surely was to come. For there, in Auntie Anusia's hands nestled the biggest triple-layered chocolate cake I had ever seen and sitting on the top were lots and lots of little colourful candles, far too numerous for me to count, when my mind is completely focussed on acquiring a generous slice of gateau.

Yelping with sheer excitement, I dared to briefly glance back and witnessed a red faced, firmly-set mouthed disciplinarian marching briskly towards me his fingers tightly clenched, his angry eyes on burning fire while, behind him, walked my mistress; her eyes were on fire too but the fire in her eyes displayed love and thankfulness and her lips were arranged in the happiest grin I have ever seen. At this point, a series of inflamed words spewed out of Mister Fender's furious, twisted mouth and these words were thrown at me, Toni, Auntie Anusia and a happy band of visitors. Then, to my utter astonishment and immense delight, I saw Toni pointing a straight finger towards the gate and stating something or other, in no uncertain terms, to her latest beau and, a few minutes later, I saw him and his books and other paraphernalia disappear swiftly out of the gate and, mercifully, out of our lives.

As you can guess, Toni's birthday bash was back on. Comfort foods were firmly back on the menu and Toni and I resumed our lives of bliss.

A Note from an Exasperated Dog Owner; More Commonly Known as the King's Servant

My dear friends,

As I address you, I am aware that I am at a great disadvantage; for, I know that you are all dear, and loyal, friends of my Kamehameha. However, I am going to jump at the deep end and simultaneously grab the nettle, so to speak, in order to get a word in and straighten some things out.

I'll get straight to the point. Kamehameha, I feel, has used his royal name to allow his thoughts and feelings run free and wild and, in so doing, he has painted a somewhat distorted picture of me and, in particular, has projected forth his absurd view that I am desperate, in his words, to harpoon a man.

Please allow me to speak the truth, and inform you, that I most certainly am not on a mission to harpoon a man and neither, contrary to what he thinks, am I desperate. As I see it, it is Kamehameha who views any man coming into our lives as some sort of threat to, what he believes, is his royal status; or, to put it bluntly, his pampered lifestyle. His sole mission in life is to make sure that any man, who dares to enter into 'his kingdom' will have to strictly conform and adapt; that is to say, he will arrive bearing gifts of endless doggie treats, be not only prepared, but also extremely willing, to tickle the 'king's' tummy for hours on end; be prepared for lots of fun times and, of course, at all times walk, at least, five paces behind 'the king.' What fellow, in his right mind, would even consider this type of nonsense? Quite frankly, if such a chap did exist, I would personally see to his head being tested, as quickly as possible.

I have had enough of dates and from now on, as far as I am concerned, if Kamehameha is still dwelling on the affairs of the heart, he can jolly well look for his own mate and leave me well out of the dating game.

Kamehameha's suffering servant,

Toni x

The Perfect Man

I am, my friends, not even going to give a hint of a comment, regarding Toni's statement. As this chapter will evidently show, my Toni is talking a lot of stuff and nonsense. She wants a man. She just can't manage to get one; or, rather, get one and keep him.

Let me go back a bit. It took days to get over Toni's birthday bash and still I can taste the gooey sweet chocolate cake and feel the wonderful silkiness sliding down my throat and into my grateful belly. How utterly brilliant is my Auntie Anusia! She's a star, and a platinum star at that, which is not how I can describe my Toni's next victim; so much for her proclaiming to the world that she has abandoned the male species for good. Fiddlesticks! Don't listen to her nonsense. Between you and I she's still as keen as ever, if not more so.

Anyway, I digress. About Toni's latest victim; actually, I don't think that Mister Edward Percival was, in fact, the casualty in this latest scenario. I'll tell you what happened, my most honest and level-headed subjects, and you can decide the verdict.

Weeks had gone by since that William fellow. You know the guy I mean; he's the one I mistakenly thought was a dog lover and ended up being quite the reverse. I honestly thought, after that unfortunate incident, Toni had come to her senses and had decided to grow old in a more sedate fashion. How wrong was I? She had no intention of growing old, let alone sedately; not in my eyes anyway.

Before I finally begin to relate this bizarre account, starring Mister Edward Percival, let me allow you in on what I consider growing old and gracefully should entail. Simply put, Toni should stay at home in her tweeds and twin-set and be utterly content with my scintillating company; she should, of course, feel highly privileged that that she has been blessed with the honour of residing with a king and, indeed, thankful that I have condescended to allow her to reside in my castle, let alone to be my companion. What more could any gal want in her life? I ask you. But no… no… no she wanted more and more is what she got, in more ways than one.

One moment this chap was off the scene; the next, he was on. To be honest with you, he seemed to have sprung from nowhere and, within a week of knowing him, I had fervently wished that he'd spring back into his box, firmly close the lid and securely lock the lid with a double padlock.

To say he was obnoxious would be a compliment. I don't know if you have ever watched that fussy detective on the television; the one with the strange moustache and funny walk; well, that's the kind of chap that landed on our doorstep and, let me tell you, he had no intention of removing himself from our castle.

Let me start at the beginning of this unfortunate nightmare. Having abandoned any further notions of sending me to behaviour classes, Toni ventured on a course of expanding her own mind, not that it needed expanding in my point of view; her head is big enough as it is. Anyway, during the long, dark autumnal months I found myself with a couple of treats and an empty castle every Tuesday evening. Where my Toni went, goodness only knows. Suffice it to say, she came back home a couple of hours, or so, later spouting something or other about the Dissolution of the Monasteries, whatever that means, and trying desperately to get some kind of obscure knowledge ingrained in her grey cells. Well, good luck to her; rather her than me. It was absolute torture listening to her hammering the information out for the entire world to hear and, I knew for a fact, just by looking at her bemused face, that her grey cells were not responding and, I must say, I don't blame them. Back to the point; Toni kept disappearing every Tuesday evening and I was left in peace to enjoy every second of my peaceful solitude until, one particular Tuesday evening, she walked in half an hour later than usual and, hot on her heels, followed a complete stranger; or, more accurately put, a strange man. I have never in my life seen the likes of his type before and, I must say, he was not Toni's run of the mill kind of guy. So, yes, he was one hundred per cent strange and not at all someone I wanted in my castle.

Cautiously I sauntered out of my den to examine this curious chap in closer proximity; to assess, ascertain and cast my verdict on this… this… specimen. Now, allow me to describe him to you, so that you can formulate your own opinions. His footwear consisted of a pair of black, highly polished shoes; in fact, they were so meticulously polished that I could see my handsome face in their shiny gloss. No problem then, if we were ever stuck for a looking glass. My eyes leisurely travelled up his well pressed black trousers, displaying neat, perfect creases in their appropriate places; his shirt was pristine white over which rested,

I think they call it, a waistcoat, of the same black colour, buttoned up to a neat black bowtie; the ensemble was completed with a smart jacket which all, to my discerning eye, looked very expensive and very black. At this juncture of the examination a worrying thought crashed into my mind; this fellow's clothes resembled the attire of an undertaker. My heart stopped beating; but, quickly revived, as I remembered that my Toni is that bit older than me and, so if this chap happened to be an undertaker, it's not me that should be doing the worrying. Back to this chap; his face was stern resembling that of the dog hater; remember William? But this particular guy had eyes that couldn't stop twinkling and a fellow with twinkling eyes, in my book, cannot be all that bad. His face, though grim looking, was on the chubby side; in fact, his whole body was rotund, a bit like mine; but, the most bewildering fact was that on his head was perfectly placed a black bowler hat from which, I keenly observed, escaped strands of black hair. So, that was his attire; but it was his mannerisms which totally unnerved, and completely baffled, me and made me question the sanity of humanity.

Before this strange character sat down, he carefully removed a starched, dazzling white handkerchief from his pocket and, to my Toni's utter dismay, meticulously wiped her kitchen chair. When he, finally, completed that particular ritual, which seemed to take forever, he cautiously and primly sat down, clasped his hands together on his knees and focussed his keen eyes on a beetroot-red faced Toni.

After I had almost recovered from witnessing this most unusual scene; and, I say, almost, as it will take me the rest of my natural doggie life to recover completely, I plunged into a deeper state of shock, when I was forcibly subjected to listen to his speech. Each sentence, coming out of the mouth of this most peculiar man, was measured; no unnecessary noun, verb, adjective or anything else was uttered; his tone firm and final. He, I quickly noticed, had a firm knowledge of many topics; but history was his love and it was the topic that brought him and Toni together in the first place; for it was, apparently, during their Tuesday evening history classes that they were, so to speak, thrown together.

After begrudgingly listening hours on end about this king or that queen, I can confidently state that I have become, somewhat, of a history professor myself; ask me anything you want about that egg, King Henry the Eighth, my friends, and I'll bestow on you a mound of information; though, I shall also tell you that, as far as superiority is concerned, I win every time, even though I can't even find myself one wife, let alone six. Needless to say, don't mention any of this to that Henry chap; after all, I don't fancy placing my intelligent head on his block any time soon. Anyway, back to this Percival fellow. His attire, speech and his endless fountain of knowledge I could just about put up with; but, his strange behaviour I could not stomach.

Things began to unravel when he decided to stay over for tea one evening; for now he was, much to my horror, becoming a regular feature in our castle; a part of our fixtures and fittings, so to speak. To tell you that Toni was on the point of inner explosion that evening would be a gross understatement. Her scrupulously prepared table, within minutes of Edward's arrival, was totally reorganized, much to her chagrin. Everything had been removed. The tablecloth was carefully straightened out and carefully re-laid and plates, knives, forks, spoons and the rest of it were re-set in meticulously measured out distances, with a small ruler Edward had extracted from the depths of his trouser pocket and, only then, was Toni's grub allowed to see the light of day. But then another painful process commenced. Precisely measured spoonsful of potato and stew were carefully placed, by this lunatic, on each plate and, only then, did he withdraw his crisp napkin, scrutinized it closely, before unfolding it slowly and carefully, as if he had all the time in this world and the next, placed it neatly over his knees making sure, of course, that it was absolutely symmetrically in line with his body. During the whole of this outrageous palaver, I watched intently, my incredulous eyes as wide as two saucers. Amusing is not the word I would have used to describe this weird scene; distressing, I feel, is a more appropriate term. My eyes, by now, were firmly glued on this eccentric for he had me totally mesmerized and he did not disappoint his truly baffled audience; for, the spectacle grew stranger by the minute. After each calculated mouthful of food chewed thirty-one times and swallowed, Edward picked up his napkin and diligently dabbed each corner of his mouth, before symmetrically placing it back on to his knees.

And so, the long and torturous evening dragged laboriously on… and on… and on. After long, painful hours I was delighted to see Edward rise and volunteer to help with the cleaning up of the table. If only I could have turned back the clock and retracted my hasty wish; or, at least wished he'd simply disappeared immediately after the repast; for this was, undoubtedly, one of the longest and most excruciating ordeals I have been forced to witness in my long life. Indeed, at one stage of the proceedings, I honestly thought the whole carry-on would never end.

Consigning Edward Percival to drying-up-dishes duty was like condemning me to suffer the tortures of an exceedingly slow dripping tap. Edward carefully picked up each washed item, from the draining rack, with the utmost care, like one would select a jewel most rare and then proceeded to dry each item. Now Toni, in her less fussy moments, would pick up a plate, dry it somewhat haphazardly and stuff it into a cupboard. Not so our pompous guest. Firstly, he scrupulously assessed the, let's say, plate; then he thoroughly dried it until it was sparkling to the eyes, with not a mere suggestion of a smear or smudge; next he would turn it this way and that, examining it in great detail before placing it carefully in its rightful place in the cupboard. The last process was not as simple as it may sound. Each plate had to be stacked absolutely straight, with each pattern of each plate placed accurately on top of the last. Only then would Edward proceed on to the next plate and then the whole process would begin again. Cutlery shone like new pins and, needless to say, measuredly and accurately placed in its assigned space. By the end of this rigmarole, it was no small wonder that they were both too exhausted for any canoodling and, for this small mercy, I thank all my lucky stars. Can you, for one moment, imagine what elaborate processes and rituals this fastidious man would go through, before he even contemplated on touching Toni's lips? I think, on reflection, Toni was mercifully spared an agonizing ordeal and one she may well have never forgotten well into her dotage.

As time went on, I learned more than I wanted to about this eccentric's idiosyncrasies. Newspapers, for example, were not opened if they had been opened by anyone else. All food that came in tins, packets and jars had to be measuredly placed into cupboards, with labels accurately facing the eye of the beholder; tea had to be brewed exactly to the second recommended and coffee ground and percolated to perfection; eggs had to be boiled for exactly three minutes, not a split second more or less; cakes and pastries had to be perfectly baked to the precise specifications of Mister Edward Percival's palate. Need I go on? Yes, actually, I do need to go on; for, I have not yet mentioned Yours Truly in all of this. Suffice it to say, every single strand of my fur be it long, short or anything in-between had to be in its correct place; my intelligent eyes sparkling; my pearly whites gleaming and smelling of mint, my nails clipped to a precise size and, as for my behaviour… All I am going to say is that during this time in my life, which seemed like an eternity, I dared not put a paw a millimetre out of place and I was, for all to see, the perfect pooch in appearance and behaviour.

It was Toni who bestowed an abrupt and swift, Goodnight Vienna, on this particular relationship, if that's what you want to call it. To put it bluntly, she had had enough. By the end of it she was worn out, had aged at least ten years and never wished to see another man again in this world or the next.

The Fun Living Guy; Or So I Thought

Joe Elkington was a man after my own heart; a man above all men in my high estimation; in other words, a rare gem indeed. If only he had not…

Auntie Anusia is to take full credit, and full blame, for this particular experience; for, it is she who introduced Toni and me to Joe Elkington and what fun he turned out to be. The ten years Toni had aged, during her disastrous encounter with Mister Edward Percival, she magically and quickly regained in Joe's scintillating company. And, I must admit, I felt at least ten years younger too. What a refreshing tonic this Joe fellow was. What a dream! What a nightmare!!

He arrived on the scene soon after Edward's sudden departure and, as I have mentioned, it was my Auntie Anusia who was responsible for bringing him to our castle door. I watched one balmy summer evening as my lovely Auntie Anusia, her hubby and Toni set off down the drive; the two females in a state of untamed excitement, while my poor uncle prepared himself for a long evening. Click… click… click. The car doors shut, the car drove off and I settled down to an evening of restful and undisturbed slumber, knowing full well that my Toni was in safe hands; blissfully unaware of the whirlwind she was about to bring into our lives.

I heard her come in a few hours later humming happily. It had been a satisfactory evening according to Toni, I mused; not bothering to raise an eyelid for fear of being subjected to a lengthy run-down of events and, so, I settled back to sleep.

I woke with a start thinking it was still dawn; whereas, in fact, it was about seven o'clock in the morning. Still too early to shorten my beauty sleep, I decided, as I eased myself back into my delightful dream. My rude awakening was due to a series of very loud and persistent bangs on the door. My inquisitive ears pricked. My wise eyes widened. My super intelligent grey cells whirled erratically around. Was this someone coming to kidnap me? The loud banging resumed and continued, making my heart bang furiously in unison with the door.

Who could this be?

Toni zoomed down the stairs almost breaking her neck; her hair in a set of ghastly rollers, secured by an unsightly garish scarf of purple and yellow intertwining swirls; her ample body tightly bound by a bottle-green housecoat and the crazy woman opened the door; a woman of her age and education, opened the door to a complete stranger at the crack of dawn! I mean, can you believe it? I most certainly couldn't. I mean to say this visitor could well have been a kidnapper or a robber; or, a serial killer! Hastily I headed back to my den as fast as my paws would carry me, placed my disbelieving head on to my paws and left her to her fate, whatever it turned out to be.

What I subsequently heard was beyond belief. Wild exuberant laughter such as I have never heard before; nor, wish to again because it was truly excruciating to these delicate ears of mine and most probably have damaged them for life, maybe eternity. Such shrieking, yelping and giggling! It was truly ghastly. Yet, there she was in her bottle-green candlewick housecoat, rollers in her hair and hedgehog slippers on her feet, laughing her head off like some demented hyena; at what? At that moment in time, I was not sure.

It wasn't long before curiosity got the better of me and out of the den I sauntered, stood at the door and gasped, as my shocked eyes nearly popped out of their sockets. There, directly in front of my astounded eyes, was a grizzly! Now, normally encountering such a vision I would run for my life at top speed breaking all world records and, most certainly, not looking back; but all I could do was stand and stare; for, this grizzly was bearing gifts and was laughing its head off at the sight of my Toni. Now, I know, she's weird; but really, there is such a thing called protocol when one is standing at the entrance to a royal domain; grizzly or no grizzly.

After minutes of standing there, in which Toni somehow managed to regain some of her composure, the grizzly, to my utter astonishment, was ushered inside and, as all the gifts he held in his big furry paws were for me, I welcomed him in accordingly even though, I had noticed, his gnashers were rather on the gruesome side. Within seconds, however, his terrible teeth, along with his big grizzly head, had disappeared, as I stared in flabbergasted amazement as the creature popped off his head and placed it carefully on the sofa before sitting down beside it. As I said, I couldn't believe my eyes! I took a very cautious, closer examination of this strange character and, slowly, I was establishing that, indeed, this weird, whatever he was, was part bear and part human. At this point

I was still about two metres away from this strange being, not daring, to come a centimetre nearer; I mean, would you? Now, I don't know if you, my dear friends, have any knowledge concerning these grizzlies; but I have. I know for a fact, that one or two have eaten a human for tea and, I've heard, that they're quite partial to poodles. I shuddered inwardly. I'm not at all sure whether they are into kings; but, the thought of ending up on his dinner menu did not thrill me at all.

My growing bewildering eyes widened to their full capacity when, a few minutes later, my Toni planted the tea tray on to the coffee table and positioned herself closer to this beast. This absolutely confirmed to me that she had now completely lost her head, a bit like the creature sitting next to her; or, maybe, she had simply lost the will to live. Anyway, there she was, before my very eyes, pouring tea and offering custard creams, to this fuzzy thing parked beside her and he was accepting her offering with, what seemed to me, immense delight. I mean, folks, have you ever heard of a grizzly who partakes of a cup of tea and cookies? My mind boggled, as I'm sure yours is doing so now. Anyway, as my mind was boggling away, I noticed, to my horror, that this creature's eyes were firmly fixed on me and his lips were positioned into a wide smile. Was he thinking about having pooch for dessert? I didn't stay to find out. Off I scampered, as fast as my wobbly pins would carry me; into the safety of my den, I climbed and buried my head where, I was certain, he could not see or find it.

After, what seemed like hours of hidden seclusion, I dared to place one cautious paw in front of the other and venture out of my sanctuary; the fuzzy thing had gone. Well, actually I tell a lie; it had not disappeared completely. His head was still residing on the sofa. This was a most puzzling scenario; so baffling was it that even my super intelligent brain couldn't solve this extraordinary mystery; especially, as where he had been, there now sat a complete human with twinkling friendly eyes, rosy cheeks and a happy grin. I stared at him. He stared at me. When we had stared into each other's eyes for long enough he rose, took steps towards me; though, by now, I thought I'd better get my pearly whites ready for potential action, and watched as, from the depths of his trouser pocket, he withdrew a piece of mouth-dribbling chocolate. I stood transfixed and stared and… stared. Now, you may well ask what on earth had come over me; for, as you know, in normal circumstances, that chocolate would, by now, be residing securely in my tummy; but, my friends, an awful thought had struck me, as I was about to take the delicious chunk of the chocolate into my dribbling mouth. What if the chocolate was poisonous? What if this piece of delight was, in fact, enchanted in some magical way, like I thought the Haupia was a while back? What then? You hear about these things, don't you? After all, this strange creature, who could transform from a full-grown grizzly, to a part grizzly, to a full human must have some sort of unique, magical powers. This entity, with the friendly twinkling eyes and happy grin, I decided, was not to be trusted in any shape or form; this bear-man thing, I concluded, had a motive to deceive me with chocolate as a bait; I mean, how low can one get? Yes, this thing was out to get me and no way was I going to be tricked; no siree! My still dribbling mouth opened and I immediately clamped it shut; though, unfortunately, the chocolate in my line of vision was still infuriatingly beguiling and was doing untold things to all my senses. And, if that wasn't enough to send anyone crazy, this chap's hand went back into his pocket and withdrew another type of chocolate which looked even more chocolaty, smoother, silkier and creamier than the last chunk to trap me. Most annoyingly I could feel a fresh surge of saliva dribbling down my face; I could taste the smooth, sweet silkiness of the chocolate and then I heard the words. "Tempt him with another bit, Joe; this is so unlike my Kamehameha. I really don't know what's up with him."

I want to live, that's what's up with me, I wanted to yell at the top of my voice as I stared unblinkingly at my betrayers; Toni, my beloved Toni, who was waiting for me to pop my clogs and Joe, who still held the tempting chocolate alluringly in his fingers and making my senses go berserk. Chocolate… survival… chocolate… survival… Blow it! If it was to be my last meal on this Earth, then so be it. Without further ado I leaped straight for this Joe creature; or, rather, his chocolate and, before anyone of us knew what was happening, I successfully retrieved the chocolate and, in seconds, felt its silkiness invade my mouth, before it slid down into my grateful belly.

After a very careful assessment of this Joe creature, I was now of the opinion that he was, in fact a full human and, maybe, not such a treacherous one at that; after all, my heart was still ticking along soundly and all my wits were still in working order and, yes, I was still alive.

My brief assurance that all was well, however, soon reversed its course as a most horrible, nagging thought crashed into my mind. What if this chocolate had, in fact, been laced with poison and this poison was of a devious, slow acting nature? What if it took hours… days… weeks, even months to act? My suspicious eyes lingered on kind eyes; but, were they really kind?

"Come on, Kamehameha." The owner of the kind eyes encouraged as he ruffled my fur on the top of my suspicious head and, before I had adequate time to plan the grand and royal rituals of my potential forthcoming funeral, we were outside in the garden and this Joe chap was throwing a colourful striped ball for me to retrieve and retrieve it I did and each time he threw it further and, like a faithful friend or absolute idiot, I played his game. Toni, I noticed stood in the background and watched then, obviously bored with the whole performance, went back inside leaving us to it. I must confess, the thought of popping my clogs flew in and out of my mind until I swiftly removed the thought completely out of my head. If the worst was to happen then, at least, I was going to jolly well enjoy myself before I reached the Pearly Gates.

The game went on and on. This was fun and, I concluded, that if this fellow was my executioner, then I couldn't wish for a more fun loving executioner. Finally, after a lengthy duration of pleasurable sport, we went inside and so exhausted and happy, in equal measures, was I that I lay beside Joe and soon fell into blissful slumber.

Hours later I was relieved to find that my heart was still happily ticking away and, after checking that all my bits and pieces were still intact and had not disintegrated away by any slow working poison, I was relieved to hear my Toni humming happily away; a sure sign that Joe was still firmly on our radar; that is to say, he was still very much on the scene; or, to put it bluntly, he had not managed to escape Toni's harpoon.

One sunny morning, while Toni and I were happily munching on our toast, generously smeared with home-made strawberry jam and sipping our coffee and water respectively, our mutual friend breezed into our castle. I must admit; though, I know it's hard to believe, I delayed the next bite of my delicious toast as I gasped, incredulously, at the vision before me. There Joe stood as cheerful looking as ever; from his toes to his head, in order, he wore a pair of sandals with no socks, thankfully; if it's one thing I detest it is human beings wearing socks with sandals… yuk! He was sporting a delightful pair of brightly coloured shorts, displaying an assortment of boats and fishes and the brightest yellow tee shirt I have ever seen, in fact, it was dazzling to the eyes; to be honest with you, I could have done with an extra polarized lensed pair of sunglasses. Anyway, back to Joe's spectacular attire. On his head he wore a type of Huckleberry hat, you know the type I'm referring to, made from straw and kind of frayed around the brim. I must admit I quite admired his chapeau. On his face, to match his cheerful outfit, was displayed one of the sunniest, happiest, widest grins I have ever had the pleasure to see. Within seconds of witnessing this cheerful scene my happy, dancing eyes abruptly stopped their dancing and my joyful heart stopped and turned to ice. There in his hand was a large pink butterfly net! Now, let me tell you my friends, there are many things I absolutely love in this wonderful world of ours: flowers, bumble bees and, though a little prickly, hedgehogs to name a few of my favourite things; but, at the very top of my list is the butterfly. I absolutely adore these little creatures. I love their cheerful colours; their beautiful, and sometimes very intricate, symmetrical patterns; I love the way they fly hither and thither without a single care in the world and the way they make everyone feel so happy in the process. And, I must share a little secret with you; I don't allow anyone but the butterfly this ultimate privilege; I allow them to land gracefully anywhere on my cuddly body: my ears, face, my long intelligent nose, my back, paws… anywhere and, as far as I am concerned, they can rest there for as long as they wish. So, you can imagine my absolute horror when I raised my eyes and saw this butterfly net in Joe's hand. I stood staring my disbelieving, and may I say hurt, eyes unblinking. How could he? I asked myself. How could this happy-go-lucky chap be a torturer of my dearest friends, the butterflies? I stood there brooding dismally. I could not be a part of his deadly mission and, moreover, I could not allow my Toni to associate with this villain; but, how to stop this cruel assignment? That was the big question and serious problem all rolled into one massive headache, as I saw my Toni, clad in a bright tee shirt and shorts and showing off her ghastly legs for all the world to see, happily linking arms with this butterfly executioner and raring to go with him to the end of the world. What was I to do? Quick… quick… It came in a flash; I am, of course, talking about my full proof plan.

Not for the first time in my lengthy life, I feigned sudden illness. Down I plopped on Toni's feet, like a sack of potatoes, and there I lay unmoving and fabricating death itself. I confess, I am pretty good at that sort of thing; in fact, my famous cousin in that place called, Hollywood, wherever it is, would have been very proud of my acting abilities; you know the gal I mean, the one who looks a lot like me; but, not half as good looking. Anyway, there I lay with my eyes closed to the world, my heart secretly beating like the clappers and not one single strand of my fur moving. I thought I was going to explode. "Kamehameha" I heard Toni's concerned voice. "Kamehameha, are you all right?" I squeezed my eyes tightly, as tight as I possibly could. "Kamehameha…" By this time I knew she had stooped down to my level, as I felt her chubby arms around my neck. It was at this precise moment that I had an almost overbearing urge to open my eyes. Why? I honestly don't know; but the urge was there and I had to rely on all my inner doggie strength to keep my eyes firmly closed and my whole body perfectly still.

"He's alive!" I heard Joe announce; though, I was truly baffled as to how he knew; maybe he had spotted a strand of fur move after all. Anyway, the next thing I heard were Toni's heart-rending litany of words, as she kept reciting my name over and over again, although what purpose that particular exercise served is anybody's guess.

I felt them before I could see them and, I am certain, you will either die of laughter or shock when I tell you what I am talking about. Can you possibly imagine how I felt, let alone looked, with a Huckleberry hat, exactly like Joe's except smaller in size, perched on my head and a dazzling pair of yellow sunglasses sitting on the end of my intelligent nose? Well, let me tell you, folks. I came alive! And the more I jumped about and yelped, the more Toni and Joe laughed hysterically.

"I knew that would be the medicine," stated Joe. "I meant to bring them in when I first arrived."

I mean, a huge bar of chocolate would have satisfactorily sufficed.

The hour long journey, to wherever it was we were going, gave me an adequate amount of time to formulate my butterfly saving plan in more detail and to weave all loose ends into a web of perfection; to stop Joe in his murderous quest, that was my ultimate challenge; to stop him on behalf of all my wonderful friends, the butterflies.

When the car finally slid to a silent stop my heart leaped and deflated; for, although I love the beach, on the rare occasion Toni can be bothered to take me there, I knew we were predominantly there to chase butterflies and not in a friendly way either.

Now, normally when Toni lays out a spread of sausage rolls, pieces of tempting roast chicken, bulging meat pies, freshly baked and thickly buttered bread rolls, cheese and cake I am in seventh Heaven. Today I was kilometers away from any Heaven; in fact, I hadn't even left the ground; for, my head was heavy with worry and you, my dear friends, know why. My sad eyes flitted to Joe and there he was tucking in heartily; stuffing his mouth with flaky sausage rolls and cheese and pickle sandwiches and swilling them all down with something red and sparkling, no doubt, adding more fuel to his energetic fire for when he set off with his butterfly net. As for me, well, I didn't touch a morsel and I was quick to notice that Toni didn't seem to care about my sudden loss of appetite as she happily stuffed her face, no doubt preparing herself for the butterfly chase too. There was movement and my eyes darted back to Joe, who was bending down to retrieve his weapon of death.

My plan was now finalized and what a plan it was! A bit daring, I must admit, especially after my episode down at the lake a few years ago; but still, I may hasten to add, as raw in my mind as if it happened only yesterday. By the way, did I ever tell you about that incident? Well, to cut a long story short, I escaped Toni's clutches and led a group of pooches to a lake where they happened to abandon me, a bit like the recent bramble bush adventure. If it wasn't for my cousin, Suzi, I'd still be stuck there. Anyway, back to the present. I was, needless to say, feeling rather cautious; but, needs must, as they say. My plan by now was firmly lodged in my head and so was the plight of my dear friends, the butterflies and, before I had time to consider the possible after-effects of my brave endeavour, I was off like the wind; well, actually more like a somewhat lively breeze. Anyway, like I said, I was off. Down the deserted beach I ran as fast as my legs would carry me and even though I was not as fast as I had been in my younger days, I was still considerably faster than Toni ever had been in her youth; for, let's be honest, a tortoise on a bad day would still outrun my mistress. So, off I went; nearer and nearer to the water I ran; larger and larger the waves seemed to appear and more thunderous too, as faster and faster my racing heart pounded. As I felt the cool water over my golden-white paws I stopped and stood perfectly still for a moment and, in that moment, I dared to look round and saw Toni and Joe following desperately in my wake. They were both shouting something or other; though, the thrashing of the waves dulled the coherence of their words; or, rather, threats. I stared wide-eyed at the looming waves before me and, I must confess, they did not look at all friendly as I started to wade in further and further; though, what I was going to do when I could no longer touch the bottom, I did not know. Swim; but, where to? France? I had heard it was a lovely place to set up a castle. The hope of Toni saving me, lest I start sinking, was a no go area; for, despite the numerous times the gal visited the Hawaiian Islands, she had never learned to swim; one can only wonder what on earth she did there. Anyway, like I said, there was no hope of her rescuing me from the perils of the sea. Would she save me from the deep blue if she could swim? This, I quickly determined, was not the time or the place to assess the situation. I waded in further and deeper with only one thought on my mind; the safety of my dear beloved friends, the butterflies with their beautiful wings. Other thoughts soon pervaded my mind. Would I ever see them again? Would they ever again rest on my intelligent nose? Would I survive? And, if the sea did claim me for its own would Joe, the butterfly chaser, continue with his merciless quest? These troubling thoughts twirled and whirled in my buzzing head as I wandered in further and further and then I could feel the bottom of the seabed no more. I, like the butterflies, was at the complete mercy of others.

Don't ask me the exact sequence of events. To this day I am baffled as to what precisely happened down at the beach. Suffice it to say; when I opened my eyes, I was convinced that I had descended to a horrible doggie place, created especially for pooches who had decided to lead a rather mischievous existence. For, when I raised my exhausted eyes, what do you think I looked at? I shall tell you; I looked at the gravest of eyes I have ever had the misfortune to gaze upon and these serious eyes belonged to the last person I wanted to see in the world. You know who I mean, don't you my good friends, the V… E… T! To say he was not amused would be the gravest lie anyone has ever told. And, as for Toni… the least said, the better.

I got to know the gist of what happened some days later when, once again, my treats did a disappearing act and Toni was reporting the whole affair, in minute detail, to my favourite auntie. I know for a fact that my poor Auntie Anusia couldn't get a word in edgeways from the rate Toni was spouting off and this is a snippet of what I heard. "So, anyway, Kamehameha has almost recovered, which is more than I can say for poor Joe. Would you believe the bravery of that man, Anusia? He waded into the sea, like a true trouper, and he couldn't swim at all, and he rescued my Kamehameha. Now, Joe is in hospital. I don't have to tell you that courageous man never wants to see me, Kamehameha or another butterfly net again. He said it will take all of his energy and all of his life, whether it's short or long, to recover from this harrowing ordeal.

My happy heart leaped when I heard this delightful news. My butterfly friends now had one less foe; or, rather, butterfly net to worry about. However, I must admit the next time one of these beautiful insects settle on my ears or nose, I know I shall be reminded of this incident. Still, it's a small price to pay for the freedom my butterfly friends can now enjoy.

Happy flying!

A Buddy Like No Other

I think I have informed you, on more than one occasion, that there is a place in Toni's heart that only one thing can fill and, sadly to say, it is not Yours Truly. I know this is incredulous; but alas it is a brutal fact. The love of her life is called Kauai; you know the place I'm talking about, it's the place from where my royal name hails from. Well Toni, as you know, takes her annual vacation there, though how she can afford it I don't know; well, actually I do know; it is by rationing my treats and she does that whenever I put a paw wrong and that, my friends, is every day and quite frequently within each day, if I'm absolutely honest. Anyway, off she pops and off I pop to Auntie Anusia's; or, that place called, the Heavenly Home Kennels. This year, however, Toni was well and truly off the ball. Oh, she'd managed to book her own holiday, of course; but, had completely forgotten to book my vacation.

Now, we both knew that, this year, I could not go to my auntie and uncle's abode because they were due to fly out to a place called… I think it's called, New Zealand; or, something like that; anyway, wherever they were going it didn't really matter; but, what did matter was the fact that I was, in effect, about to be made homeless. Can you imagine a pooch of my royal status… homeless? It doesn't bear thinking about and, yet, that was the situation I was facing. Toni was booked, packed and ready to go and I wasn't.

After a series of frantic phone calls, and severe head scratching, on Toni's part, we were, finally, about to set off on our respective vacations. Apparently she had, eventually, managed to find some sort of sanctuary for me where I could lay my intellectual head; though, I must admit, I did wonder where I would end up. Soon the mystery began to unravel before my very eyes.

Toni was her usual excitable self the day before her hols. Her suitcase, packed weeks ago, was now standing to attention at the door and she was rushing about our castle in a very agitated state, without one single thought in her buzzing head of giving me a final pampering session, let alone any farewell treats. At that stage I felt as if she'd already abandoned me and left me to the wolves, so to speak and I miserably concluded that, if that was the case, the sooner we went off in our separate ways, the better. Where I was going, I still did not know and that thought played heavily on my mind and caused all of my senses to spin around in a crazy whirl.

After checking and double checking all the doors and windows ten thousand times the bulging suitcases, heavy bags, my Hawaiian duvet and plush cushions, Toni, I and, hopefully, my sack of assorted treats, were all crammed into Toni's small car and we were, finally, off!

To say I was puzzled, bemused, excited, shocked, delighted and surprised are all understatements and, I am sure, a good language expert, I think linguist is the correct term here, could find a more suitable descriptive word for the topsy-turvy whirl of emotions I found myself being invaded by. All I can say, with true conviction, is that I thought my fast pounding, excited heart would, at any second, jump out of my chest and I would die on the spot of sheer happiness; for, here we were, standing outside Auntie Anusia's door!

I didn't know how this unexpected turn of events came into being; but here we were and just in case I was dreaming I blinked once, twice, three times and when I opened my hopeful eyes there, we still were. I was no fool. I was certainly not going to question why we were stood there; not when my heart was brimming with joy and I was ready to explode with pure happiness.

I can't stop telling you that my Auntie Anusia is my favourite person in this whole world. I apologize, folks; I tell a lie, my excited thoughts have run away with me; oh gosh, let me correct myself, if I may. Of course Toni, when she is in her right and generous state of mind, is my absolute favourite person; but my Auntie Anusia comes a very close second and, if Toni happens to pop her clogs any time soon, I fervently hope my Auntie Anusia will adopt me; even though I would have to, somehow, put up with my dastardly cousin, Suzi. Anyway, back to the present. Here we were and, in seconds, out pounded my auntie with a handful of treats and a warm welcoming cuddle. This is going to be Heaven, I thought. Sheer bliss! How wonderful, I mused, that my auntie and uncle had seen sense and given up their holiday to that far flung place, I think, they call New Zealand and had decided that looking after me was a far more delightful option. A sudden black thought crashed into my mind; Toni hadn't given up her vacation to pamper me. There and then I allotted my Auntie Anusia and her hubby into the privileged number one spot, of my favourite people in the world and, as for Toni, I had banished her way down my list.

In to the house we went with my hoard of comfy cushions, my king-size Hawaiian duvet and all the other paraphernalia a king needs, in order to maintain his equilibrium and reside in first-class luxury. I noticed, on entering the house, a bulk of suitcases and bags at the door and my admiration of my auntie and uncle went into orbit; in other words, there was no higher esteem I could bestow on them. They are stars, I concluded; platinum stars, which is more than I can say for my Toni.

How wrong can one be? Well, in the space of ten minutes and to my utter dismay, I found that my heart had plummeted down to earth at record speed, crashed and fragmented into a thousand pieces. Can you imagine my shock and horror when, soon after our arrival, Auntie Anusia and her hubby, together with their bulging suitcases and big bags, disappeared down the drive in a black cab and out of sight. Where? New Zealand, my friends, and in their place, some thirty minutes later, walked in two total strangers. I say strangers; I think I have actually clapped eyes on them before in this same house. Cheerful and friendly looking at first sight, I mused; but, that's not the point, my friends. The point is I was left with these two elderly humans; for, in less than five minutes of their arrival, Toni had vanished into thin air too.

Well, this was one for the books, I glumly thought, as I sat prim and proper-like on my hind legs and very carefully scrutinized this highly suspicious pair, with my super penetrating eyes. I have stated that they were friendly looking and I would also state that they were well into their eighties, though I am not a brilliant judge of ages; after all, I sometimes think Toni looks a hundred plus and that's on one of her good days! The lady, I noticed, was quite cuddly, a bit like me, with short, grey, curly hair; her eyes were friendly and twinkling and she had a smile to die for. The gent was a tall man with grey hair too and he had a long and intelligent nose like mine; his lips seemed to look as if they were on the point of smiling. So far; so good, I surmised. But what they were doing here in my Auntie Anusia's house was still a baffling mystery. This mystery became more puzzling when off the chap trotted to his car, brought back two suitcases, went back out and returned with a weird shaped wicker basket of sorts. I must say I was quite intrigued with this last odd looking object and, deciding that I'd had a reasonable rest, got up and strode over to this peculiar contraption to examine it in more detail. What I saw made my fur curl and my head spin. I had to look again, and again, just to make sure I wasn't hallucinating. There it was as large as life! I stood absolutely transfixed, my four paws glued solidly to the plush cream carpet beneath, while my whole body froze and my eyes were hypnotized by this… this… CAT!

My dear beloved friends; please give me a few minutes to recover from the memory of this devastating shock.

My friends, I think I have told you before that, as much as I absolutely adore butterflies, I detest cats; all of them. I don't care whether they are black, white, ginger-striped or green with purple dots; I don't care whether they are tidy looking, scruffy or anything in-between; I don't care whether they have the inclination of getting to know me on a friendly basis; or, whether they want to don their armour, gather their spears and go to war with me; I hate them all! If Toni was here, instead of abandoning me and gallivanting half way across the world, she would tell you what a difficult time we have had with these obnoxious creatures. In fact, Toni's life has been in the balance on more than one occasion when, on one of our leisurely strolls, I suddenly espied a feline on the other side of a busy road; ran for it at top speed, with Toni hanging on to the end of the lead and pleading for her life. There but for the grace of some fast thinking motorists, we would be lying side by side in the mortuary. I digress. Anyway, I stood mesmerized by this dastardly thing in the wicker basket as eyes locked with eyes. I did not like what I was staring at. I did not like it at all, I thought, as I quickly made an assessment of this thing. A pompous, over pampered pet which was, I knew, summing me up and, no doubt, deciding that I was well beneath her status as I continued to stare unblinkingly at her gleaming eyes, her beautifully groomed brilliant white fur coat and her well fed, over indulged body. There we stood like two warriors ready to do battle; there we stared and weighed each other up and there I yearned to leap at this fiend, devour her for lunch, lick my chops and savour the memory. My daydream came to an abrupt end when Bertie, that was the name of the chap, swiftly removed the basket, with its annoying contents, placed it well out of sight in the kitchen, sat down on the sofa with his wife, Claire, and ushered me to his side. This was indeed a brilliant sign. I did not need to be asked a second time. I snuggled in-between Bertie and his missus and gratefully received the pieces of doggie chocolate they offered me forgetting, for a blissful while, about that pesky gal stuck inside the wicker basket and banished into the kitchen.

My state of bliss was rather short-lived. When I awoke from my happy slumber I gasped, my horrified eyes resting on the fluffed up furry ball lying comfortably in Claire's lap. My initial reaction was to leap at the thing, have my murderous way with her and think about the consequences at a later date. One fleeting look at Bertie's stern eyes told me, in no uncertain terms, that that would not be a wise move on my part and so I abandoned my attack, saving it for a more opportune time.

I kind of detected, the wise old pooch I am, that Claire and Bertie belonged to my uncle; or, rather my uncle belonged to them as he was their offspring. I also perceived that they had come to stay at their son's house for a spot of house-sitting, while he and my Auntie Anusia went off on their jollies; I gathered, therefore, that I was stuck with Bertie and Claire. That wasn't, I thought, a bad thing; if only I wasn't stuck with their over pampered, beloved pet, who I now know is called, Queenie! Queenie!! Of all the names in the whole world, this vain, obnoxious looking, pompous feline has ended up with a royal sounding name. Well, I decided there and then, if Queenie thinks she is going to queen over me, she can jolly well think again; there's only room for one royal here and we all know who that is.

Our relationship, if that's what you want to call it, was on very rocky ground right from the start and one unwise move on her part, I decided, would most definitely see her demise. However, to my utter astonishment, this Queenie character displayed excellent behaviour; at least, she displayed such first-class behaviour when Claire and Bertie were in sight. She would sit on the plush cream carpet, looking all high and mighty, daring to look at me, while I sat and, from my vantage point, looked down at her as I questioned, what right had she to blatantly stare into the eyes of royalty and not quiver beneath their gaze? But, quiver she did not. And, so, we sat and stared at each other, while all the while Claire and Bertie bestowed on us both an equal amount of attention and treats, favouring neither of us. Each of us was equal in their kind eyes and on each of us, I knew, they would bestow the same sort of punishment, if either of us dared to step out of line. So that was the situation I, King Kamehameha, found myself in, my dear friends. I kind of had to tiptoe around this feline creature and I had to remain on my very best behaviour, which was not an easy thing for me to do.

One afternoon the truce ended. The pampered beauty dared to venture stealthily, like a common thief in the middle of the night, into my personal boundary and, would you believe, while I was snoozing away, she performed a dastardly deed that, in the end, saw us both punished severely. I was, as I have mentioned, in a state of blissful slumber when, suddenly, my eye popped open and there she was! Not only was she there in front of my super intelligent nose, she was actually in the process of stealing a bit of strawberry gateau, Claire had kindly left for me. I narrowed my fast awakening eyes, just as the last bit of cake went inside Queenie's greedy mouth and then, without a second thought, I pounced!

There were paws all over the place; fur was flying randomly hither and thither, fuming eyes glaring dangerously and gnashers gleaming. At one stage of the proceedings, we rolled about in one big, fluffy golden-white ball and the whole performance would have been a star act in any reputable circus as round and round and round we rolled. I felt her treacherous pointed claws digging into my handsome face and my cuddly tummy and, let me tell you, the terrible bramble bush prickles were a mere tickle in comparison to those vicious talons. Anyway, round and round and round we continued to spin, like some kind of whirling dervish when suddenly…

"Enough!"

We froze in a solid ball and, some seconds later, began the elaborate task of unfurling ourselves. Slowly… slowly we unwound, with a good proportion of our fur lying scattered on Auntie Anusia's plush carpet. Up we gradually rose and side by side we stood, like two naughty schoolchildren; no disrespect to you my dear young friends. But you know what I mean, don't you? When you're in trouble for some minor offence and you are stood there trembling, at the head-teacher's door, waiting to be sentenced and, consequently, punished. It is not a good feeling, as you may know, and in the long seconds Queenie and I stood there, it felt like an eternity. Waiting… waiting for our inevitable punishment which, we both knew, would surely come.

It came!

Stern black looks were imparted on us both and reinforced by sterner stares; all treats were withdrawn with immediate effect and, to top it all off, we were subsequently abandoned; left to put up with each other while Claire and Bertie left the building, to enjoy themselves at some ice cream parlour.

To say this fiend and I glared viciously at each other would be stating it mildly. I don't know about this Queenie character, although I kind of presumed she felt the same way about me; but I wanted to tear her guts out. Now, as you know my dear subjects, I am not a violent king by nature; if I had of been then Queenie, along with her dazzling white coat and shining eyes, would have been in my tummy long ago; but you have to understand, that because of this pompous, thieving gal I lost out on a piece of delicious, mouth-watering strawberry gateau and I can never get that piece back; well, not unless I devour Queenie in the process. This devious act of hers is both unforgivable and, most certainly, unforgettable. And, so we stood there, like two warriors on the verge of a murderous war where any type of attack would be permissible, as we waited for the other to take the first strike. No way, I thought, was I going to be the chief perpetrator and, as a result, never be offered another slice of cake again. I am not daft. And, so, I waited and… waited while, all the while, making sure my beady eyes did not leave the gal for one split second. I've come across her type before; one split second of daydreaming and I would be dead meat because these claws of hers are more lethal than any gleaming spear I have ever seen. So, we stood and stared and stared and stood; sat down and stared; lay down and stared; roamed about the room and stared and, not once, did we avert our respective eyes from each other. At one point, I thought, I espied Bertie in my line of vision, looking through the window and grinning inanely. I must have been imagining things because I dared to look again and he was gone. And, so the stand-off continued. By now my empty tummy had started to rumble, knowing full well that all thoughts of strawberry gateau or double layered chocolate cake were futile; neither was there any sign of boring, dry doggie food, which I would have gratefully devoured at this point and wouldn't complain about the flavour either. The bowl remained empty. My tummy continued to rumble, sending my nerves into wild arrays of severe irritation. It took all of my self-control to maintain my resolve; but, maintain it I did and Queenie did not crumble either.

Minute after minute passed us by; hours slipped away and eventually Claire and Bertie reappeared, no doubt their tummies full of strawberry and vanilla ice cream, with chocolate flakes added to the delightful mix; bestowed on us smiles of an ingratiating nature while Queenie and I remained in the Purgatory of our own making.

To cut a very long and boring story short, we both tired of each other's manoeuvrings and, in the end, planted ourselves down on to the carpet and eyed each other warily from our vantage points until exhaustion took us both over.

When I awoke, to my horror, I found this Queenie gal had dared to place herself by my tummy and there she blatantly lay, as if it was her rightful place. My heart stirred and so did all of my doggie senses. This was my chance to have cat for tea; after all, I was dying of starvation at this point of the proceedings. Once again I scrutinized her very carefully. There beneath the fluff and nonsense was potential for a good few mouthfuls; how tasty they would be I couldn't tell;

for, as you and I know, outward appearances are so often deceiving and disappointing. Maybe, I thought, as I licked my dribbling chops and prepared my pearly whites to ease into her ample flesh, I would get away with it. As I opened wide my ravenous mouth, uninvited black thoughts barged inside making me rapidly slam it shut. Treats would be gone forever and, if Toni ever found out about my treacherous act, which she surely would… it didn't bear thinking about; for, there was the possibility of finding myself homeless; I mean, a royal king on the streets… And, what about Auntie Anusia's verdict on the murderous act? But the thought which kept me from actually committing the act of murder was poor old Claire and Bertie; their kind hearts would be broken and, in the end, I could end up with three murders on my conscience and most definitely a gruesome death sentence hanging over me, with the prospect of a rough noose around my royal neck. That last thought put an immediate end to my wavering thoughts and Queenie was saved and so, probably, was my own precious skin.

Mister and Missus Bertie Wróbelowski found us, sometime later, snuggled close to each other and I must admit, though with a touch of hesitancy, this Queenie gal was not such a bad sleeping partner; for, one thing she was certainly soft and cuddly and the way she jerked her head up, looked at me with immense approval, and settled back down against my tummy told me that she liked me too.

The upside of all this, and there was a very big upside, was that Queenie and I were rewarded with an array of delicious mouth-watering delights to savour; Claire tickled Queenie's tummy, while Bertie tickled mine and cuddles and praises were not only of the highest calibre but overflowing in their generosity too.

So, there you go. One never knows what's going to happen in life which is, maybe, just as well; but, one thing I do know for sure, although Queenie is now on my Christmas card list, she is the only feline in the entire world that is the exception to the rule and a fine specimen of a feline she is!

The Dreaded Diet

On arriving home from her annual vacation to that far-flung island of Kauai, somewhere in the midst of the Hawaiian Islands which, if you don't know, is somewhere in the midst of the Pacific Ocean, Toni put herself and me on a diet. Now, I have been on numerous of her diets before and, let me tell you, they are no fun at all; neither has one single one of them worked; both Toni and I, I'm happy to state, are still as cuddly as ever.

I can well understand, though, why she put herself on this strict starvation regime. Toni had indulged; she'd gorged herself with far too much Haupia, drank too many Mai Tais and, now, she feels, her podgy face, arms, legs and other bits and pieces need to shrink. Well, all I can say is good luck to her; she'll need it. But the thing is, my dear friends, I am forced to join her on this madcap venture. Claire and Bertie overindulged me due to my, eventual, outstanding behaviour towards their beloved Queenie and Toni has, therefore, decided that it is time for me to shrink too. Personally, I fail to understand why I have to be punished; not only that, but I don't look good when I lose some of my fabulous self. I need to be big, fluffy and cuddly; it suits my lovable nature. And, besides that, a skinny king, I feel, loses his authoritative air; but, try telling Toni that. Well, I did try telling Toni in many doggie ways but she ignored all of them and now I am on a diet and have, begrudgingly, resigned myself to weeks, possibly months, of physical torture, not to mention a good measure of mental anguish.

It was a regime I had, mercifully, never been subjected to before. Everything seemed to be organized in sixes. There were six rules and, within each rule, there seemed to be the number six included. Now, if that wasn't enough to convince me that my Toni had lost the few marbles she had left, nothing else would. Anyway, these are the six rules I'd like you to browse over and tell me what you think.

<u>RULE ONE</u> Only six doggie mini treats allowed each day. (Six! I have barely started to taste them after forty-six; sixty-six would be more like it.)

RULE TWO Six walks a day. (I could live with that particular rule.)

RULE THREE Six grooming sessions a day. (To be honest, I didn't know where the grooming business fitted in with the diet scheme of things, except that it might have been some weird workout to extinguish Toni's wing bats; or, bat wings, whatever they're called. You nice ladies, of a certain age, might know what I'm talking about because I certainly don't; except that, I think, they are the fleshy bits under the upper parts of your arms. Yuk!)

RULE FOUR Six sessions of retrieving a ball. (I know with that chap, Joe Elkington, before he showed me his butterfly net, I could have gone on for ever; but normally, I find this exercise boring and this tedious rigmarole I could have well done without.)

RULE FIVE Six special treats, for example, a piece of succulent roast chicken; or, a tiny morsel of doggie chocolate a week. (Six minute treats a week! Was she for real? I would never survive; I would end up like my Toni, a nervous, gibbering wreck.)

RULE SIX Only six tiny morsels of toast, with thinly scraped strawberry jam or honey each morning. (Six; I usually enjoy one whole round and that's on extra thick bread, with generously spread honey or jam spread over it and oozing deliciously over the top.)

And there it was, folks. I was going to end up skin and bones; a mere shadow of my former royal self; a skeleton. Unrecognizable, undistinguished, undernourished and very un-royal if that was the correct word to use; you see, the mere thought of it all was already having a profound effect on my thinking process and use of the appropriate terminology. What was I going to be like in six weeks' time; for, that was the time schedule Toni had allowed for this regime to take effect and produce eye-watering results. It would certainly produce eye-watering results, I didn't know about anything else though; except to tell you that, by then, I would be well on my way to joining my ancestors and that, I thought, would be a blessed relief!

By day two of the regime, I was flagging and so was Toni. She was munching on her cardboard-like cereal, splashed with a thin coating of watery milk trying, no doubt, to take her mind off the ghastly meal while she read the newspaper. But I knew how she was feeling because I felt the same, as I munched on my dry reduced-fat doggie food. After we had finished our meagre meals, we set off on our lengthy walk. Yes, our walks now were lengthy and brisk, not at all like our pleasant leisurely strolls of yesterday. Brisk walks were the order of the day, with no excuses to stop a while and ponder on life; or, even to extract a stray twiglet, which happened to get entrapped in my beautiful fur coat. On and on we marched to places I'd never been to before. And, what was the point of it all? When we, finally, got home I lay in a state of complete exhaustion near Toni's feet, which were placed in a steaming bowl of water, containing some sort of secret soothing additive, and all I could hear were moans and groans emitting from her lips, when she managed to summon enough energy to emit them forth. What kind of life was this? I asked myself, resigning myself to another day of torture once dawn had arrived.

And it arrived; with a vengeance. After a restful night of much needed beauty sleep, Toni had, from somewhere, found a renewed source of energy, vigour and determination and she was raring to go, though I knew not where, and forcing me to accompany her on yet another gruelling ordeal.

While I was marching on, like an overzealous soldier on a vital mission, my mind was preoccupied with another thought; for let's face it, any thought was substantially better than the detestable thought of unnecessary exercise. Anyway, my mind drifted and I mused on the fact that, just lately, I had not witnessed Toni attempting to reel in any new guy. Had she, I wondered, abandoned her futile mission? Had she, at last, seen sense? Or were all the available bachelors, of sound mind, hiding? It was a mystery; for, since Joe the butterfly chaser, none had ventured on to our horizon and I must secretly applaud them for their sensible thinking; after all, there is only room for one king in the castle and that king will always be there for the lady of our castle, Toni. Little did I realize, while I was musing on this profound fact, how my allegiance to my Toni would be proved in the not-too-distant future.

Suddenly, I was rudely thrust out of my reverie. We were sprinting! Yes, I know it's hard to believe when Toni and I are well past our sprinting days; but there we were pounding the tarmac, so to speak, and a sight many unfortunate onlookers, I know, would rather not have witnessed. On and on we went increasing our speed with each step; though, when I took a swift backward glance, I noticed that Toni's face was beetroot-red and the gasps, moans, sighs and groans emitting from her mouth were not at all delightful to my delicate ears; not that I bothered to take them all in as I also found it hard going. On and on we went until… FLOP! Down she went. To be honest, so intent was I in reaching our finishing line I kept going, failing to realize I was running solo, with only my dangling lead for company. Eventually I looked back and, to my immense horror, glimpsed a most unsightly, crumpled bundle on the ground. After regaining my breath, I sauntered towards my mistress who, by now, was acquiring a string of admirers who were bending over her, peering closely; one was even taking out his mobile phone to, no doubt, tell his best mate about my Toni falling at his feet. From somewhere came a deafening, shrieking sound and the bewildering sight of blue flashing lights. Within minutes my Toni was gone and I was on my way, to goodness knows where, with a total stranger.

All I knew was that I was in the back of some sort of van and shooting off into the distance somewhere; my head was in a whirling state of unrest. Where was my Toni? Why was she taken away in a big van with flashing blue lights and loud sirens? Had she, finally, been taken away to a lunatic asylum; and, more importantly, what about poor me? Who was my kidnapper? What grand sum was he demanding for my ransom? And, was I ever going to get out of this ordeal alive? All sorts of thoughts and scenarios good, bad and indifferent flashed in and out of my buzzing mind until, finally, exhaustion took over and I fell into an uneasy slumber.

I awoke with a sudden jerk. Click... click. The back door opened and my cautious eyes peered at a largish, jolly looking face. I wasn't going to be fooled; no siree. I have heard about his type. You know the type I mean, my dear friends, the kidnapper who looks all jolly and easy-going, only to will his victim into a false sense of security and then secure his neck on to a block. My highly intelligent eyes narrowed into suspicious slits as I observed this chap's grin grow wider. I must admit, he did have a friendly smile but, I stoically determined, I was not going to be taken in by it. Oh no... no... no. I scrutinized him, like I would examine a piece of chunky cod on the fishmonger's slab, not that I'm into that kind of thing; but you know what I mean. I surveyed carefully his rosy cheeks, his ginger hair, his large body; my eyes following as his big hands reached out for a long rope. Was this a noose for me? I think I would have preferred Henry's block. A black thought crashed into my head. Was this cheerful looking chap actually a cheerful looking hangman? I continued to assess the situation in all its minute detail and came to the sad conclusion that I didn't much care for his choice of noose. It looked rough, grainy in texture and would surely be most uncomfortable; I would much prefer a velvety type or even a noose made out of pure silk. A common rope; why, that's for villains and I know I've stolen a treat or two; but, a common old rope... As if to add to my dismay, a series of past misdeeds came crashing mercilessly into my already jumping, erratic mind: pinching Toni's smelly slippers; making delightful holes in her socks, tights, leggings, trousers; running away with her oversized pants which ended up on a pole in our neighbour, Mister Frobisher's garden for all to see… Oh, the list of my crimes is endless. And now… and now, it is payback time and it looks as if I'm going to be denied a judge, jury or any hope of a reprieve and go straight to the gallows. With a heavy saddened heart, I allowed the coarse noose to go around my delicate royal neck and took my final bold steps towards meeting my Maker.

As I have mentioned, I haven't been good all of my life; in fact, Saint Peter will, no doubt, shake his sorrowful head as he stands at the entrance of the Pearly White Gates and inform me, in no uncertain terms, that I can't step inside and then, where will I end up my friends? The thought doesn't bear thinking about and, so, I have forcibly banned it out of my head and meekly followed the cheerful hangman to my final destination on this Earth.

What soon became apparent was that I was actually going to be given one last meal. Well, I thought, at least this executioner was following the necessary protocol; though, I know it's hard to believe, I didn't feel much like tucking in heartily into my final meal; I mean, would you if you were about to stick your head into a noose? But then, after quick reflection of the matter, I decided I might as well try and enjoy my last repast. And, what a meal it was! Excuse the pun, folks; but it truly was a meal to die for!

Now, don't forget, that by now I was well into Toni's strict diet regime; so, you can well imagine the sight of a large bowl, full to the brim with delicious looking succulent dog food, mixed with generous pieces of crispy bacon and grilled sausages, made my heart leap to the highest Heaven and I, consequently, devoured the entire lot in three minutes flat, gave my chops a grateful lick and forgot the hangman for a few blissful minutes. As for the hangman, he decided to grant me a final rest on this Earth; I expect he wanted me to ease into my fated ordeal in a relaxed mode and, with the death sentence still hanging over my head, I fell into a deep sleep.

My ears pricked to the burst of excited screams, sighs and chuckles and slowly everything came back to me: Toni sprawled out on the pavement, like a sack of potatoes; the cheerful hangman with his noose ready and waiting for me; or, rather my neck; my last meal and now, an excited audience getting themselves ready for the ghoulish performance of my exit out of this world. Slowly I opened my frightened eyes and looked cautiously around at the faces peering down at me. This was not the type of audience I was expecting and I'll tell you why. When Toni and that Percival fellow; remember him, that strange guy with the even stranger mannerisms? Well, when they had focussed their attention away from me and on to the subject of the French Revolution, I had snatched snippets of information regarding that subject. Apparently, many aristocrats had lost their heads on that gruesome contraption called the guillotine; anyway, some old hags at the time decided to turn up and watch the macabre proceedings and, not wanting to waste any precious time, they knitted themselves scarves and bobble hats and gossiped about their neighbours and laughed their heads off when other heads rolled. Well, anyway, that's the kind of audience I had expected to turn up and witness my sad demise. My astounded eyes nearly popped out of my head when I raised my heavy head and gazed upon my gathered, and still gathering, audience; for, they were made up of little humans just like you, my dear friends. The excited group consisted of the very young variety, you know about four or five years of age; the slightly older lot of seven- and eight-year-old with gaps where their teeth should be; then there were the nine- and ten-year-old and one or two that were, perhaps, fifteen and sixteen. But all had one common expression; curiosity. Now, I must admit, that at this stage of the progress of events my faith in you, my little people, was diminishing fast; that is to say, it was whittling away at great speed. Never in my wildest and darkest of nightmares, did I ever think that one of you lot would heartily rejoice and probably start knitting and cheering at my execution. Never!

And so, I was led out, my heart heavy and sad, by a young girl of about seven or eight; ghoulish followers hot on our heels, to face my executioner.

He was stood there straight as a rod; proud looking with an added look of vigorous determination. In his clenched hand he was grasping tightly something that looked long and dangling. Was this a much stronger noose for my cuddly head and extra intelligent brain? I exhaled a deep, heavy sigh and allowed myself to be led further; though, I must admit, my feet felt like four wobbly jellies.

I felt a thick, what seemed like a leather band, being secured around my generous furry neck and heard my executioner's voice which, I must say I felt, was rather too cheerful for this sombre moment in history. "That should do it."

So, this was it! This was going to be the end; the final curtain. Desperately I tried to get my scattered thoughts into order and was left severely unimpressed with my airhead, at this most important of times; for, I should have known the drill inside-out by now because, as you know, this is not the first time I was preparing myself to meet my Maker; remember the incident by the lake a few years ago? But, try as I did, I could not get one clear thought into my wandering mind as Toni, Mister Frobisher, Toni's oversized pants, lakes, bramble bushes, Toni's old beau slipping on a trifle and landing in casualty, holey socks and everything else went round and round and round in my fuzzy head like an out of control, crazy roundabout.

The tug of the leather strap around my neck brought me back to the here and now. Perhaps, I pondered, this would be a good time to say a prayer. A sudden thought crashed into my head. What about my worldly possessions: my plush and comfortable Hawaiian duvet and cushions set, my uneaten treats? Another thought overrode the last; what about my special friends, the butterflies? Who would allow them to rest a while on their nose; certainly not Toni? And then, there was Toni and Auntie Anusia; how would they survive without me? But it is you, the little people of this world, that I would miss the most, because when everyone else came and went, you were always there; I could always have a natter with you. Oh well, my dear friends, the time had come to say, goodbye, as I felt my trembling body being led to…

And there I stood; at deaths door. Slowly, I opened my eyes; this was, after all, the perfect time to show the world the bravery of a king. What I saw made me instantly freeze on the spot. I moved my eyes from side to side and back again; but, no, I was not mistaken; there were no gallows in my line of vision, no matter where I looked. I was, in fact, standing in the middle of a large circle of… little people, just like you at home folks. Can you, for one moment, imagine how I felt? I don't suppose you can because I can't even begin to explain. Suffice it to say that my iced heart thawed out in seconds and it leaped to the pinnacle of Heaven and when the little girl, you know the seven or eight year old I mentioned earlier, threw a ball at me, I caught it and dutifully, and proudly, walked up to her and placed it gracefully at her feet, to the rapturous applause of all her mates who then all wanted to have a go. I was happy; ecstatic. I wasn't going to die; not yet, anyway. I had miraculously found a host of little friends and, no way, was I going to let them down with a tiredness attack.

We played for hours; all sorts of different games. Some with balls, others with sticks; sometimes we just trotted along together going nowhere in particular and, finally, we all sat, or lay, down on the cool grass and revelled in the warm afternoon sunshine. What bliss!

And what about Toni; you may well ask? I must admit her whereabouts did fleetingly flash through my mind now and again; though, her actual whereabouts were still a complete and baffling mystery; but I knew deep inside my guts, that wherever she was, she would survive; she always did!

In the meantime, bits of very interesting, and very welcoming, bits of information were drifting into my head. The cheerful hangman wasn't a hangman at all; this fellow was, in fact, a sheep farmer. I had actually noticed lots of sheep scattered around and wondered what they were doing here; but, as I had more pressing worries, like the looming noose, I kind of dismissed the sheep from my head. This cheerful man was also the father of the seven or eight year old.

The girl, who was called, Jamie, immediately took to me and I to her and, as soon as it became apparent that I was going to be staying with this family, for reasons I did not understand, I decided that I was going to make the most of it. But there was a dark shadow looming on the horizon and I soon came face-to-face with my cousin, Suzi's, double! Can you imagine, in your wildest dreams, how I felt when, suddenly, I was eyeballing this double? Suzi, or her double; it was all the same to me. In fact, so nearly identical was this pooch to my cousin, Suzi, that for one treacherous moment I thought it was Suzi; a fate worse than the gallows, I can tell you. Anyway, we stood there for long minutes eying each other up and down, lengthways, sideways and every other way conceivable; I, the important King Kamehameha, and this double of Suzi's, who was obviously the king or queen of this farmyard; both trying to establish our rightful sovereignty in the eye of the beholder when, suddenly, I heard the sound of a whistle and the pooch had disappeared, like greased lightning. Where it had gone, at that precise moment, I could not ascertain as I darted my puzzled eyes around and then, there, I spotted it, at some distance, chasing the sheep. I noticed that this double of Suzi's was obeying a series of whistle commands and that, at times, she moved with remarkable speed and, at other times, she seemed to move around the sheep in a stealth-like manner as she gathered them all together. Well, this looked like fun; too much fun for Yours Truly to miss. Off I went; into the delightful fray I galloped with all of my senses on fire. And, as Suzi's double finally tucked in the last sheep into the fold, I jumped into the middle of the happy family and drove them all apart. My fast beating heart was leaping with joy. I couldn't remember ever enjoying myself so much. I heard a burst of rapid whistles, saw the double chasing the sheep this way and that and Farmer Bill running all over the place, stopping every few minutes to take off his flat cap and, with it, wipe the beads of heavy perspiration off his tortured brow; his face a vivid beetroot-red, his eyes shining but I don't think they were shining with happiness; while all the while I was running round and round in large circles until, from somewhere, Jamie appeared and managed to miraculously catch me and, with the aid of her mother, harpoon me in. Now, I can honestly say I know exactly how Toni's dates feel.

I had loads of fun on the farm and, to be absolutely frank with you, I had placed my Toni on to the back burner of my thinking mind; for, as I told you previously, she is quite capable of looking after herself and there is no doubt in my mind that, when she is good and ready, she will come to collect me… I think.

Anyway, days turned into weeks, at least, I think they were weeks, they could well have been months or even years in doggie time; time had become a blur in this happy place. I had noticed, though, that there had been no sign of Toni on the horizon and so I kind of resigned myself to the possibility that she would remain a happy memory and that this happy farm was now my new home.

Now, you may be wondering how I adapted to Suzi's double whose name, incidentally, was Spot, due to some small blemish on one of her cheeks. Remarkably Spot and I got on very well, which is just, as well as she wasn't going anywhere anytime soon and neither was I. I soon learned to work the sheep and together Spot and I became an admirable pair of doggie workers and as for Jamie, we shared her between us.

On one particular day, as we were herding the sheep, I noticed Farmer Bill's wife talking to a couple, way down below us in the farmyard. Now, at that point, I thought I was seeing things, because the couple I was staring at resembled my Auntie Anusia and her hubby. I tried to banish the absurd idea out of my head. It couldn't be them; what on earth would they be doing on Farmer Bill's farm? Reluctantly I abandoned my sheep herding duties, turned my back on them, and took a few cautious steps forward and then I decided to run. I ran faster and faster, gathering speed all the while until I reached the boundary of the extensive field and there I stood like some grand statue; transfixed. There before my very eyes stood Auntie Anusia and my uncle, deep in conversation with Farmer Bill's wife. Auntie Anusia had not seen me at this point; but I had seen her and off I bounded again, at full speed capacity, until I finally stood at the very tip of her shiny black shoes. After all-encompassing hugs and a thousand kisses bestowed on me, we were all led inside and there I learned the full story of Toni's absence.

Apparently, Toni had been residing in hospital for a long duration of time. Remember our sprinting session? Well, she'd gone down like a sack of potatoes and managed to break her leg in two places; I tell you, my Toni certainly doesn't do things by halves. Anyway, to cut a long and boring story short, there were complications, she had to stay in hospital and now she is being released out into the world.

A heavy dilemma, like a black cloud, hung over me. I was very happy in my new home. I was fully aware that it was not in the style of a kingdom I deserve; but I was very content here. I could run around at my heart's content; there were no strict rules and absurd regulations; no dastardly diets of Toni's creation to worry my intellectual head over and, more importantly, here I had little Jamie as a very special friend. True, I had to share her with Spot; but, somehow, between the three of us we managed very happily. Wrapped heavily with the burdensome weight of my dilemma, I felt the softness of two warm arms around my neck bringing me closer and then, as I looked up at Jamie's tearful face, I felt her tear drop on to my nose and there, like the butterflies, it rested making my heart break into a thousand pieces. I didn't want to go; I didn't want to leave Jamie, Spot, Farmer Bill, his wife and all of their sheep; but then, I desperately wanted to see my Toni again. My poor heart was torn in two and then I heard Auntie Anusia's words as she spoke to Bill and his wife; her voice full of heavy concern. "I feel Toni shall never get better if she doesn't see her Kamehameha." What? My ears pricked. My heart felt it had already died. She continued. "Since our return from our vacation, Toni has come to stay with us; but she has totally lost her appetite and, we fear, if she doesn't see Kamehameha soon, she will simply fade away." Was I hearing things correctly? Did Auntie Anusia say Toni had lost her appetite? Things must be drastic! She's fading away… from a broken heart? Fading away because she's missing me? My heart was crumbling now into a million pieces; for, here was Jamie with her cuddly arms lovingly wrapped around my neck, with Spot sitting next to her and my Toni kilometres away and, by all accounts, fading away. I wish, my friend, King Solomon himself was here to personally advise me on this dilemma of mine; for, at this point, I didn't want to go and I didn't want to stay. Oh, if only there was two of me!

And so, I sat and I pondered and so did everyone else, while the clock on the kitchen wall kept ticking away the miserable minutes. Finally, I felt Jamie's plump arms and hands begrudgingly leave my fluffy neck and I watched her kneel before me and look solemnly into my sad eyes. I thought my heavy laden heart would explode as I stared straight into her young, innocent, glassy eyes; knowing exactly how she was feeling because I was feeling the very same. Words cannot explain; but I think you know what I mean; it's that tugging of the heart feeling that's painful, sweet and bitter all rolled into one and it gnaws and… gnaws and… gnaws…

"You have to go to your Toni, my dear Kamehameha." I heard her softly spoken quivering words and, momentarily, I looked away from her tear-brimmed eyes as it hurt so much to look at them. "You have to go, Kamehameha," she reinforced, "and we all have to let you go." Spoken like a true trouper for one so young, I thought. And there it was; my fate sealed by a seven or eight year old girl.

I left with a bulging sack full of assorted mouth-watering treats; lots of waves, smiles, tears and fervent promises of future mutual visits and, with that, I was gone.

Cautiously I walked into the gloomy sickroom. Everything was perfectly still and quiet. Had Toni already popped her clogs? Stealthily, I placed one foot in front of the other and as I approached her sickbed, I found her in the land of nod. I sat on my hind legs for a while gawping at my mistress and, from where I was sitting, I could kind of see that she had, in fact, faded away a little; her face seemed smaller and more drawn and I could see veins under the skin of her hands, which were placed on top of her duvet. It's a jolly good thing I came, I mused, whining a little to alert her to the fact that she was, once again, in the presence of royalty. I thought I saw an eyelid flicker. I whined a little louder. An eye opened. Two eyes popped open, followed by the biggest smile I have ever seen.

After a generous number of kisses and cuddles were bestowed, I heard Toni's delightful words. "And, Kamehameha, I promise you and I shall never go on another diet regime again." Then she hollered, "Bring us three very large slices of double layered chocolate gateau, Anusia; one for you, one for me and the largest slice for my Kamehameha."

And, lest she forget her promise; or, the going gets tough in my castle, I know there is always Farmer Bill and his brood I can run to and claim permanent sanctuary.

The Love Rivals

Well, my dear friends, you will be pleased to know that Toni made a remarkable recovery due, of course, to my invaluable presence by her sickbed night and day and soon we were, once again, firmly established in our own kingdom. But things had changed; or, so I had mistakenly thought.

As promised, mercifully there was no more talk of diets and things seemed to have got back to normal. You know the kind of things I am talking about; the tedious six grooming sessions were reduced to one a day; walks resumed their leisurely pace and generous portions of succulent roast chicken, with golden crispy skin; fat sausages and mouth-watering chocolate gateau were reinstated back on to the menu and regularly placed into my bowl. In no time at all, Toni was back to her old podgy, cuddly self and so was I. And so, we plodded happily along. I had also noticed that Toni had regained her marbles and I was most delighted that I was now the only male figure in her life, on whom she could bestow her full attention. Yes, things were sailing serenely along on a nice even keel. And then – I should have known, my dear friends; that this was too good to be true; too fantastic and blissful to last. The warning sign came one afternoon when Toni had arrived home from one of her occasional supply teaching assignments, in some obscure village, and the out of tune humming began. My ears pricked. I wasn't hearing things. I tried to bury my tortured ears into the depths of my luxurious Hawaiian duvet; but you know me and, as always, burning curiosity got the better of me. I raised my head and cast my suspicious eyes on to my mistress. I blinked hard and then blinked extra hard; but, no, there was no denying it, the grin on her face said it all. My Toni was once again ready to harpoon some poor, unsuspecting, unfortunate victim.

Now, as you know, my mission in life is, at all costs, to live a peaceful existence but that, of course, does not mean there should be no fun. On the contrary, my peaceful life must include loads and loads of undiluted fun; I absolutely insist on a joyful, fun-loving life and anyone getting in the way has to be eliminated by whatever necessary methods spring into my super intelligent mind, whether by fair means or foul. I must admit I have been quite successful in the past and Toni's hopefuls, by one process or another, have been swiftly dispatched into the hopeless category and our status quo has been fully resumed. But you and I know that this has not always been an easy task to accomplish and, to be honest with you, I think Toni and I are too long in the tooth now for this type of nonsensical caper. I mean, I don't like to admit it but we are both past our prime; or, to put it bluntly, past our best. Between you and me, my Toni is quite frazzled around the edges, so to speak, though, of course, that does not certainly apply to me and she has, I feel, long ago lost most of her marbles; yes, I think it's high time she joined her peers, started to knit jumpers and think about growing old gracefully. But, yes, she was most definitely humming and so I prepared myself for the fallout which would, I knew, would inevitably come. And it did come, bringing with it an outcome of events neither Toni, nor I, expected.

He appeared on our doorstep all spick and span, bright eyed and bushy tailed, as they say, and immediately, at first sight, I fell in love with this guy. His bulging bag of treats not to mention his friendly smile, twinkling eyes and cuddles attracted me towards him like a magnet and there I stuck, like a limpet, never leaving his side.

And neither did Toni. To my utter dismay, she stuck to his other side like glue and, as you can guess, a love rival war commenced with this Graham chap firmly in the middle of it all, whether he wanted to be stuck there or not. Neither Toni, nor I, asked his permission to be his shadow; neither Toni, nor I, was going to relinquish our determined positions.

Why she clung on to him, I'm not sure. Perhaps it was the bunch of colourful roses he brought her every time he came; I'm thinking it was more likely to be the endless box of chocolates and the delicious cakes with gooey cream oozing out of the sides; maybe it was the fact that this Graham chap was so easy-going; or, perhaps being the perfect, and most willing, cook clinched the matter; for, there was no doubt about it, Graham's culinary skills were first class; he was a sensible chef who did not tolerate this ponsy-wonsy nonsense, where one ends up with a measly stick of celery on one's plate and not much else. My friends, you are going to be green with envy when I tell you that my new love fried sausages to sizzling perfection; his golden roasts were crispy on the outside and succulent within; his cakes to die for. What a man! What a gem!! A rare treasure indeed and so I decided that there was no way this jewel would have the chance to escape our clutches and if things turned sour between him and my Toni, as things inevitably had a habit of doing where Toni and guys were concerned, I had a back-up plan; I would personally, by royal command, appoint Graham as my royal cook.

Both Toni and I eagerly awaited Graham's visits. Toni spent hours in the bathroom though goodness only knows what she did in there. All I can say is that she looked much the same when she, finally, re-entered the world. I spent much the same time picking out miniscule bits of garden debris, I had accidentally picked up whilst leisurely roaming about my garden, out of my fur coat. I was aghast to see that Toni had gone back to wearing her shorter skirts again and, I must say, that if her tree trunk legs didn't put the man off than nothing else would. Her smile was now a permanent fixture on her chops and her singing, well; you know what I think about that. If only I wasn't subjected to the torture of listening to the tuneless din while she groomed me rigorously. But, to be honest, I would have put up with anything as I was out to impress Graham myself and I needed a shiny, smooth, beautiful coat for the job.

Anyway, we both seemed successful in our attempts to impress our man; for, the poor bloke didn't know which way to look; that is to say, he didn't know on whom to bestow most of his attention because, if he favoured Toni then Yours Truly's nose would be out of joint and vice versa; so, you can understand the dilemma the unfortunate chap had found himself entangled in. I didn't envy him, I must say; but, having said that, I couldn't quite understand why he simply couldn't make a cut-throat choice; after all, I was the sovereign in the castle and it was I who would ultimately grant, or deny, him the green light to stay; plus, I had got the cute factor, which is more than I could say for Toni, bless her. So, quite frankly, I didn't understand his problem; it was a simple choice in my highly esteemed point of view. The guy was in a fix of his own making.

Now when all three of us went out together on one of our jolly jaunts, things ran smoothly. But, my dear readers, I am sure you will understand that, at times, it was impossible for all three of us to go out together; for example, as much as I'd love to have gone to that place they call the cinema, the guy at the door firmly put his foot down and wouldn't allow me in, no matter how much I gazed on him pleadingly with my begging eyes. Neither was I allowed to enter the place called the restaurant, which was a great shame; I simply didn't comprehend why I couldn't sit at the table with Toni and Graham and be allowed to tuck into a generous slab of a juicy steak with, of course, all the trimmings. And, as for the leisure centre, where various exercise classes were continually in progress; well, I never was, and never will be, keen on going there anyway. The problem, however, was that when, on occasion, Toni and Graham were gallivanting about town and having the time of their lives, I was stuck home alone brooding for England; for, whereas in the past, I couldn't wait for Toni to vacate our castle, so that I could clock up a few good hours of kip, now I yearned to be with her; or, rather to be with her beau who, incidentally, had managed to, somehow and miraculously, survive five weeks of Toni.

I don't know what exactly it was that lured me towards this guy, apart from his generous treats and cuddles; it was just him. So, when I was abandoned for the evening, I did not ease into blissful slumber. On the contrary, I was bereft of all joy and was left in a state of total unrest. Tortured thoughts raced in and out of my mind, bringing with them unwanted scenes of Toni and Graham tucking into thick slabs of succulent steaks; or, Toni and Graham canoodling together in the back row of the cinema, without my royal presence close by Graham's side. The hours without them; or, more precisely, without Graham were like one long, torturous, never-ending eternity. I tossed and turned on my Hawaiian duvet; I paced the length and breadth of the kitchen, wearing Toni's highly polished wooden floor out; I didn't eat a single morsel out of my bowl or slurp a single mouthful of water. All I could do was to pickle in my self-inflicted misery until click… click… the door opened and in they sauntered without a care in the world; without a gram of regret or remorse of having abandoned me. How could they? Slowly, I raised my pained eyes to them and let me tell you, my dear friends, in that moment in time, I did not feel the slightest bit of love for either of them as I watched them laughing and, later, canoodling on the sofa without a single glance, or treat, thrown in my direction. I closed my eyes tightly and fervently wished Graham, at least, would quickly regain his sanity. There was, I sadly concluded, no hope for my Toni.

My prayers were answered the next day when, to my utter delight, Graham took me, and my ball, out on our own and Toni was left indoors to suffer the misery of a treacherous hangover. I must admit that I am not a vindictive type of pooch; but I did feel that I was justified in feeling a sense of satisfaction that she had received her come-uppance.

As I have previously mentioned Graham found himself torn apart, so to speak, and as the weeks turned to months, I found him flagging; his energy levels had sapped; his enthusiasm to keep both Toni and I amused, and entertained, was somewhat waning and I began to feel that he longed to be somewhere else. But, still, he kept coming; continued to divide his attention between Toni and myself and he started to be boring. He knew it; Toni knew it and I certainly knew it.

Instead of taking Toni out, he now planted himself down on the sofa and spent endless evenings ogling the box. As for me, for some inexplicable reason, his treats were not bountiful anymore and neither was his enthusiasm to take me out for a run around. We became the boring threesome.

What to do now? I wondered. I scratched my puzzled head with my paw at this point; scratched it harder and waited for some sort of enlightenment to descend over me. None came. I lay and brooded but no solution loomed on the horizon. Graham seemed to be a permanent and annoying fixture in our castle and a very dull one at that and I began to seriously question the entire human race; for how, I mused, could one human being change so drastically from being an attentive, generous, fun-loving creature into a tedious, uninteresting, intolerable bore in whose company I wished no longer to reside? Even his sausages had lost their taste and had become dull and boring like their cook. I also knew, for a fact, that Toni had lost interest in this particular male specimen too. No longer did she spend hours in the bathroom, five minutes was the maximum duration; the short skirts were replaced with tweeds and twin-sets and on her face, which incidentally had not the slightest trace of make-up, was pinned a permanent line of pure sufferance.

And so it went on and I began to think that that place called Purgatory would be a far happier place for us to dwell in because, even if one has the misfortune to land there, at least there is a hope of an escape, sometime in the distant future.

It came; the end, I mean. Suddenly, without any warning, the end mercifully came.

He sauntered in with a huge bunch of roses, double the usual size and twice as beautiful, and I didn't know whether to cry with happiness, or dismay; for, at this stage of the proceedings, I didn't know what the flowers symbolized; love, or the merciful end of torturous love. Did they mean a return to our happy threesome days; or, would I have to mop Toni's tears away with a king-sized handkerchief? And, if Toni wept tears would they be happy tears or tears of doom and despondency? Carefully, I watched the interesting scene unfold before my very eyes as, momentarily, Toni's eyes lit up at the sight at the colourful, blooming bouquet and then, just as suddenly, the light went out as she was asked to sit down and our man sat on the other side of the kitchen table. This formality,

I thought, did not bode well for my Toni; for, as all gals of experience know, it's one thing when a gal tells a chap to sling his hook; but, when the table is turned and the chap dumps the gal, then be ready for a mighty catastrophic fallout. I prepared myself accordingly; though, in hindsight, I should have saved myself the energy, effort and my precious time.

My Toni was ditched; but soon after he had deserted our kingdom, she danced with sheer joy, hugging and kissing me and thanking her lucky stars for the happy turn of events and, I must admit, I thanked all the gods I could think of too. The bore had gone and so had Toni's tuneless humming!

The Harpoon Escapees

I dedicate this chapter to the harpoon escapees; or, to put it mildly, and between you and me, the ones that got away from Toni's clutches; in other words, the lucky ones. And there were many, too many for me to mention each one individually; but a few carefully chosen ones are worth a special mention.

There was the doggie psychiatrist. No need to guess how that episode went down with me. Suffice it to say it didn't and, in the end, Toni decided that she knew what's inside my intelligent head better than anyone; though, why she didn't get her own head looked at, when she had the chance, I don't know. After one date we couldn't see the loony doctor for dust.

Next came the neighbour. He was not a great candidate either. He, I felt, was far more interested in securing his mug of sugar than being a brilliant stepdad to me; so, he had to go too.

Then there was the bookworm. Now, to be honest, I thought there could have been a chance with him; I honestly thought he could be a successful candidate because, as you know, there is nothing my Toni likes better than getting her nose stuck into a heavy tome. However, as a result of their mutual interest in books, the pair sat on opposite sides of the sofa, more interested in the plots they were immersed in than each other; so, that kind of fizzled out.

The sergeant major! Don't ask me how he ever got a look in; I am reeling from the effects to this very day. I mean; a real sergeant major! Toni had obviously lost her head, together with every single marble in it. I mean to say, I have already got one sergeant major residing in my castle and one is more than enough for any king to bear. Anyway, to cut a long story short, he must have been the first, and only, sergeant major in history to have given up on bestowing discipline on his inferiors. We saw him, and his discipline cane, off in no uncertain terms; though, the stern look he bestowed on me on his exit makes me shiver, inside and out, to this very day.

They came and they went; but they did not conquer. And now, even Graham the bore is off our radar; apparently he is now with another poor unfortunate, no doubt, boring the socks off her too.

And so you have it in a nutshell; the list of some of the escapees and all I can say is that, I am jolly well pleased that my Toni failed so miserably in all of her ludicrous ventures.

A Note from the Long-Suffering Servant

Remember me?

Yes, it's Toni, Kamehameha's; sorry, let me correct myself before His Majesty takes umbrage, 'King' Kamehameha's long-suffering servant.

I feel I need to set some parts of His Majesty's account straight; for, I feel, my Kamehameha has spoken way out of turn and made me look like some kind of raving lunatic, desperate to catch; or in his words, harpoon a hubby. I know you are all loyal fans, and faithful friends, of my Kamehameha; or, 'King' Kamehameha, as he has so generously bestowed on himself the sovereign address; but I am begging you not to take all that he says as gospel truth. I am not out to catch; or, as he says, harpoon a man; but neither am I going to throw one back into the ocean, so to speak, if one miraculously ticks all of the appropriate boxes. So far, unfortunately, between them all they have managed to tick only three out of sixty-seven.

You, ladies, will know how hard it is to secure someone, who is half decent, that belongs to the male species; let alone someone who, somehow, manages to fit adequately into all of our numerous, and detailed, specifications. The ones that take up the challenge are brave men indeed; the ones that succeed are extraordinary to say the least and I have, as yet, to find such a delightful specimen.

Now, with respect to my exceedingly high standards, a guy who is courageous enough to take up the gauntlet and venture forth for my highly scrutinizing consideration must be in possession of certain attributes of his own; above all, he must be honest and kind. I am not too bothered about his intellectual standards, so long as he can add to one hundred and his conversations don't bore me to death, as Graham's did during our last excruciating days together. Neither am I too bothered about his looks, so long as he doesn't resemble a creature from the black lagoon. Now I know Kamehameha; I've ditched his so-called royal title here, hopefully he won't notice; where was I? Oh yes, my Kamehameha always insists on a fun-loving suitor for me; but we all know my pooch is thinking of himself here. To be honest with you, I find fun-loving guys quite exhausting; remember Joe, the butterfly chaser? So, a stay-at-home kind of guy is okay for me, so long as he has a bit of get-up-and-go; I am not bothered about an excellent cook either; though, I know Kamehameha would have something to say on that point. No, as long as the chap is caring, honest, kind, trustworthy and God-fearing he has a spark of hope; though, the most important ingredient he must possess is that special something. Now, don't ask me what that special something is because I'm not sure what it is myself; but, when I do know I will, of course, let you in on it.

As well as passing my list of strict specifications, this potential hubby would have to pass one final test with flying colours; the poor guy would have to subject himself to Kamehameha's close and detailed scrutiny and we all know that would certainly be no picnic. All I can say, is good luck to any chap who decides to take the challenge; he is a brave man indeed and would be a most outstanding specimen if he, somehow, manages to acquire my pooch's approval because, after all, he is the king of the castle!

Toni x

An Important Address to My Faithful Subjects from Your King

I'm flabbergasted!

Yes, my dear and loyal subjects; I am absolutely flabbergasted. I had to reread Toni's statement nine times for the words to fully sink in and register. You are my witnesses, my dear friends; my mistress has announced that I am the king of the castle; so, if we happen to have any more disputes in the future, regarding my sovereignty over our castle, we now have undeniable, solid proof who the true, and only, sovereign really is.

On to the second subject of importance; I and you, my loyal subjects, know that if, by some phenomenal stroke of luck, a dashing knight in shining armour should happen to knock on our castle door, my Toni would follow him to the end of the world; however, we also know that the chances of that miracle happening are very thin, very thin indeed; so, I am certainly not going to worry my super intelligent head over such a trivial matter.

As for my mission; well, it was complete before it ever started. All I ever wanted was a peaceful life, with lots of scope for sporadic adventure and, so far, this has been successfully accomplished.

Toni's intrepid attempts at harpooning herself a man, and presenting me with a stepdad whether I wanted one or not, all failed miserably and for that I profusely thank all the Hawaiian gods I can possibly think of; for, now we have both come to realize that there is no room in our castle, or our hearts, for anyone else.

Long may we both reign!

PS Yes, you have read correctly. Long may we BOTH reign! For I have bestowed on my Toni the highest honour; the title of Queen!

Good health and happy, sunny thoughts to my Queen and to ALL of you, my dear friends.

Long live the king!
King Kamehameha x

Part Two
'King' Kamehameha in... Lockdown

Lockdown Preparations

Lockdown!

My dear loyal subjects, please forgive me for my uncharacteristic hesitancy; but, would you believe, it has taken me a whole day and most of the night, in which I was forced to sacrifice my essential beauty sleep, to get my super intelligent head around this ominous word… lockdown?

Well, you'll be pleased to know that I have now, got the gist of it and the gist I have got, I most certainly do not like at all. Apparently, my dear friends, there is a most detestable thing called a virus going round; spinning around and around our beautiful world and now the boss of our country, that lovely chap with the white hair, has decided that if we want a good chance of seeing our next birthdays, we need to adhere to some pretty severe, not to mention boring, lockdown rules.

After a careful; nay, scrupulous assessment of the situation, I have come to the conclusion that I, King Kamehameha, am going to be imprisoned inside my castle for a whole three weeks. A whole three weeks with my Toni! Can you imagine that scenario, folks? To be honest with you, I think I would rather have a serious dose of solitary confinement; but sadly, I don't think that's an option which is, I feel, a regretful shame. Anyway, suffice it to say, I am not looking forward to this hibernation period with my mistress; though, I must confess, she is getting things ready with a certain amount of zest and a generous dose of energetic vim. At this precise moment she is out of the castle and in the process of purchasing macaroni or pasta, whatever it's called; you know what I mean, the little dry, curly-wurly shapes you put into boiling water and serve up with some kind of delicious smelling sauce; not that I have had the pleasure of sampling such a delight. Anyway, she's out collecting provisions, like a grizzly preparing itself for a severe winter and I should be making the most of this precious time snoozing away and dreaming pleasurable dreams. Instead, my intelligent head is whirling with nagging worries and prickly anxieties and the gruesome thought of three whole weeks in lockdown with nobody but my Toni. Do you think I will survive?

Now, don't get me wrong. You, my friends, know I love nobody more than my Toni; well, maybe my Auntie Anusia; but, that's between you and me. But, three weeks incarcerated with my Toni, with nothing to do but look into each other's eyes, would send any pooch, no matter how tolerant, to the very brink of despair. So, you can see the predicament I am in. It is not a good one. I placed my whirling head on to my paws but sleep evaded me, as my stark eyes stared into the depths of a gloomy future ahead, and then I heard the outside door click.

I saw the cumbersome mounds of bulky packages, and overflowing grocery bags, before my eyes met a grim, flushed faced Toni, with her hair askew making her black floppy hat all lopsided, crash into our castle and plonk herself down on to the nearest kitchen chair, her bags and packages falling to the floor, causing a solitary toilet roll to fall out and roll delectably along the floor. My instinct was to pounce on this rolling roll; Toni's no-nonsense eyes made me seriously reconsider. Instead, my inquisitive eyes lingered on the sight of overflowing bags, hoping to catch sight of some tasty treats; but, not one single morsel did I spot; only a mound of toilet rolls were in view. Now, I think I have mentioned on a previous occasion, that I think my Toni has lost a marble, or two and I don't mean the rolling variety; but, now, I am certain she's lost them all! I mean, who in their right mind, would buy loads and loads of toilet rolls? I rose and cautiously ventured forth allowing my long, intelligent nose to sniff out any potential treats; instead, it made one contact after another with shiny packets of pasta; or, whatever you call these dry things in shiny packets, or the inevitable toilet roll. I raised my eyes to my exhausted looking mistress. Yes, I sadly concluded, she had most definitely lost every single one of her small grey cells and the evidence was right there in her shopping bags. I strolled into my den, curled up into a tight, fluffy, golden-white ball and pondered on my dismal future.

Week One of Lockdown

Now, if you think that was bad; that, my dear friends, was nothing compared to things which were to come; for, while I half watched and half listened to a toffee-nosed man on our television set, I heard that this lockdown session could be extended if we did not behave ourselves and observed the rules and, just in case I thought I was in the midst of some kind of weird nightmare, this guy repeated this grim possibility three times, as if once wasn't enough. My heart sank. We were only in our second day of this lockdown business and already I was plotting a series of intricate escape manoeuvres.

Strict rules had already been swiftly processed, and firmly established, and they were rules made by very important people, in that big, old place called, I think, Parliament; rules which, for example, stated that I was only allowed one walk a day. I decided to reflect on that particular rule a little later; another rule was that Auntie Anusia and I could no longer enjoy any more tête à têtes; in fact, she was banished from entering our castle and we were banished from entering her humble home. Toni could no longer go socializing, which was a kind of blessing in disguise, because, at least, I would be saved from the horrors of any potential stepdads; on the downside, however, there was no hope on earth that I could engage in a spot of socializing with my furry friends either. Neither would my Toni be doing any of her supply teaching work. It was going to be me and Toni and already, on day two, we were starting to get on each other's nerves.

For a start off, the menu had changed. This did not put me in a jovial mood at all. My tummy rumbled and a horrible, grizzly feeling invaded my heart and soul and made me severely question why Toni was punishing me for a virus I had nothing to do with. Let me explain the situation further. Instead of receiving my standard extra thick round of toast, with a generous serving of honey or strawberry jam; I received half a round of some new variety of unappetizing bread, thinly spread with some type of inferior. nondescript jam and the words, "In case we get rationed, Kamehameha." So, as you can well imagine, my spirit was firmly deflated before I even embarked on the day. And, it got worse.

Our one walk of the day was painstakingly torturous, to say the least. Gone were our leisurely, long strolls; now, Toni had decided we had to avoid all other humans like the plague and, as soon as she spotted one in the far away distance, we would dash across the road at breakneck speed and that wasn't without its flaws because, frequently, there happened to be a human on that side too; then, Toni and I would find ourselves zigzagging from one side to the other, weaving this way and that until I seriously didn't know whether I was coming or going and, as for Toni; well, I feel, she never truly knows whether she is coming or going anyway.

Now, if that was the end of the torture it, perhaps, wouldn't be that bad; but, no, my dear friends, a new rule has come into place and this particular rule is most distasteful and disagreeable to me. How would you like it, my beloved subjects, if after a gruelling and torturous walk you ventured into your kingdom and your paws; sorry, I mean your lovely feet, were subjected to a vigorous scrub and not just with mild scented lavender soap and water? Before I could place one royal paw into my castle, it had to go into a bowl of water, filled with some horrible smelling stuff called, disinfectant and not only that, it had to be arduously scrubbed with a not too soft scrubbing brush, then thoroughly dried and so did the other three paws. What a rigmarole! I decided there and then, as I was stood one quarter in and three quarters out of the bowl, that I was not going on any more walks. And, hence, our war commenced.

On the morrow, day three of lockdown, my resolute mind was made up; my paws were firmly tucked away beneath my cuddly body as I feigned heavy slumber.

"Right, Kamehameha; walkies!" Chirped Toni in her still, cheerful voice; though what she had to be cheerful about was beyond my understanding.

I don't think so. I stated silently though firmly.

"Kamehameha; come on."

Not on your life. I reinstated steadfastly; the image of the bowl full of that pungent liquid planted fixedly in my mind.

"Come on, Kamehameha."

I felt her plump, smooth hands on my fluffy neck and the soft leather collar go around my generous royal neck. Fervently I urged my acting prowess not to fail me at this crucial time, as I lay still as a horizontal rod.

"Kamehameha."

Not a minute move.

"Chocolate!"

I leaped!

"Gotcha!"

I stood, my eyes narrowing as I stared at my deceitful mistress. I mean, how low can one get deceiving me in this way? I continued to stare blatantly at her. My answer came. Obviously, three days of lockdown were affecting her badly. I let her off… this once. And off we marched and, needless to say, on my return the bowl, with its awful smelling stuff, came out again.

Apart from the rationed breakfasts, and the torturous walking experiences, there were other problems to deal with and as the days progressed, so did the problems. I will get back to these in more detail later and concentrate on the start of lockdown for now.

In the first week I noticed that Toni was becoming lazy. No longer did she rise at the crack of dawn, thankfully. Instead of rising at five forty five precisely, she would now start clattering about upstairs at seven o'clock, eight fifteen or even nine o'clock and, not only that; she was taking a longer duration of time in accomplishing her daily tasks. For example, instead of gobbling down her breakfast and rushing out to work at top speed, she would take a leisurely forty-five minutes to devour and savour her repast; instead of taking five minutes to wash her pots, it would take her fifteen minutes; instead of sweeping the kitchen floor in seven minutes, it would take her thirteen minutes and so on. I also noticed, and this my friends was a very bad sign, that my Toni was losing her sense of style; not that she had a great sense in the first place. So, instead of sprucing herself in a boring tweed skirt and twinset of a ghastly shade; or, short skirt and fashionable top, on the rare occasion she had harpooned a man; she descended the stairs in a pair of baggy jeans and oversized top, with her hair askew in all possible directions and, if that wasn't enough to make me shake my royal head and wince, her hair was changing colour on top to some despicable, ghastly grey shade. I tell you, she looked like some hippie who had, obviously, seen better days. The sight was most certainly not pleasing to my most discerning eyes; in fact, I had to look away, so horrifying did she look. But, to top it all off, she had the nerve to look down on me and have the audacity to say, "Ooh, Kamehameha, you look so scruffy." Can you imagine how I felt; a royal sovereign being criticized in this shameful manner while she, herself, looked like a scarecrow on a bad day. I tell you, my ancestors would have had her untidy head on a pole for a far lesser crime. Needless to say, we stared at each other and we both looked away in sheer disgust.

As the long week wore on and we only had each other for company, I noticed that my Toni was not her cheerful, happy self anymore. No, her cheerful, happy self had disappeared and was replaced by a quieter, a more thoughtful and serious Toni, who now couldn't even be bothered to talk to me all day long; though, if the truth be known, that was actually a soothing relief to my ears, as three-quarters of the time, I don't even think Toni knew what nonsense she was rambling on about.

As time wore on, we kind of withdrew into our own little worlds; our own desert islands and, instead of being a unit, we were islands drifting apart. I knew this did not bode well for our well-being and, one evening as she barely acknowledged me as she abandoned me for the night, I decided to formulate a lockdown plan of survival.

Lockdown Plan of Survival

So, here we both were in our second week of lockdown. We had, somehow, miraculously survived the first week and to say it had been torturous would be wishful thinking. By the end of it, not only was I willing to abandon my castle, and all of my worldly possessions, namely my plush Hawaiian duvet and cushion set and my bag of treats; but I yearned to zoom into space, at top speed, out of our solar system and as far away from Toni as I could possibly get. That, I soon learned sadly, was an impossibility. No rockets were available. All travel, except essential travel, was banned; although, I must admit, I had a concrete, full-proof argument to put forward to the chief astronaut; but I had to get to the space station in the United States of America to put my argument forward and that posed a problem.

And so, alas, my space dream became an abandoned project; at least, for the time being and I, and a sad eyed and miserable faced Toni, embarked on our second week of imprisonment.

Now, I mentioned at the end of the last chapter that I was planning a lockdown plan of survival; well, now I'd like to share it with you and see what you think. Any feedback from you would be most welcome.

King Kamehameha's Lockdown Survival Plan

1. A solo trip to the furthest part of space one can reach, as soon as travelling restrictions are lifted.
2. Swiftly remove, from Toni, her title of Queen and send her packing.
3. Completely ignore all new rules and regulations and start an anarchy.
4. Allow for nothing less than a castle full of fun and laughter.
5. Insist on the rule, Kamehameha's way; or, no way!
6. Curl up and die and go to Heaven where I can rule in peace. (Though, technically, this is not a survival rule of this world; but, my future home.)

So, what do you think, guys?

Mmm, I'm not too sure which I'll go for first; I still kind of like the first one; though, I am also leaning towards the castle full of fun and laughter rule; but, then, I do quite like number three rule too. Toni, I feel, will not take kindly to number two rule. Let me ponder for a while, my good friends.

Grooming Time

As the days merged and rolled into one Toni and I, to my absolute horror, began to acquire resembling characteristics and mannerisms. No longer did we rise up with the lark; no longer were we spruced up and looking the picture of beauty and elegance; though, I'm not sure I would ever have called my Toni elegant, let alone beautiful, bless her; no longer did we enjoy delicious bits of chocolate or cake and no longer did Toni dream of harpooning a guy. Neither did we play with our ball in the garden or even exchange glances. We were, as I have mentioned, drifting apart and each day the drift became wider and deeper.

As I have stated, one startling characteristic we shared was that we were starting to look the same; scruffy. Yes, you have heard it from the royal lips of Yours Truly, King Kamehameha. *Scruffy* is the word. My Toni was staring to look like an aged wizard, with kind of weird shades of hair colour. It was kind of grey on the top; yuk! Then, it sort of changed into a darker, chocolaty brown colour with lighter patchy shades and, I must say, she looked a proper spectacle, especially as she wore no make-up to camouflage her drained, pale face. To be honest, she looked like death warmed up, as they say, and she looked as if she felt it too.

I, my friends, was far… far from feeling myself. My fur was tangled with little bits and bobs of garden debris enmeshed deeply into my coat; the shiny gloss had all but disappeared and, instead, I wore a dull, drab, tangled coat; my nails desperately needed a manicure and, now, even my eyes had lost their sparkle.

Toni and I were like two miserable bedraggled ghosts of our former selves and, although I have never been a great fan of the grooming brush, I must admit, I wouldn't mind a little tickle of it on my tummy now.

My friends, you have heard of the saying, be careful what you wish for? If only, by some magic power, I could have extracted this last wish of mine. Too late. As I was lolling about, my empty tummy rumbling in eager anticipation of my meagre half a round of toast, with a thin scraping of some inferior jam, my eyes widened with horror. Instead of breakfast, out came the paraphernalia of brushes, combs, nail clippers, scissors, bottles of lotions and potions and a host of other unpleasant looking things, I care not to mention, and the dreaded words, "Enough is enough, Kamehameha. It's time for action!"

My bewildered eyes glared at my mistress and in her eyes, I saw a devious, determined gleam and, I must say, I did not much care for the gleam as, I knew from past experiences, it did not bode well for the status of my equilibrium. I braced myself, my eyes scrutinizing intensely the grooming utensils. This is not going to be a barrel of fun, I dimly thought; my hope regarding any kind of breakfast diminishing by the second. Closing my eyes, I began to psyche myself for the gruelling ordeal.

As I stood waiting for the chop, I began to reconsider the whole grooming thing; after all, Toni would be getting rid of all the nasty little prickles and annoying bits of leaves which had invaded my coat and, if I was to succumb, I would end up looking like the grand 'old' royal king I am.

My dear subjects, I beg you, never ever trust a gal with shiny nail clippers, let alone a pair of shears and especially if she has a suspicious glint in her eye; it spells TROUBLE!

I am not going to bore you with the intricate details, regarding the manoeuvres my Toni put me through, in order to achieve my eye-catching look and what a look it was!

The second she packed her paraphernalia away, I bounded to the mirror to take a good look at my gorgeous, handsome self, my excited heart beating loudly for my country and threatening to jump out of my chest as I stood and stared, my eyes growing wide as two round saucers. I blinked; blinked again and blinked a third time and when I opened my eyes I was still there. My friends, if I hadn't had been staring at myself, I would, by now, have been dead from a fit of uncontrollable laughter; for, what I saw was, undoubtedly, the funniest thing I have ever seen in my entire long life.

My intellectual beautiful head, thankfully, still remained looking super intelligent and beautiful; as for the rest of me… Forgive me, my friends, while I take a little while to compose myself; for, even now, though this is a memory, it is still as clear as crystal.

As I said, my head was still there and intact; but, everything else on me had changed; or, to be accurate, disappeared. If a deep, dark hole had claimed me for its own at that point in time, I would not have minded in the slightest. However, being the brave king I am, I faced what I was staring at and gave myself a careful and very detailed examination. My observant eyes looked down at my generous body; it was still fluffy but my fur was considerably shorter and no lingering bits were lodging there anymore. My eyes lowered down to my legs and there they stayed and, no matter how many times I blinked and how fervently I wished, my pins remained exactly the same; pins without fur; or, at the very most, the minimum amount of fur. Yes, my legs resembled four spindly pins with no luxurious fur adorning them.

So; as a quick résumé, profile, update or whatever you like to call it, I had a beautiful looking super intelligent top, namely my head; a body which, I guess, was passable, and four pins which were profoundly ghastly. I looked, my friends, like that Santa fellow you see in shops, at a particular time of the year and it is not the first time Toni has subjected me to this particular type of horror. And, no matter how long I stood and stared; stared and stood, the image remained exactly the same. I, King Kamehameha; a king of great stature and honour; a laughing stock more like.

There was, however, a tiny grain of comfort. At least, I concluded, we were in lockdown!

King Kamehameha on Strike

It took me another full day of lockdown to start recovering from my grooming ordeal. To be honest, I got to wishing that lockdown would be firmly held in place, until the day came when my ugly looking pins started to look like royal legs again.

Toni, on the other hand, couldn't wait for this lockdown business to end; I know this because I heard her rabbiting on the phone to my favourite auntie, Auntie Anusia. In fact, at this present time, my Auntie Anusia has far superseded my Toni on, My Favourite Person in the Whole Wide World list. Never ever, I know with absolute certainty, would my lovely, adorable Auntie Anusia subject me to such a humiliating and demoralizing grooming experience; never! So, yes guys, I am now wishing for a lockdown eternity, in which Toni can stew over what she has done to me; or, rather, what she has done to my royal legs.

Needless to say, I was not on cosy, pally terms with my owner. Two can play at her silly game, I decided and with that decision planted firmly in my mind, I decided to send my Toni to Coventry; unfortunately, not literary speaking, due to lockdown restrictions; but, the Coventry where one is ignored. And so, I set to work and it wasn't as easy a job as I first thought it would be, because ignoring Toni would, regrettably, mean ignoring her food. Nevertheless, I stuck to my principles and stuck my important head in the air, ignoring all her offers of toast, jam, honey, doggie treats and anything else she tried to tempt me with. I was on doggie strike!

Now, at the completion of the first day of downing my tools, so to speak, I was not at all impressed with this strike business. Before you start having your own ideas of going on strike, let me tell you, it is not much fun and it seemed to be rather all one sided; also, to top it all off, the only one in our castle that seemed to be suffering was me, the sovereign.

My strike was definitely not going according to plan. I was not presented with a bowl of roast beef with lashings of thick gravy, big chunks of chocolate or even the odd doggie chocolate digestive; in fact, the whole thing was backfiring; Toni, my friends, was quite content to just ignore me; but, how to rectify the situation and get my own way; that was indeed a very baffling puzzle. I'd seen news bulletins in the past where disgruntled workers stopped working, stood outside their factories and got a reward of more pay. All I got when I refused to eat Toni's boring food and went into a deep sulking session in protest, was the cold eye from my mistress and a rumbling tummy. Her heart had gone. Where? I don't know; all I am certain of is that it had left her premises leaving behind a moody, bad-tempered, boring and lethargic Toni. And I don't even know what she was so miserable about; after all, it was me who ended up with the stick legs!

But I was a brave, strong willed king and fight on I would. However, there was a matter of great importance; how could a great and honourable king march onwards at full throttle on an empty, rumbling tummy? This was indeed a problem because, as you know, I had refused to eat and, even more worrying, was the fact that Toni was blatantly accepting and complying with my self-imposed hunger strike, as if it was the most natural thing to do. What was I to do? To eat; or, not to eat was the troubling question and the more I thought about this dilemma, the more baffling the whole thing became, even in my super intelligent brain. For, to eat would be to succumb and not to eat; well, you my dear friends, know what that would ultimately mean. I lay in my den and brooded and whilst brooding, I decided I most certainly would not be going out into the world with these ghastly pins of mine. No way! Toni could ask, cajole, attempt different methods of cunning persuasion; try and drag me off, although I'd like to see her try; furiously hop about from foot to foot; or, jump up and down like a Jack-in-the-box; but no way was I voluntary going out into the Great Outdoors to be ogled, teased and heartily laughed at. No way!

"Chocolate!"

I sprang up like that Jack-in-the-box I have just mentioned and stood, completely forgetting my resolve, mouth wide open and saliva dribbling uncontrollably down my cheeks, as I waited expectantly for the smooth, brown chunk as it hovered about in Toni's podgy fingers. And then, my excited heart plummeted a stark realization invaded every one of my senses, making my watery mouth clamp tightly against the tempting, delectable chocolate, which was still luring me into a tempting point of surrender. With all of my doggie might I forced my eyes to abandon the inviting brown junk of sheer loveliness and switched my attention to Toni, staring unblinkingly at my devious mistress, as a fresh spring of saliva threatened to expose me for the weakling I was now beginning to portray. I closed my eyes tightly to muster a new, stronger determination as the alluring image danced enticingly in my mind until… I could stand the torture no more. Opening my mouth as wide as I possibly could, I felt the piece pop in and immediately felt its smooth, silky-like texture. It was sure bliss. I closed my eyes to savour the melting creaminess which, by now, was invading all of my senses. I also felt the familiar collar being attached around my neck and the no-nonsense words, "We're off, Kamehameha." And, before I could gather all of my wits around me, we were indeed off, out of the house, down the road and into the throes of a purposeful walk. At this stage of the proceedings, I was not in a good mood at all. If the truth be known, my friends, this particular king was in the midst of a very deep sulk as he, that is I, walked begrudgingly on; or, rather, was pulled along with my royal head bent low, eyes downcast and my ears and tail definitely drooping. As for my heart, it was a wonder it was still beating at all; for, it was shattered in thousands of fragments and each fragment was a symbol of disappointment; for, I asked myself, how could Toni betray me in this way? How could she stoop so low, knowing full well that I would sooner pop my clogs, than say *no* to a piece of delicious, mouth-watering chocolate? I must admit, I started there and then to see her in a new light; I saw her as a cunning deceiver. Well, I pondered, two can play at her game and I planted myself in the middle of the pavement and refused to budge, even one tenth of a centimetre, while my mistress smiled, tugged, grimaced, pulled, scratched her multi-coloured head, threatened me with untold revenge and eventually stood staring icily at me, while I repositioned myself more comfortably. Now, I was sitting mighty proud on my hind legs, my head held high as I portrayed an image of imperial status, excellent breeding, honour, pride and respectability; for, no one messes with King Kamehameha, not even his mistress.

Long minutes went by as, regally, I sat. I must admit, I felt a twinge of sympathy for my frustrated servant as she shuffled uncomfortably from foot to foot, while my delicate ears were subjected to a barrage of threatening words of the most unsavoury nature, I dare not repeat. As for her glances thrown my way; suffice it to say, a thousand sharp pointed needles would have been less offensive to the eye. I continued to sit elegantly; a most becoming image of extreme beauty, apart from my ghastly pins, while my red-faced Toni stamped, shuffled, sighed heavily and continued to pull and tug without the slightest trace of success for her effort, except a great deal of frustration adding to her already ruffled equilibrium and as for her blood pressure…

And we would have remained there until kingdom come, if her ears had not been subjected to the continuous tooting of car horns and the gasps and tut-tutting of passing strangers. My heart leaped. I recognized the sound of a particular horn; there is no other like it in the whole wide world, possibly the universe. It's a kind of a squeaky, high-pitched sound which often goes off-piste and into a kind of whistling, oozing reverberation; it is the sound that belongs to the horn of my Auntie Anusia's battered old motor and it is the most joyous sound in this world. And, here she was, as large as life and laughing her head off! In fact, so loud and uncontrollable was her laughter it threw her into a fit of choking.

I continued to sit haughtily, not moving a single muscle; though, I must admit, my eyes flitted over to my most favourite auntie in the world and lingered on her, somewhat, red, flushed face while she coughed, spluttered and tried desperately to cling on to life. By now, Toni had left my side and was doing something, or other, to my Auntie Anusia's back. I moved a few cautious centimetres in order to assess the situation more scrupulously. I moved a few more centimetres. I stopped; a sudden flash of instinct telling me to THINK. What if this was some kind of an elaborate ruse to trap me? What if somehow, magically, while I was sat there all high and mighty, my Toni had informed my auntie of what had happened, called in the cavalry and they were both in cahoots? I sat back down and narrowed my suspicious eyes. I must admit my poor Auntie Anusia did not look to be in a good way; for, by now, she was gasping for some much needed air.

Like a wildcat I sprang and was by my auntie's side and, miraculously; don't ask me how but in the midst of barking, jumping, gasping, spluttering, crying and sighing between the three of us we managed to bring my Auntie Anusia back from the brink of deaths door.

Now, you may wonder what my auntie was thinking of, escaping lockdown procedures and driving about the place in her battered old contraption. Well, when I found out, my heart almost broke with love for her. She, my friends, was on an important personal mission, an errand of mercy, to make sure that I, King Kamehameha, continued to be ensconced with a bountiful supply of luxuries, by bringing me a king-sized bag, rather like a sack, full to the brim with my favourite doggie chocolate bars and other yummy delights. Wow! I still can't believe what a pure gem of an auntie I have got and when I think back to what treacherous lengths my Toni stooped down, to bribe me into going on a walk, one measly bit of chocolate, it doesn't bear thinking about.

Anyway all I am going to further say on the subject is this, if I could have predicted my auntie's admirable intentions, I would never have subjected myself to the efforts of enforcing a strike in the first place!

Retirement Plan

Needless to say, these are not my retirement plans no… no… no. A king of my great stature and presence cannot, for a split second, think of any form of retirement; for, the moment he succumbs to that particular notion, he is on a very fast downward spiral and then, my dear subjects, a great king becomes merely a memory and who wants to be a distant memory? I ask you. Certainly not I; for, I intend to rule over my castle, and Toni, until I pop my clogs and, if things go well and according to plan, I aim to rule in doggie heaven too.

Anyway, back to the retirement subject. It is no other than my Toni who is thinking of retiring and I have got to do everything in my power to deter her from such an unsavoury notion. I mean, can you for one moment imagine my Toni and I, together in the same castle, with only each other for company, forever and with no hope of a respite? Well, I can't; the trials and tribulations of lockdown have already been an insight into this potential disaster. You know the tribulations I mean; getting under each other's feet; having nobody else but each other to gawp at day after day, after day; encroaching on each other's valuable space and so on.

You see, well before lockdown my Toni was already kind of semi-retired; that means some of the time she was at home but most of the time, thankfully, she was out earning pennies, in order to keep me in treats and the royal luxuries I am not only used to; but, of course, expect. Now, during the days she is not called out to one of her schools; I think I've told you that my Toni is a supply teacher, we put up with each other's moods and whims; but frequently, she is called out to these establishments called schools and being quite a popular teacher she's here, there and everywhere; a bit like that pimpernel fellow. Actually, my dear friends, you may have come across her; you know, when your usual teacher is a bit off colour and needs a break. Let me describe her to you again and then, if you come across her in the future, you'll know she's attached to me and refrain from placing a repulsive frog on her chair. She is kind of short, a bit on the plump side and her hair; well, when she's on the prowl to harpoon herself a guy, its long, blonde and quite glamorous; when she is not on a harpooning mission, it is dark and neatly secured into a tight bun and she also dresses accordingly; she's either in short skirts and fashionable tops or twinsets and as for her nails; well, she's either sporting stubs or talons; you get the picture? Anyway, now you may not come across her at all, if she decides to go through with this retirement nonsense.

It still baffles me how exactly she got this retirement notion into her silly head. I am, though, pretty sure the idea grew during our lockdown and has now mushed up the few brain cells she had. But what to do with this particular problem; that is my greatest concern, and, at present, I am truly perplexed. Indeed, at this moment in time, I am summoning up all of my super intelligent cells to come to the rescue; however, uncharacteristically, they seem to be somewhat elusive.

I tossed and turned all night and at the break of dawn I was feeling un-refreshed, gloomy, irritable and not at all my sparkling self. Toni, on the other hand, came pounding down the stairs at top speed, breezed into the kitchen and bestowed on me a wide, cheerful smile and humming tunelessly, instantly making me quiver all over. If this was a taste of what was to come, I am seriously thinking of taking drastic measures of abandoning my castle and finding a full-time job myself.

This new idea of mine grew and grew until I could think of nothing else. I think I have told you previously about my first rate sheepdog qualifications. Remember; when I ended up on Farmer Bill's establishment; or, more accurately speaking, his sheep farm and I ended up being a sheep herder alongside another pooch called, Spot? So, yes, I have got excellent qualifications in that area of work.

I could, I feel, be an expert food taster; for, as you know, I love to indulge in the tasty things somewhat; hence my rather rotund tummy and, let's be honest, I have sampled various culinary offerings of Toni's creations some good, some of a medium standard and some; well, all I am going to say, it's a pure miracle I'm still alive to tell the tale. So, yes, I have some experience in this area and would, I feel, qualify as a high-class food taster for our wonderful sovereign who, I believe, lives in quite a grand palace. So, yes, I would even consider forgoing my own castle to reside in the monarch's abode, just to be on hand; that's how utterly selfless I am, folks. Yes, I am definitely thinking of sending my outstanding résumé to the palace.

Then, there is a chaperoning job to consider. Let's face it, I have had more than enough experience in this line of work; sifting out many a bad egg who would, by now, have been Toni's hubby, and my stepdad, if I hadn't have ventured in and saved the day. So, yes, a chaperoning job, providing the treats are in plentiful supply, would be okay with me.

There are many other jobs I would be extremely proficient in; but, the job of all jobs; the ultimate top job I would most certainly apply for, and let me tell you there would be no worthier candidate than I, King Kamehameha, is the job of hiring out my royal self for a period of time. I would, of course, NOT consider being hired out to all and sundry; in other words, if any old Tom, Dick or Harry applied for my services they would be sorely disappointed. Only clients of a very superior status need apply; for, if I am to be hired out to an establishment, whether it's for an hour, a day or a week, I expect top-notch luxuries and nothing less. In exchange, the successful and very lucky applicant would receive my excellent company, the delight of looking at a most dazzling image of elegance and, most importantly, my royal presence. Now, this last attribute, as you and I know, is invaluable; there is not a high enough price in this world for this unique privilege and the lucky candidate must be prepared to give it the due respect it deserves.

So, there you have it; Toni is preparing to slow down and I am preparing to rev up; so, our time together will soon be very limited, thus decreasing the possibility of killing each other. Time will, of course, determine our ultimate fate.

As I was pondering deeply on the above Toni announced cheerily, "So, Kamehameha, it's going to be you and me from now on. I shall give in my notice and then we will start our retirement together; but…" She threw me a gravy bone which I snapped up immediately; which is just as well, for her next words made my heart sink. "We'll have to tighten our belts." I did not like this last statement of hers at all and, instantly, began to think furiously about what job I was going to opt for.

Now, let's go through my options again, my dear friends, because I am definitely going to be asking for your input on these ideas of mine.

Number one job, making my way back to Farmer Bill's farm; the mere idea of that delicious possibility sends hundreds and thousands of exciting goose pimples around my body; for, as you know, I had an absolutely fantastic time on the farm with Spot and Jamie; so much so, I was in two minds whether, or not, to return to my own kingdom and, if it wasn't for the fact that my Toni had ended up on her deathbed, and would have gone through the dastardly dying process, if it wasn't for my scintillating company, I would still be residing happily on the farm to this very day, running joyously after my sheep friends.

One thought deters me from gathering my Hawaiian duvet and cushion set, and my hoard of treats, and setting off at top speed, and that is the thought of young Jamie. She is settled with Spot and with the possibility of Yours Truly turning out of the blue; well, that would upset the apple-cart, so to speak. It's a dilemma I'll have to ponder over very carefully in the next few days, as I scrupulously assess my future.

Job number two, working for our present sovereign; the prospect of being employed as our dear sovereign's chief food taster would, I feel, be a most delightful job; the mere thought of it is, uncontrollably, sending dribbling saliva down my face. Imagine, if you will, your king sampling mouth-watering delicacies and luxuries all day long: fat sizzling sausages, thick slabs of beef steaks fried to ultimate perfection and I am certain that some kind of pheasant would be on the menu too, and, what about the endless variety of cakes and gateaus and posh ice-creams with tiny umbrellas? A stark, black thought crashed into my head as Akoni, my Hawaiian friend, came sharply into focus, and the memory of what I thought was his poison-laced Haupia. And, with this memory, came the shock realization that the job of the sovereign's chief food taster would be to identify any hidden poison. What if I popped my clogs in the line of duty? No; on second thoughts, this was not the job for me.

On to job number three, the job of chaperone. Now, I have told you before that I am expertly qualified in this area of work; for, unfortunately, I have had heaps of experience in sifting through my Toni's disastrous dates and, let me tell you, it was no fun at all. Can you remember me telling you about that guy with the ghastly socks; or, Joe, the butterfly chaser; or, indeed, that finicky, pompous chap who took hours in arranging the crockery in its place and who nearly bored me to death in the process? Another round of that sort of thing would definitely send me into orbit which, on reflection, would be much preferable than living through another similar, excruciating ordeal. No, my chaperoning days are well and truly over!

That leaves me with job number four, the hiring of my good self. Now I have to seriously ask myself; do I really want to end up in any old common establishment, where royal protocol has no place, let alone meaning? No, I most certainly do not want to end up in a place that does not cater for the high standard of respect and luxuries I am accustomed to, and expect; not even for the duration of five minutes.

So; where does this leave Toni and myself? I ask you. Back to square one; that's where. And, the last time I looked, Toni was still humming happily, and tunelessly, away busily planning our mutual retirement.

Now, can you honestly imagine Toni and I ensconced in a happy, cosy bubble in my castle? Can you; because, I certainly can't? I am looking at the bigger picture, my dear subjects; I am looking forward in time, when the novelty of this retirement business has evaporated away and we are left with the bare bones of the after-effects. I imagine a dull, rainy autumnal day and Toni is bored out of her skull; when she's arduously scrubbed in, and out, of her kitchen cupboards ten thousand times; when she's rummaged through her extensive wardrobe a dozen times sorting, and resorting, her ghastly attire; she's scrubbed me until I'm so meticulously clean I gleam and now we're tripping over each other and getting on each other's fragile nerves. My friends, I think you understand me, when I tell you we need our individual space, at least ten metres apart and we are not going to get it, if Toni embarks on her retirement scheme. Quick! There is no time to lose; something has to be done, post-haste. A concrete, full-proof plan needs to be swiftly formulated, and set to immediate action, before… it's too late!

All night my intelligent grey cells worked overtime as they whirled and swirled, mingled and intermingled until, finally, as the first speck of light filtered through the kitchen blind, I came up with a sensational plan. I was, my friends, going to make life in my castle unbearable for Toni and, soon, she would be running, at top speed and breaking all world records in the process, to one of her schools.

There was no time to lose. I set myself to work immediately. making my way to Toni's door of entrance of a morning and spreading myself out leisurely. Sure enough, I heard her plodding down the stairs and striding towards me. I feigned deep sleep.

"Aloha, Kamehameha." She chirped happily. "Kindly move."

I don't think so. I replied silently and most defiantly.

She knew I wasn't dead because, as I raised one involuntary eye, our eyes locked.

"Kindly move yourself, Kamehameha."

I narrowed my eyes. King Kamehameha, if you please, I silently corrected her; but move, I did not.

I could sense her hovering over me; wondering, no doubt, what had got into me. Instantaneously and spontaneously, she raised one hedgehog slippered foot over my head. There it lingered while she waited for me to move. I didn't; not at that point, anyway. Her foot remained dangling precariously over my head which, of course, contain my super intelligent cells, until I decided I had had enough of this carry-on. I moved. Unfortunately, at that precise moment, she moved too swaying this way and that until she lost her balance, stumbled and was about to fall on top of me. Now, as you know my Toni, bless her, is no featherweight. Too late, I tried to escape her fall; but, before I could run for my life, she fell on top of me and we were both frantically scrambling for our lives and, let me tell you, I flashed a gleaming gnasher, or two. Of course, it was only a defence mechanism; I would no sooner hurt my Toni than hurt a fly. It worked. She espied my flashing pearly whites and moved rapidly away, banged her head on a cupboard door and ended up seeing a trillion shining stars. I, on the other hand, raised my regal self, shook my fur back into its place and strolled casually into my den, where I closed my eyes and smiled to myself. Battle one to me.

Battle two came the day after battle one. It came during breakfast time which is normally a calm, pleasurable experience; but, not so that particular morning; at least, not for Toni. This battle was won so easily, and so quickly, it is hardly worth mentioning. One minute I was eating my thick round of toast, smeared generously with yummy strawberry jam; the next minute, as Toni's eyes were glued to something or other on the moving screen, the television set I think it is called, I stealthily crept up to her plate, placed my dribbling mouth on to her fine china and took her toast away and, before she knew what had happened, it was settling happily in my grateful tummy and I was licking my chops in thankful appreciation.

"Kamehameha!"

I was fully ensconced in my den when I heard my name; but I knew the sharp tone well enough to know that my Toni was not amused. Off she went to make herself another round. Back she came with the tasty, jam laced toast on her plate. This time my challenge was even easier to accomplish. The silly gal held her breakfast precariously in her fingers, while she was gawping once more at the screen. I think you know how it went.

Some minutes later, I began to ease myself into blissful slumber, with a very content tummy and my ears attune to the gnawing rumblings of my mistress's empty tummy. Such is life!

Ah well; so far, so good. But, my dear subjects, this was not the time to start being complacent; this was not the time to lay leisurely back in one's den and dream of sizzling sausages. Oh no… no… no. Strike while the iron is hot; isn't that what they say? I had to set my paws firmly back on the warpath, especially after I had listened into the conversation my Toni was having with my favourite auntie the other day and this is how a snippet of it went. "So, yes, in answer to your question, Anusia, I am still en route to a blissful retirement."

En route… en route, I pondered, but not there yet. There was still hope. In that moment in time, I decided I would have to up my game, if I was to ever succeed in sending my Toni back to work. Once more I propped my intelligent head on to my fluffy, golden-white paws and pondered deeply and, once more, my super-duper cells worked their magic!

In the meantime my mistress decided that she was, once again, going to try and lose some of her podgy self. Out came the scores of fitness videos she had shoved to the very back of a cupboard wishing, at the time, never to clap eyes on them again; out came her shorts, T-shirt and sweatband; the exercise bike, rowing machine, the mini trampoline and some other contraption, with strings that you hang on to a door knob. I dread to even think how the last thing works; just one fleeting look at it makes the mind boggle. Anyway this time, unlike the previous times, I was delighted to see the sight of all these things because, with them, came potential opportunities for chaotic mayhem; though, I must admit, the thought of seeing Toni's tree trunk legs did not thrill me at all.

The first exercise session commenced, and I looked on in complete awe, as my mistress jumped up and down, stretched and curled tightly into a ball; danced, trotted and bounced about like something possessed, whilst looking as if she was about to catch her last breath and expire from sheer exhaustion. But no, not my Toni; like a true trouper she carried on puffing and panting, red and sweaty, sighing and gasping for breath and, to be honest with you, not looking a pretty picture at all. I was mesmerized; truly hypnotized as I continued to enjoy this very unique, and rather ghastly, spectacle.

A thought crashed into my mind, rudely interrupting my pleasant state of mind and ruffling up my equilibrium. This was the time to act; not to sit pretty and enjoy oneself. Toni's retirement was looming. It had to be stopped. Up I got and wandered into her space.

"Excuse me, Kamehameha." She panted, jumping on the spot like some frightful, oversized jumping bean.

I stood as still as a rod, my eyes lured to the young guy moving agilely on the screen his movements, unlike Toni's, perfectly in rhythm with the music. My eyes flitted to my mistress who was now gasping for much needed air. This was no time to stand and ogle, I admonished myself severely. I moved closer to Toni's uncoordinated jumping feet as she stumbled to one side.

"Kamehameha; move out of the way; now!"

I raised my eyes to my panting, red-faced owner. That was no way to address a king. My feet remained firmly and stubbornly in place and my shrewd eyes remained steadily fixed on Toni. She could budge if she wanted to; I was not a king for budging. There we stayed in a static pose until Toni decided to prance around once more and so did I. The slower she went, the more I jumped about; the faster her tree trunk legs moved, the faster my paws moved about the floor until we were both going hither and thither, whirling and twirling; going round and round and round and round; round and round and round and round until… CRASH!

I heard an ominous creak; then another creak; then everything went black and still. Only the energetic voice belonging to the guy on the screen, and his lively music, could be heard and then… everything became a blur.

Eventually, when I opened one cautious eye, I immediately closed it. I did not see what I saw, I told myself. But… I did see it. Slowly, I opened both eyes and, let me tell you, to this very day I see the image as large as life and twice as clear. There… there was my Toni and she was in the midst of the most incredulous act, of laboriously trying to manoeuvre her doubled up torso, which resembled a unique snake, so twisted was it; but each time she moved a mere centimetre a gruesome, agonizing wail emitted out of her twisted mouth. Was this some new fitness manoeuvre she was trying to conquer? I asked myself. If it was, then good luck to her; I was certainly not about to join her in this one. I continued to stare as she slithered, sighed and gasped. My eyes narrowed as I ruminated. On second thoughts, this could be fun. I made a move. Agh! Another move. Agh! Agh!!

Gingerly, I manoeuvred my left paw. It was all right. I must have been imagining things. Confidently I began to unfurl my right paw. Agh!!!!!!!! I not only saw stars; I saw comets, meteors, black holes; the sun, the moon and an odd looking astronaut. Had I popped my clogs? My bemused eyes flitted here and there and rested on Toni who was, incidentally, still slithering along the wooden floor and gasping for England. Had she, finally, gone completely raving mad? Without thinking I moved my torso. Agh! Had I gone mad? Had we both landed in some weird twilight lunatic zone? I stared after my slithering mistress and my question was answered. Yes, we had both, finally, arrived there. At that particular moment she looked around and I so wish she hadn't. The icy glare she threw me, my friends, made me shiver and quiver inside and out in equal measures. We both looked away. I can honestly say, without any exaggeration on my part whatsoever, that at that point of the proceedings, if we were situated on opposing polar caps, we would still be much too close for comfort. Unfortunately, we had to make do with opposite sides of the kitchen and there we continued to lay and glare at each other until, finally, we both closed our eyes and we must have dozed off respectively.

After a blissful, but all too brief, escape into oblivion I cautiously opened one eye; I opened two. Could I be seeing what I thought I was seeing; or, was I still ensconced in some dream, or other? Narrowing my puzzled eyes, I peered closer. There was my Toni hunched over me, with my right paw in her chubby hands, whilst she was diligently wrapping something white, soft and long around it; around and around it went until she finally, and to me relief, secured it with a neat little bow. Now, at this stage of events, my friends, I daren't look into her eyes; for, I was not feeling the tingling of love for my mistress. On the contrary, I was still reeling inwardly with the after-effects of her icy eyes on me. Still, I had to admit, my precious paw was feeling more comfortable and did no longer hurt so much when I moved it; though moving it, I soon found out, was not a straightforward act as my paw was stiff and wouldn't bend properly.

As the minutes ticked away, my heart started to mellow towards my Toni. She had definitely made my right paw better and, when I thought about it logically, the whole sorry affair had actually been propelled by Yours Truly. As my mistress with one bandaged up leg grabbed the side of a kitchen unit and, laboriously, tried to stand I saw that her face was contorted with ugly creases and her forehead beaded with sweat and my heart melted further. Maybe she wasn't such a bad old soul, after all; however, that admission of mine does not make it all right for Toni to go ahead with her retirement plan; oh no… no… no! This round, I conceded, should go to us both; but, it's onwards and forwards to the next stage; for, there was a war to be won and we all knew who was going to win it!

The following battle was the last; at least for the time being, because I was getting mighty exhausted, not to mention bored, with this retirement nonsense. So, I decided, if this was going to be my last attempt at preventing Toni from venturing into blissful retirement, it had to be a battle worth its salt. And, I must say, my super intelligent brain cells were tossed this way and that; I planned and unplanned; I schemed and then threw my schemes out of the window; I plotted and nearly gave up entirely. And, if it wasn't for the little voice in my very clever head telling me that I, King Kamehameha, always persevered no matter what; I would have given up and made detailed preparations for my own retirement.

Now, I'm not going to tell you about the intricate details of the plan I had formulated, my dear subjects; as, I feel, that you'll think I'm an excellent candidate for the loony bin. Suffice it to say; this was a plan like no other. It would either work brilliantly and I would reap its rewards; or, I would have gone to an awful lot of trouble to no avail. I will, however let you in on the bones of it. Simply put, I was going to stick to Toni like glue; wherever she went, I would follow her like her shadow; whatever she did I would be there by her side, whether she wanted me to be there or not. This is how the whole thing unfolded.

Day one; Toni breezed into the kitchen and immediately, like a flash of greased lightning, I rose, sauntered to her side and stood as close as I possibly could get to her tree trunk legs, as she popped our rounds of bread into the toaster. "How are you, Kami?" She cheerfully enquired.

King Kamehameha, if you don't mind. I admonished her severely.

Sitting primly at the table, I placed my paw lightly on her podgy lap and looked endearingly into her eyes. She looked down at me in a somewhat bemused way, making lots of little fine cobwebby lines form around her puzzled eyes, her brow wrinkling and causing more lines to appear. "What's got into you this morning; you're not normally this good mannered, Kami?"

King Kamehameha. I corrected her once again, becoming fed up with this particular rigmarole. And, if you don't mind, my manners are always a spectacle to be admired! She moved to the worktop and refilled her coffee mug. Swiftly I moved to join her. She sat down. I sat down close by her side, attached to my Toni with invisible glue.

"I don't know what has got into my Kamehameha, Anusia," I heard her say to my favourite auntie over the telephone, sometime later, "but, he will not leave my side. I think he may be coming down with something; he hasn't eaten anything either, as he's too busy gawping at me as if there is no tomorrow." And, then to my ultimate dismay, and utter horror, she mentioned the dreaded word; the most odious word in the English dictionary; not to mention the whole wide world, V… E… T!

My eyes shot to my bowl. Indeed, it was still heaped to the brim with my doggie food. For the first time in my long distinguished life, I had completely forgotten about my precious tummy; after all, I had more pressing issues to think about, namely a lifetime of retirement with my Toni. My eyes drifted back and forth, from my breakfast to my mistress, back to my breakfast and so on. V… E… T………. V… E… T…… V… E… T…… The word crashed mercilessly in and out of my mind…… V… E… T…… Without another thought I approached my bowl as fast as my three healthy, and one poorly, bandaged leg would carry me, gulped down my breakfast in record speed, and without actually tasting one single morsel, and hastened back to my mistress's side where I, once again, stuck to her like a faithful limpet.

Placing her receiver down she cast her bewildered, and somewhat worried, eyes on me and shook her head slowly from side to side, then she turned and took steps out into the garden and I abruptly followed.

Gardening was a most entertaining experience and, my dear friends, I most fervently recommend it. Actually, not only do I recommend it; I insist all my subjects should become little gardeners and report back to me on your progress. Perhaps you could share with me some of your gardening tips. I would highly recommend planting a purple buddleia; it is a favourite of my special friends, the butterflies; they love it. I must say, I thoroughly enjoyed my first gardening experience and can't wait for the second one to come along; although, my friends, I can't say the same for my Toni.

She had embarked on pulling out the weeds and so did I. Being a novice in this line of work, I scrutinized her very carefully as she pulled out long dangling green stems with little yellow flowers and I copied her; only, I went a step further, being the diligent worker I am; I eagerly pulled out the long green stems with purple, red and white flowers too and thought, what a lot of work I had saved my Toni and how very grateful she would be.

Grateful, is not the word to have described my Toni. One glance at her furious eyes, her firm set mouth and her furrowed brow told me, in no uncertain terms, that she was not only angry with me; but she would dearly like to see my head on the end of a pole, preferably detached from my body. Obviously, I concluded, I was not doing enough work. I averted my eyes from her and dug my paws in deeper; digging out more green stems with cheerful colourful flowers and, haphazardly, threw them hither and thither not caring where they landed.

But, care I did sometime later, when Toni frogmarched me up the garden stepping stones and commanded me to sit, without moving a muscle, outside the door of our castle. As I dared to move a muscle, with the intention of venturing inside and sticking to my Toni like glue, the door was firmly slammed in my face; the loud bang of the slamming door producing disturbing effects in my delicate ears. There I sat and there I pondered. Was I about to get some kind of great reward for my gardening services? Delightful images of sizzling sausages, large portions of succulent roast chicken, mouth-watering slabs of textured chocolate loomed large in my mind; pleasantly weaving and interweaving with each other, until the door opened and my wide, expectant eyes dropped to a bowl of water, an unfriendly looking scrubbing brush and a large bar of disgusting looking soap. As I raised my perplexed eyes, I looked upon a scowling face, which promised unpleasant things to come; certainly not things that would make my tummy perform happy somersaults. I blinked. I blinked harder and blinked harder still; but the image remained exactly the same; the bowl of water, the scrubbing brush, the soap and the scowling face. To say I was bemused would be the understatement of the year. I was truly at a loss and the more I tried to unravel my puzzled thoughts, the more utterly confused I became.

Within twenty minutes it all, however, became perfectly clear, the confusing mist lifted and the error of my ways; though, well-intentioned, became clear. In the midst of vigorously scrubbing my paws Toni stated, "And, for pulling out all of my beautiful flowers; the flowers I have tenderly grown from seed and bulb; nurtured and watered and sang to… (Well, I wouldn't call her screeching singing)… you… YOU, Kamehameha; well, you see how you like going without a single treat for a whole day."

I fell into a deep lapse of silence, while I pondered the grim thought of a whole day without a single treat. I sighed heavily. It was a bad outcome; but it could have been worse; the ban could have lasted a week. I might just survive, I concluded as Toni scrubbed and rubbed with all the zest she could muster and I resigned myself to my fate and resolved to redouble my efforts in re-establishing my role as Toni's personal shadow; her retirement scheme still firmly hovering in both of our minds.

I was scrubbed until I positively dazzled, after which I sat obediently close to her side and would have gazed lovingly into her eyes until kingdom come; but my Toni was having none of this lovey-dovey nonsense. There she sat, looking down at me as if I was some despicable worm and then, would you believe, she had the audacity to state haughtily, "I am not amused, Kamehameha!"

Well, neither am I, I wanted to tell her in no uncertain terms. In fact, I was eons from being the tiniest bit amused. Imagine, if you were a royal sovereign of great esteem, being scrubbed most robustly without a plush, soft towel anywhere in sight and then given such an icy glare, making all your bits and pieces shrivel up. Well, let me tell you, I am still reeling from the injustice of it all especially as you and I know; I only wanted to give my Toni a helping paw in the garden. Well, all I can say is, never again!

As I sat there brooding on my miserable state, I espied Toni's hedgehog slippers resting in the corner of the kitchen. Quick as lightning I was up, had one smelly slipper clenched firmly in my pearly whites and was bringing it over to my annoyed mistress. Carefully I planted it down, employed the same routine with the other ghastly slipper, sat down on my hind legs and waited patiently for some kind of a reward. I waited and waited. I noticed that she had put on her slippers and there I sat waiting. But as I have told you before; my Toni's word is her bond and no treats meant exactly that; no treats. My heart sank, as did my eyes and soon my whole body followed.

When I awoke my Toni had disappeared; but, not her slippers. With a heavy laden heart, full of the burden of sadness, I picked up her foot attire and retreated with them into the sanctuary of my den. In I dismally entered and down I lay and I didn't care if I popped my clogs.

Dawn broke and I awoke to find that I hadn't popped my clogs; but, when my still sleepy eyes looked around my sleeping quarters, I fervently wished I had. All over my crumpled Hawaiian duvet, and luxurious tropical cushions, were tattered pieces of something, I couldn't quite recognize. I peered closer and closer still. I was in a complete state of total bewilderment. I lifted my healthy paw and moved it among the unidentifiable bits and pieces. I froze. Slowly, my eyes widened to big saucers as icy realization struck me with the full force of a thunderbolt and a horrific jigsaw began to emerge and formulate an image; or, rather, two images. What I saw in my mind's eye made me quiver at the knees, like a wobbly strawberry jelly, my dear friends. I saw… I saw… Toni's tattered hedgehog slippers. Toni's slippers! Can you, for one moment, imagine how I felt? I can't adequately describe the feeling myself, except to say that my whole body, not just my knees were now shaking and trembling not like a strawberry jelly, as I previously mentioned; but, like a whopping big trifle shaking in all directions, as if they were shaken by a fierce gale force wind; as for my little brain cells in my super intelligent head; well, they were furiously whirling about with nightmarish images of a permanent empty bowl and all the cupboards bereft of goodies; not to mention Toni's black, thunderous face.

All was silent. All was perfectly still. This was, I knew, the calm before the storm, as the saying goes. And, what a storm it was going to be! Of that there was no doubt. After all, I dismally concluded, Toni's favourite slippers were now in ten thousand bits and we all know who the culprit was. Slowly, I turned around and crept back into the depths, and relative safety, of my den and as I lay my remorseful head on my paws, closed my eyes and wished slumber to quickly take me for its own, I felt a piece of Toni's slipper fall on to my nose.

Blissful sleep evaded me and forced me to examine the facts which had brought me to this miserable state and, gradually, a picture began to emerge. A disgruntled Toni had departed to her bed chamber for a few hours kip and I had departed into my own bed chamber, clinging on to Toni's smelly slippers. (Yuk!) Now, you may question my sanity at this stage; but, remember, I had vowed to stay by my Toni's side and once a king makes a vow then, in my book, a promise cannot, under any circumstances, be broken. And so, as Tony strictly forbade me to venture out of the servants' quarters, namely the kitchen, I was left alone with a determination that I would, at least, stick to one of her precious possessions. And, let me tell you, I think my Toni would have eventually gone to meet her Maker in those ghastly, smelly hedgehog slippers of hers if... well; I think you know what happened.

I remember drifting off to sleep with her odious slippers resting by my paws and then the... dream. And what a delightful dream it was. There was, I remember, a poppy field full of happy hopping rabbits and what a pleasure it was to run and hop with them; what fun! Until, in the midst of our carefree frolicking, I espied a... CAT! Need I say more? That was it! As quick as lightning I abandoned the rabbits and I was off. Nearer and nearer to the dastardly ginger and white furry creature I got and, at the point of opening my mouth as wide as I possibly could, in order to acquire a generous portion of the creature, I momentarily stopped, my mouth opened wide, as I remembered another feline who I had befriended called, Queenie. At that point I would have allowed the cat to escape but, would you believe, the feline turned and snarled at me, displaying a set of quite awful looking gnashers. Well, that was unforgivable; I mean, to snarl so viciously at a king! My old friend, Henry, would have had that fiend's head on a block in no time at all. I, on the other hand, couldn't be bothered with all that chopping block paraphernalia. I pounced on the thing and I will allow your imaginations to run wild on the scene that followed; a clue; Toni's tattered slippers. So, there you go. Not my fault at all. The fault lays entirely at the feline's door; but, how to convince my Toni? I lay and pondered and pondered and lay but nothing sprang to mind; nothing that would save my bacon, so to speak. I continued to lay and ponder. And, I would have pondered into the next millennium; but, for the sound of ominous stirrings upstairs. Yes, a chirpy voice was coming from the radio, followed by a chirpy tune, which did not make me feel chirpy at all.

The toilet was flushed, there was plodding about and then I saw them from the security of my sanctuary two bare feet, minus their hedgehog slippers and they were purposefully coming towards me. I closed my eyes and fervently wished a big hole would gobble me up.

I heard before I saw. I squeezed my eyes so tightly they hurt. A thousand simultaneous claps of thunder would have been more pleasing to my delicate ears, my friends. Toni ranted and raved; stamped about the place and jumped frenziedly and threatened me with a LIFETIME ban on ALL treats, while I curled my body tight and contemplated my misdeeds. For, yes, when I thought about it in more detail, it was all my fault and not the fault of the cat, the rabbits or the dream. It was all my fault entirely and now, being the brave king I was, I had to face up to the consequences of my actions. But, my dear friends, I didn't want to face up to them. I wanted to forget that the whole dastardly deed had happened; but, as I looked forlornly at the debris of Toni's favourite slippers, I knew, that wasn't to be.

Toni and I were at war. But, my friends, this was the most bitter war any king has ever fought; for, it was a silent war; a war of grim set mouths, downcast eyes, heavy laden hearts full of gloom and despondency; a war of avoidance. Our castle became our grim prison and Toni and I were its miserable prisoners in total lockdown. The cold war went on for days and would, I fear, have gone on for decades if it wasn't for an unexpected intervention.

One bright sunny morning the doorbell rang. I raised my sullen eyes to see Toni plodding to the door, opening it, scanning the periphery and, seeing nobody in sight. She was in the process of closing the door, and would have done so, if it wasn't for my superb powers of observation.

From the corner of my observant eye, I had espied something on the doorstep. Agilely I rose and moved as quick as my bandaged paw would allow, grabbed the parcel by the string with my strong pearly whites, dragged it inside and plopped it by my gloomy mistress's bare feet. There she sat, her mystified eyes staring down at the mysterious, brown, bulky package; there I sat staring up at my miserable looking Toni until, curiosity got the better of me and I could stare no more. I pounced and, just as I was about to ravenously tear the parcel apart with my eager pearly whites, I stopped and stood there like a solidified doggie statue, moving not one centimetre as I suddenly remembered that it was my spontaneous, erratic actions that had brought about our full-scale war. In that moment our eyes locked and, I felt, she knew how very difficult it was for me to control my inquisitive urges and to try and be a super good pooch and maybe, just maybe, I had learned from my past mistakes. I am sure I saw a flicker of a smile dance about on her lips.

I looked intently as she withdrew her eyes from me and proceeded to untie the string of the parcel; her eyes bemused as she carefully unwrapped the brown paper. Mightily intrigued I continued to look on and saw two boxes, a smaller box resting on top of a larger box. By now every vein in my body was wildly pulsating with excruciating curiosity. What could these boxes contain? I wondered. I nudged in a little closer and peered more intently, as Toni carefully raised the lid off the larger box, unwrapped the white flimsy paper and brought a funny shaped object out. Toni's eyes widened and, I must say, mine stretched wide too; her lips broke into a happy smile and my mouth displayed a most engaging doggie smile. My friends, we were both staring at a new pair of hedgehog slippers! She clasped one slipper tightly to her chest, sighed and cast me a warning look; but my gaze was on the second, smaller box where, eventually, Toni's eyes turned too. Opening it, she rapidly closed the lid and all I could hear was a bout of hearty laughter escaping her happy mouth. What on earth could be inside that box? I silently speculated. And the more she laughed, the more I wondered.

Finally, all was revealed and what a surprise, and shock, I got. Out came another hedgehog slipper, much smaller in size and was followed by another three. My happy doggie face abruptly transformed into a doggie horror face, as

I sat on my hind legs and stared and… stared and unable to think any thoughts at all.

My favourite auntie, Auntie Anusia, who had miraculously saved the day, by sending her sister a pair of new hedgehog slippers, after hearing about the hedgehog slipper tragedy, was about to ruin my life; for, I knew exactly what was coming.

It came!

While an ecstatic Toni roamed about our castle sporting her brand new hedgehog slippers, I looked down at my new set adorning my four paws and pondered miserably. Yes, they had solved the cold war between Toni and myself; but they were a hard punishment to bear; or, rather, to wear for my past misdemeanours.

Toni's retirement plan, as far as I was concerned, was most definitely not going my way. My Toni was well and truly comfortably ensconced in her new slippers; now all she needed was a pipe!

A Police Cell for a King

Well, if you think that episode in my life didn't go at all well for me; that was nothing compared to what was to come. I ended up in a police cell!

Yes, my dear, beloved friends you have misread not a word of my report. Just to reiterate; I ended up in a police cell!! And, not only did I end up in a police cell; I ended up in the tiniest, darkest, gloomiest and most miserable looking cell you can imagine. I was a king of famed repute, in the midst of a virus lockdown, in a common local police cell and I was not a happy pooch.

Try not to shed a tear, my loyal subjects, as you imagine this miserable scenario, I found myself in because, boys and girls; young and not so young subjects of mine, I know this is hard to believe; but there is nobody to blame for the unfortunate predicament I found myself in but Yours Truly. I, King Kamehameha, take full blame for the dastardly outcome I am about to relate to you.

Since time immemorial, my dear friends, my mistress has tried to instil in me the advantages of being a well behaved pooch at all times and with her encouragement came a set of strict warnings and with these warnings, a set of consequential promises regarding unacceptable behaviour. My Toni has told me, until I am blue in the face, that I have options in my life and that bad choices bring with them punishments. Well, since time immemorial I have listened intently to these remonstrations and, well, the thought of being a bit mischievous, now and again, always conjures up the delightful image of happy, carefree, sunny days interlaced with loads and loads of fun. So, you can guess which direction I often went in and how it all panned out in the end.

The thing is, my friends, since this lockdown business my Toni has decided that the field is no longer good enough; or, in her words, safe enough for us to have our strolls. Strictly adhering to the two metres social distancing rule, she has got it into her head that if she comes within ten metres of any other human, pooch or any other living creature she'll end up on her deathbed and, being on it once before, she is not taking any chances. So, we have changed our walking route and now we walk sedately along the pavements where, as soon as she espies someone on the horizon, we are crossing to the other side of the road at Olympic record speeds. So, you can imagine, along the course of our half hour walk, we end up zigzagging across the various roads around thirty-seven times per road and don't ask me how many roads we travel along. Now, as tiring and tedious as this is, this is nothing compared to the ghastly, and most terrifying, establishment we pass by on each of our nerve-racking walks, namely the police station. Now, my friends, I know my Toni wouldn't mind harpooning a guy in uniform; but, to be fair, I don't actually think she chose this route with this kind of nonsense in mind. No… no, she has chosen this route as a constant warning to me, to mend my rascally ways; to bestow on me a daily reminder of what could, and probably would, happen if I choose not to live the life of a perfect pooch and, let me tell you, that place gives me the goose bumps every single time I pass it by; it also makes my feet turn to wobbly jelly and as for my guts, I can't even begin to describe what they do as we pass this most horrific establishment. Suffice it to say, I don't even have to look at the place to feel the pimples invade my trembling body and, lest this is not torture enough, Toni never fails to say, "Now, Kamehameha, one paw out of place and you'll be going in."

Once, or twice, I dared to have a peep at the imposing structure and my heart dropped; for, the building looked old and grimy; an institution, I concluded, of stern faces and even sterner discipline and, most definitely, not a place of fun. No, my friends, I did not yearn to end up spending a night in there, let alone a life sentence, under any circumstances. But, end up in there I did and it all happened like this.

As I have mentioned previously, this lockdown business was getting us down. Toni only ventured out into the wide world when absolutely necessary, for things to keep us going you know like bread and treats. She was going nowhere else and everyone else was banned from setting their foot into our castle and I, King Kamehameha, didn't even have a say in the matter. Toni and I were imprisoned in our kingdom; our fortress, with only each other for company. Gone were the days when we strolled leisurely by in the park; gone were the days when Auntie Anusia came visiting with her hubby, bearing a huge bag of delicious treats; gone also were the days when Toni and I would go visiting. Toni and I were now stuck together and, let me tell you, we were starting to get on each other's nerves.

The first days of lockdown, as you know, were all right; we were quite cosy on our island. By the eleventh day; well, let's just say we were ready for the grand escape! But, escape where? There was nowhere to escape.

I watched, as Toni scrubbed and polished every nook and cranny in our castle, until everything sparkled; I sat by her as she read for England, ploughing through her entire library of books and, let me tell you, they looked a formidable lot; I also sat patiently by her side as she watched the television, until her eyes were fast becoming square; I witnessed her experimenting with various strange recipes, I'd rather forget but cannot, due to my new role as chief personal food taster. After my recent escapade in the garden, I dared to only watch my Toni as she forced all the blooming flowers and every blade of grass to stand to perfect attention and where there was no place for a single weed. Finally, we sat and stared into each other's eyes. But, enough was enough! I wanted fun and fun was what I intended to get, by fair means or foul and so I set off on my joyful mission.

At first, my escapades were of a subdued nature. I dared to place a cautious paw on one of Toni's hedgehog slippers; however, the disdainful look my mistress threw me, as I was caught in the act, put an immediate stop to any further notions I had regarding her precious slipper.

Next, I moved on to playfully nipping Toni's toes, when they were in her slippers and out. Now, I thought this particular game was fun and I thought Toni did too; after all, all the indications were there. I nipped and she jumped into the air; I nipped a little more and she jumped higher and squealed delightfully in the process; or, so I thought. She must be enjoying this game, I thought, and so I nipped harder and, true to form, she jumped higher. The more I nipped, the higher she jumped. This was great fun!

So, you can imagine, my friends, how truly baffled I became when, after a vigorous bout of our nipping, jumping, squealing, shrieking game, I ended up with some sort of ghastly mask over my beautiful face and was banished into my den. Try as I did, I could not fathom out the error of my ways and, in the end, I came to the sad conclusion that my Toni is at a very strange age and I decided to give her toes a well-earned rest.

I rapidly moved on to greater things and more exciting antics. Let me share with you the episode regarding knitting wool. Wow! That was indeed fun and funny. During this lockdown period, my Toni decided to take up a new hobby; actually, it was a challenge she had long ago wanted to have a go with and then something or other always got in the way. Now, she firmly decided, it was D-day, whatever that meant. What a ghastly sight I encountered when, begrudgingly, rousing myself from a delightful snooze, I saw Toni's ugly ankles sticking out of a cupboard and the rest of her torso, arms and head, plunged deep... deep into the same mentioned cupboard. All kinds of missiles were randomly flying hither and thither out of the unit: knitting needles, a battered sowing basket, drapes of some sort, glossy patterns, another pair of knitting needles; followed by a little hook of some sort which landed on me, almost poking my eye out. I ducked my head my ears attune to Toni's gasps and sighs, as she squeezed her head, arms and the rest of her torso further inside stating furiously, "Where the dickens is that jumper of mine?" I left her to it, planning my next move.

I needn't have wasted my precious energy, effort and time on futile planning; my opportunity of seizing fun by the scruff of the neck came to me in a most simplistic, surprising and delightful way.

By now Toni had found what she had been searching for and when I saw it, my shocked eyes nearly popped out of my super intelligent head. It was, my dear friends, the most ghastly, ugliest, appalling bright yellow, oversized jumper I had ever had the misfortune to clap my eyes on and, believe me, I have seen some odious items draping over my Toni in my time. I stared incredulously as she pulled this thing out of the cupboard and my heart froze instantly, when her happy, sparkling eyes darted in my direction and a wide smile spread over her chops. I shuddered whilst all of my inner guts writhed, twisted and turned as I continued to ogle the thing she was holding up. Surely she was not thinking of, somehow, using this article she was holding up with me in mind? The glint in her eye told me, however, she was. And then came the brutal confirmation of the fact; her ghastly, out of tune humming commenced. Now my Toni only ever hums when (1) She is on the brink of harpooning some unfortunate soul; or, (2) She has something truly awful lined up for me and, since there is no new chap on the horizon; or, likely to be during this lockdown duration, there is only one conclusion; she is planning something horrid for me and, without a doubt, it was something to do with that unsightly yellow jumper, if you can actually call it a jumper.

I was, as always, right in my assumption; but I was still puzzled as to what it could be. Gradually the whole mystery began to unravel and in more ways than one.

On a rainy, gloomy Tuesday afternoon we found ourselves musing respectively on this and that. After a hearty breakfast, I was just about to ease myself into a nice nap when I heard the dreaded words, "Right, Kamehameha, this is no time to laze about; we have work to do." Of course, she was using the royal *we*; though, to be honest, I can't remember giving her my permission. Anyway, I knew what she really meant was that she was going to engage in some pleasurable activity and I was to be as good as gold. Well, I thought, that suited my plans and so I sprawled out leisurely on my plush Hawaiian duvet.

If only I had closed both my eyes instead of just one; for, with that one eye, I espied something which made my closed eye open abruptly. Toni was pulling out the wool of that ugly yellow article, she calls a jumper and, now and again, she scrutinized the growing mound of yellow wool very carefully and, by her sheer intense examination, I knew she meant business; her words brought an icy shiver to my very bones. "Kamehameha, my dear friend, we are going to have new matching yellow jumpers!"

I stared wide-eyed at my mistress. Did she mean I was going to get one too? And any hope of my Auntie Anusia coming to my rescue was dwindling too. Remember the hedgehog slippers episode? Quick… quick… I had to formulate a plan at top speed. This was no time for cosy doggie naps. Time was of the essence and a full-proof plan was needed; now!

First, I had to observe intently and assess what course of action my Toni was about to take and, folks; it wasn't long before my heavy heart felt like a solidified boulder; for, my worst fears were coming into fruition before my very eyes. I watched stunned, amazed and petrified of what was to come. And, it came.

Diligently, excitedly she continued to undo the jumper, stopped, drew up a high-backed chair, attached some wool around the chair and proceeded to wind the wool around it. I watched in utter amazement; my eyes glassy, as if hypnotized, at the magic that was happening before my very eyes. For, would you believe, my friends, the jumper was shrinking fast and the wool around the chair began to grow and my heart began to thaw; for, the ghastly jumper was now disappearing at rapid speed. However, Toni's threat still rang loudly in my ears and her tuneless humming meant she was on some ghastly mission of great importance. This was no time for a king of my standing to be complacent; this was the time for a sovereign, worth his salt, to act. And so, into action I sprang.

I must admit, from the corner of one of my observant eye, I saw the treacherous look Toni threw me; but, needs must, I told myself firmly and the thought of an odious yellow pullover adorning my royal back and generous belly, making me look like some super-sized bumble bee, made me think logically no more. Into the string of wool, Toni was handling, I pounced and, before she could put a stop to my caper, I found the end, secured it firmly in my pearly whites and was running around and around Toni and, as I ran, I found I was creating a delightful yellow cocoon around my mistress, while she was in the midst of some daydream or other. I stopped for a while and admired my unique handiwork, then around and around I continued to go; around and around and around. I went with such speed it all became a yellow blur and, when I stopped for another brief assessment, all I could see were my mistress's glaring eyes staring starkly at me, telling me she was not amused. But I was. This was fun of the highest calibre and I increased my speed rapidly, as I caught a glimpse of Toni's tree trunk legs trying to break out of the cocoon. Around and around I continued to go. I froze. Her words, though muffled, were as clear as crystal in my ears. "It will be the police station for you tonight, Kamehameha." Faster and faster I worked, imprisoning her into her cocoon more securely before she had a chance to imprison me. Finally, all the jumper had disappeared and I stopped and admired, in more detail, my artistic sculpture; a big, yellow, bulky, cosy looking cocoon and two furious eyes glaring back at me. I smiled my doggie smile. If my caterpillar friends ever needed a helping hand with their cocoons, I would most certainly be the best candidate for the job.

I strode leisurely into my den, made myself comfortable amidst my plush Hawaiian cushions and continued to admire my wonderful creation. I even had a title for it; you know, like they do in these posh art galleries, 'A Bug in a Yellow Rug!' Yes, I beamed feeling very satisfied; I most certainly possessed a great, exceptional artistic talent.

By now I could hear Toni's muffled vows of revenge and, I must admit, that part of the proceedings was not too delightful to the ears, especially as I happened to hear the words, "… police station… tonight… cell…" I closed my eyes. I was safe… for the time being.

How my Toni escaped from her cocoon, I shall never know, except that her escape was made during one of my happy naps. Anyway, escape she did and she was not a very happy escapee. I heard her before I saw her; or, more truthfully, I heard the crashing chair against the kitchen table and, when I dared to open one eye, I saw the chair, complete with the bug in the rug, thrashing madly against the table. I snapped my eye shut. Finally, when I plucked up the courage to open both my eyes, the angry bug, now minus her rug, was looming threateningly over me and, let me tell you my dear friends; it was not an aesthetically pleasing sight to one eye, let alone two. She glared. I stared and an ominous, heavy silence reigned over our castle; the calm before the inevitable storm, as they say. This, I thought glumly, was not going to be a happy scenario and my foresight came to fruition, as I stared unblinkingly at my mistress's chubby, wagging finger and her burning, angry eyes and heard her words, "Tonight, Kamehameha, you and I are going to the police station; but, only one of us will be spending the night there."

Well, I guessed the prison guest was not going to be my Toni and so I prepared myself for what was surely to come; for, Toni's thunderous face told me, that my sweet doggie smile would be of no consequence whatsoever; I might as well save myself the effort. The only minute light at the end of this particular tunnel was that Toni had threatened me with the police station a million times before and nothing ever came of it. Maybe – that evening, we walked side by side in grim silence. One surreptitious sideway look at her sullen face told me, that Toni hadn't seen the funny side of our knitting wool episode; she meant business. We plodded on. From afar, I glimpsed the grimy carbuncle and all that it represented and, I must admit, my heart skipped a few beats at the horrible sight. Step by solitary step the place of authority and discipline became larger and larger, until it was upon us. Toni stopped. I stopped. My fast beating heart stopped. Two pairs of eyes turned and stared at each other, before darting back to the horrible looking, grey stoned building which was, my friends, Her Majesty's Constabulary. At this point I felt my knees quiver and my heart freeze over as my eyes strayed to my Toni, who was still staring unblinkingly at the distasteful sight before us. My questioning eyes narrowed. Surely, Toni had not been serious? Slowly I opened my eyes wide to take a better look at my mistress and what I saw I did not like. I was staring at a grim-set, determined face with one solitary thing on her mind; revenge! I felt my guts treacherously writhing and shrivelling inside my belly and my paws, including my poorly bandaged paw, turning into four blobs of quivering jelly, don't ask me the flavour, as my eyes flitted and stared at the imposing, unfriendly, cold looking building before me. Should I run? I asked myself. I wouldn't get far with my poorly paw, a little voice in my head told me. Should I plop down and lay perfectly still feigning death? Done that; worn the T-shirt, so to speak, and to no avail. A sudden idea struck me; an idea that could save my bacon.

Solidly I placed myself down on to the pavement and refused to move a fraction of a centimetre. I was, in other words, on strike; determined to stay on my plot of terra firma all night, and well into the next week, if I had to. I felt the tug of my lead and then a rougher tug, to no avail. There I sat my super intelligent, royal head held high and proud; my body upright and perfectly still, with not the slightest inclination to move and my shrewd eyes set firmly on the entrance to the foreboding building before me.

"In you go, Kamehameha," urged Toni as she tugged at my lead once more.

I don't think so. I silently, and obstinately, stated without flickering an eyelid.

"Come on; we're here." Another tug. "Kamehameha!"

It's King Kamehameha, if you don't mind. I silently admonished her. And, you move if you want to; but this king is staying put.

I felt my mistress's eyes burning into the depths of my very soul; I felt them drill into my little, super intelligent marbles and, still, I moved not a single muscle as I looked straight past her and into my bleak future.

To my utter amazement after some quiet, and some not so quiet, mumblings and mutterings Toni abandoned the hold on my lead, allowing it to fall on to my generous body, and off she marched up the winding path and straight through the constabulary door.

I sat and pondered for a while. I could make some sort of dash for it; maybe my poorly bandaged paw wouldn't let me down. I pondered a little more. No, that was not the thing to do; after all, a brave king does not simply run away from things, no matter how bad; he encounters them face-to-face, rises up to the challenge and… wins! I stayed firm, the great sovereign I am; unmovable, invincible and waiting… waiting.

A motley gathering of people walked in and out the doors; the majority casting their admirable, though somewhat curious, eyes my way; a couple of them chuckled, which I thought to be a mighty distasteful thing to do; a little person, like you my dear friends, walked by with a grown up, stroked my beautiful coat; but, for most of the time I sat alone and lonely, waiting for what was to come.

My heart skipped a beat when out walked a calmer looking Toni and, hot on her heels, was a large man with a most unfriendly looking face. He was dressed up to the nines in a smart pair of black trousers, a posh black jacket with shiny silver buttons and the most becoming black helmet, with a dazzling silver badge of some sort on the front. I stared and stared at this badge and wondered what it represented because, as you know, I am a curious type of pooch. My musing, however, was cut short abruptly with an attention grabbing cough and the sternest set of eyes I have ever had the misfortune to gaze upon; for, they were black as coal and shiny and they meant serious business.

A sudden enlightening idea struck me. I gave this fierce looking man one of my best, friendliest doggie smiles; the kind of smile where I show off my gleaming pearly whites to the best of my ability and then I waited patiently for my compliment. Instead, I heard the cold, stark words, "Is this the culprit, Miss?"

My shocked eyes opened wide; my smile still trying, without any success, to dazzle the stern looking individual before me.

"Yes, this is the culprit, Officer." Toni answered firmly, unwaveringly as my eyes darted from one to the other and my doggie smile died a slow death.

For long seconds, which seemed torturous hours, they both gaped down at me and, let me tell you my friends, by now, my hope of winning this guy over with my cheerful smile was fast diminishing, as I heaved heavily and stared at his no-nonsense façade. This, I glumly thought, was not looking good at all. And there we sat, or stood, in a strange lopsided triangle, adhering strictly to the two metres social distancing rule; three minds whirling erratically, with all kinds of thoughts of what was to come.

My thoughts, my dear loyal subjects, despite the formidable appearance of the grim looking officer, were not that grim. I know he was hesitating, wondering what to do with me; otherwise, I would have already been dragged inside and standing at his desk. And so, I thought, while they were making up their minds, about what kind of mild ticking-off to give me, I would make myself comfortable by sliding down to the pavement, placing my royal head on to my paws and having a little snooze.

Never presume; or, assume in this life, or the next, my dear subjects. I think I have given you this stark advice in the past and, to be honest, I should have adhered to it myself on this occasion; for, next thing I knew, I felt a hard tug and, before I knew what was happening, I was frogmarched, by Toni and the Police Officer, through the police station doors and up to a formidable looking desk, behind which stood an equally formidable looking chap. Needless to say, the friendly smile was missing from this fellow's face too. I stared ahead. "Name?" Barked the policeman.

"Kamehameha," stated Toni.

"Address?"

It was duly given.

"Any personal belongings?" Barked again the horrible individual, looking at me so sternly, I thought my blood would either curdle or freeze.

"Only the bandage around his paw." Toni announced, without any sign of compassion in her voice whatsoever.

"He can keep that."

Well, thank you for small mercies, I thought dismally as I stared unblinkingly at this despicable chap.

To be completely honest with you, I was still half thinking that this could be some sort of an elaborate game that Toni had conjured up; some kind of joke she was playing on me, I dared to cast my hopeful eyes on her. My friends, she was still looking as thunderous as ever, making me tremble inside; telling me, in no uncertain terms, she meant raw business.

My worrying eyes flitted from my mistress, to the chap behind the desk, to the fellow that escorted me in and all three sets of eyes told me they were not amused.

Well, neither was I, my loyal subjects. I was not amused at all. For, what king, in his right mind, would allow himself to be hauled into Her Majesty's local constabulary, like a common criminal, and then allowed himself to be looked down on, and frowned upon, as if he was a contemptible worm, instead of a highly esteemed king? I must be losing my marbles, I concluded. What other explanation was there? I sighed heavily; reflecting upon the fact that, I would now probably have a lifetime of solitary confinement to ponder on this puzzling query. I raised my eyes to the egg behind the desk and awaited, with bated breath, my dismal fate.

It came; my dismal fate, I mean; but not before I caught the formidable looking officer winking at my Toni! Was I seeing things? Was I, indeed, losing my marbles? Or, was I facing a fate worse than a stint of solitary confinement? Had Toni harpooned this chap for a possible future date, once she had me ensconced in the cell? I closed my eyes and allowed myself, willingly, to be taken away and out of sight of any prospective stepdads. The cell it is for me, I smiled resignedly to myself, and long may I reign there!

My resolve evaporated as soon as I stepped into my new home. My friends, it was the most ghastly, bleakest, coldest, dampest, gloomiest place I have ever imagined; or, had the misfortune to experience in my darkest nightmares. Begrudgingly, I sat down on the hard, cold, damp floor and looked up at my cell warden. Immediately I looked away; one fleeting glance at his stony countenance was more than enough for me. And so, I sat and wondered where Toni had got to; for, I hadn't seen any sight of her and I hadn't heard a single sound from her, since I departed the policeman's desk.

Slam! Bang!! I was alone in a dark, unfriendly cell with only my thoughts, and a solitary, determined spider crawling across the grimy floor, for company. My inquisitive eyes followed the spider's zigzagged journey, as it travelled obliviously along. I felt my heart warming to this creature and wondered why Toni found these interesting insects so frightening; screaming our castle down when she happened to clap eyes on one. And thinking of Toni; where was she? She had abandoned me; thrown me in the clink without a second thought and now she was probably planning her date with the policeman. Such is life, my dear subjects. And now I have to face a potential life sentence of existence in this grimy cell, with nothing to look at but four grimy walls, one small iron barred window, a thick solid door and one spider; not to mention, the thought of tasteless cell food, without any hope of treats coming my way and the stern, inhospitable glares of the constabulary. Well, the thought of it all made me want to curl up and die, there and then, and so, my friends, I made plans to do just that.

I lowered my generous torso on to the hard floor and placed my royal head on to my soft golden-white paws and I waited to die, my ears finely attune to the echoing of voices and laughter. My ears pricked. I was sure I'd heard my Toni's exuberant laughter. My body froze. Surely not! I was hearing things; this ghastly cell life was already damaging my super intellectual brain cells. I must be going mad! What on earth would my Toni still be doing here? And, why would she be laughing her head off, when her beloved king was stuck in a police cell? No… no… no… It was my wild imagination; it was playing tricks on me. I closed my exhausted eyes. Abruptly they snapped open stark and wide; my ears standing on end once more. It was my Toni; without a doubt it was my Toni and, folks, she was definitely laughing her head off. Well, I wished it would come off; then, at least, I would no longer be tortured with her odious laugh. Once more, I closed my eyes to the world, my heart broken in ten thousand fragments. How could she? How could my Toni get rid of me in such a horrid way and rejoice? How could she? But, she did. And now, I was here and she was there and I couldn't wait to pop my clogs. I lay my sorrowful head on to my bandaged paw and waited… hoping for a swift, imminent release from this sad world.

The clanking of the heavy door forced my eyes to open and I stared unblinkingly into the darkness. The door slowly opened. The light came on and a scary looking policeman stepped inside, planted down a bowl of distasteful looking grub, and another full of water, and vanished, switching off the light and clanking hard the door behind him. I rose and approached the bowl with the food, sniffed and strode back. I lay down, closed my eyes and, mercifully, fell into a deep, dreamless sleep.

The clattering of the door, a good while later, did not make me stir. I couldn't be bothered to see what it was all about. My eyes remained firmly shut; but… not for long.

"King Kamehameha." I heard the majestic words and my heart leaped to the highest heavens. Was I hearing things? Or, had I popped my clogs and was I now reigning in Paradise? I raised a curious eye. My heart spiralled swiftly down to Earth. I was, my dear friends, still ensconced in my dismal cell with the four grimy walls, the one small iron barred window and, my friend, the spider; but the heavy solid door was partly opened and I could see black trousered legs moving hither and thither. I dared to raise my head to the hovering figure before me and my curious eyes widened, like two gigantic saucers, as they looked upon a most friendly looking face. The terrifying looking policeman with the black shiny eyes and grim face had now, somehow, miraculously transformed into a sparkling eyed, cheery faced guy with the widest, and friendliest, grin I have ever seen.

Bemused, I stared at him while he continued to beam down on me and there we stood and sat respectively, staring and beaming at each other. And, while I stared, a most disturbing thought crashed into my head. Was this chap a cheerful executioner? Was I about to be led to the gallows? Now, I know my dear friends that we have travelled along this similar scenario before; remember when I mistook Farmer Bill for a cheerful hangman? But, this time, what other reasonable explanation was there? I was, after all, already a condemned pooch, residing in Her Majesty's quarters and, not long ago, this cheerful chappie, I am now staring at, was the most treacherous looking character, I had ever had the bad luck to set my eyes on. My mind was in a whirling, swirling turmoil; in other words, I was truly flummoxed.

"Your Majesty," my cheerful executioner grinned inanely, as he extended his arm, "after you."

My intelligent eyes narrowed; then narrowed further to mere slits. Was this dubious character mocking a highly esteemed king? I assessed and scrutinized and, try as I furiously did, I could not get to grips with this particular human specimen. My eyes switched to his extended arm and, I guessed, it was time to move my royal self.

Proudly, I followed him on my three healthy legs and one bandaged, poorly leg; my regal head held up high and my heart beating like the clappers. Where we were going, I did not know; but, I decided, that if I was heading towards my execution chamber, then I would step in boldly and proudly; the true king that I am. In I went and the heavy door slammed hard after me.

Down I flopped. I snapped my eyes shut. Was I dreaming? Hallucinating? Where was I? What was I doing here? What on earth was happening? Slowly, I opened one eye, then another and what I saw around and beneath me made my heart sing with joy.

My dear friends, my eyes feasted upon a plush room, most befitting for a king of mighty stature. My wide, surprised eyes rose to one wall and, there, I saw her; my Toni beaming down on me from a glass picture frame, wearing one of her brightly coloured Hawaiian Mother Hubbard's. My eyes switched to another picture frame and there was my Auntie Anusia, smiling down on me like a ray of sunshine. In another frame loomed my cousin, Suzi. My eyes swiftly moved on from that particular image and on to Queenie; the one and only feline I have ever befriended. I was surrounded by the ones I loved; but what, I wondered, were they doing in picture frames, hanging from walls in a plush police cell? My eyes dropped to the floor and my heart soared to Heaven; there, beneath me, were stacks and stacks of my colourful, tropical cushions and my king-size Hawaiian duvet! Had I, indeed, popped my clogs and arrived in Heaven? And then – I heard the unmistakable voice. No, I most certainly had not arrived in Heaven unless… unless my Toni had followed me there because that was most definitely her voice; it could not possibly belong to another human. Her feet sauntered in; well, actually, it was her odious black pumps that I saw first of all. My eyes rose to her tree trunk legs, her awful tweed skirt and up to her garish pink twinset and rested on her beaming face. On the very point of bestowing on her one of my delightful doggie smiles, I firmly checked myself. What if this was some kind of an elaborate ruse, to throw me off my guard? What if she was in cahoots with the Chief of Police and in the midst of plotting something dark and sinister, throwing intricate traps my way, to lure me into a false sense of security? What if… what if…?

"Kamehameha; my dear, dear Kamehameha," Toni cooed as she planted her plump body down on to the floor and gave me the tightest of cuddles and, I must say, the feel of her chubby arms around me made me feel all warm and fuzzy inside.

But, try as I did, I could not shift the feel of unease away from me because, my honourable friends, hadn't she abandoned me at the police station? Hadn't she left me in a grimy cell with four grimy walls, one small iron barred window, a heavy solid door and one spider? Hadn't she laughed rapturously while I was stuck, alone and lonely, in that frightful cell? So, what had changed? I asked myself. I was truly and utterly baffled.

It all came to light in the next few minutes. What also came to light, was the fact that I was not going back to my castle; not yet, anyway; maybe, not ever!

She cuddled me tighter and then, abruptly, let me go; knelt directly in front of me and looked intently into my soulful brown eyes. "Kamehameha," she said softly; but, being the intelligent king I am, I noticed there was a trace of seriousness in her voice. Still, I listened; it is, after all, my duty as a king to listen to all his subjects, no matter what sort of rubbish they may spout off. "Kamehameha," she repeated, "you have to mend your ways." I must admit, I did feel like nodding off at this juncture of the proceedings; for, I have heard this boring speech twenty-five thousand, nine hundred and ninety-nine times in the past. I pricked my ears and forced myself, with all of my doggie will, for the torture to come. "You are stopping in a cell until you have learned your lesson," she stated and planted a feather-like kiss on my mighty intelligent forehead and vanished out of the door, clanking it shut.

My eyes wandered around the sumptuous surroundings, taking the overfilled bowl of delightful looking doggie food, mixed generously with bits of sausage and chicken, and I smiled my doggie smile as I approached my banquet.

That night, while Toni tossed and turned; fretted about me and made umpteen mugs of tea; wandered aimlessly about our castle and stared into the empty space, which should have been occupied by my good self; I sprawled out luxuriously on my plush Hawaiian duvet, with a host of comfy cushions around me and my tummy full of delights and closed my happy, sleepy eyes.

If this was punishment for having a bit of fun then, bring it on; the more, the better. I dozed off with the delightful thought of the next bout of glorious fun, whirling happily around my happy head.

'King' Kamehameha Breaking in and Out

I soon learned, my dear friends, that my happy little holiday in the police station cell was a one-off and that the establishment of Her Majesty's Constabulary was not a destination I could plan next year's summer vacation. I heard the ins and outs of this, while Toni explained my recent police cell adventure to my favourite auntie. "And so, Anusia," she chirped on the phone, "Ken, you know, Sharon's husband, is a policeman and we decided to teach my Kamehameha a lesson in obedience; however, Kami decided he liked the cell and didn't want to come back home. In the end Ken told him, in no uncertain terms, that his cell was no hotel. Still; I thought it was good while it lasted."

"And so, apparently, did our lovely Kamehameha," chuckled Auntie Anusia, after which they both burst into a fit of rapturous laughter. Now, it was while she was chatting away on the phone that my Toni was attacked by a cough; to be honest, she'd had this cough for a day, or two, and she also revealed to my auntie that she was feeling rather hot.

Well, before you know what was happening, my Auntie Anusia was standing outside our bay window and glaring in, with a set of deeply serious eyes; her hubby, my uncle, was standing at least two metres away from the opening door, whilst my Toni had been bundled on to a stretcher and was swiftly whisked away, in a white van with blue flashing lights, at top speed. Before I could get my little intelligent brain cells to work to full capacity, I was bundled off and whisked away too.

I was totally and utterly baffled as to what on earth was happening, especially as Toni was taken off in one direction and I in another. I didn't, however, worry for too long, because I was in the delightful company of my Auntie Anusia, my most favourite person in the whole wide world; well, that is apart from my Toni, of course. Anyway, off we went; Toni to goodness knows where and I to my auntie's castle where I knew, without a doubt, I would be spoiled rotten.

I was not disappointed. Out came all the treats, the soft cuddly toys, the colourful bouncy ball and out came Suzi. Now, for those of you who are not familiar with Suzi, let me tell you a little bit about her. She is my cousin. She belongs to my auntie and uncle and she feels their castle belongs solely to her. In fact, my dear friends, she mistakenly thinks that she is the boss of the whole wide world and she thinks… she THINKS she can boss me about too. Well, she can jolly well THINK again. No one; but, no one is the boss of me, except ME!

Well, anyway, I took one disdainful look at her and she, as she boldly strode past me, threw me one of her ghastly glares. We were at war; but that, folks, was nothing new. We were never really the best of mates even though, I must confess, on one occasion she had actually saved my life. However, now she thinks I should be eternally grateful to her. Grateful, of course I am; after all, she pulled me out of a potential watery grave; eternally grateful, most certainly not; I have more interesting and important things to do with my precious time.

Anyway, we lay in our respective corners of the kitchen, glaring at each other, until I decided that enough was enough. I had stared at her ugly mug long enough; I needed my beauty sleep. But, as I luxuriously spread out my generous body, something niggled me annoyingly and, I knew, if I didn't sort it out, my guilty conscience would not give me a moments peace; not to mention the stark reality of being sued for deformation of character. Allow me to put the record straight, my dear subjects. The fact is, my cousin Suzi is not that ugly; really, she's not ugly at all. Secretly, I think she's quite beautiful; though, she's got a long way to go before she comes anywhere near to my beauty status. For those of you who are not yet acquainted with Suzi, let me describe her to you. She is a border collie who sports a very fine black and white coat and she is annoying. For example, she does all in her power to get all the cuddles, treats and attention; she craves to be the centre of attention and to be in the centre of all things at all times; but that is nothing compared to her worst crime. Oh no… no… no; her worst crime is that she has the sheer audacity to think that she is better than I, King Kamehameha. Now, I know that you, my faithful subjects, would never for a moment dare to even consider such a notion; the notion that you are superior to me; but, Suzi; well, she has no qualms in that particular area and, hence, a war over true sovereignty frequently ensues between us.

At the present time I had more urgent things on my mind. My Toni had been hauled away, in a van with flashing blue lights and a blaring siren, that was none too pleasing to the ears, and I was beginning to wonder whether she was, once more, laying on her deathbed and, if she happened to pop her clogs, where would this sovereign end up? My eyes flitted around my current lodging premises and,

I must admit, they were very comfortable. I had a nice comfy bed and cushions, with the thought of lovely treats to come my way on a regular basis and, of course, my Auntie Anusia to fuss over me at any given opportunity. But then there was… Suzi.

Suzi… Suzi… Suzi… I looked across at the sleeping, fluffy black and white ball and pondered. Would I, in my right mind, want to spend the rest of my days with this fiend; or… should I start searching for a new castle? This was indeed a dilemma and, after long minutes of fretful tossing and turning I fell into an uneasy, and equally fretful, sleep where Suzi was chasing me, black and white fur flying in all directions; eyes glaring, gnashers gleaming and she, ready to pounce. My eyes shot wide open and darted this way and that. The rascal was blissfully snoring and, after careful examination, my bits and pieces were still all intact; but, for how long? I asked myself. During a sleepless night I began to concoct a plan.

To be honest with you, I honestly thought that my resolve of escape would be considerably weakened by the first light of dawn; but, if anything, I was firmer in my resolve. There was, after all, no other way of maintaining my superiority than to leave this particular castle and rule supremely in my own kingdom. But; how to leave and, more importantly, where to go were indeed problems which weighed heavily on my mind and then, as if by magic, as I was heartily tucking into my doggie food, sprinkled generously with pieces of roast lamb, and the odd roast potato added for good measure, the idea loomed and what a superb idea it was! I was going to escape to a kingdom where, I knew, I would be the rightful and ultimate king.

Stealthily, in the middle of the night, I eased myself out of the partly opened window. Now, don't ask me how I did it. At one horrible moment, I seriously thought I was going to end up being a permanent fixture in the opening, with my head and paws sticking out in the breezy night air and my generous belly, and the rest of my bits and bobs, well and truly stuck in Auntie Anusia's kitchen. I was, I know, not a pretty sight. Still; needs must. I pushed, shoved, struggled, heaved, panted, sighed, gasped, said a word I shouldn't have said; shoved, gasped and panted some more and I was out! True, I'd left a good proportion of my glossy golden-white fur coat behind; but that was a small price to pay for my freedom. Now, it was onwards and forwards to my destination.

Fleetingly I looked back at the opened window and thought I'd heard Suzi yap. Without further ado, off I went like the wind; actually, it was more like a lively breeze; on and on I ran as fast as my poorly bandaged leg would allow; on and on I went; on and on…

After precisely half an hour I was stood in the grounds and admiring the kingdom I knew so well. Swiftly I scrambled on to the bistro table at the back of the house and in through the loosely opened window I clambered; honestly, my Auntie Anusia and my Toni need to get their respective heads tested; leaving their windows open for all and sundry to wander through; not that I am all and sundry, of course. Anyway, back to my account; in I went and down I plopped on to my Hawaiian duvet and plush tropical cushions and gave a deep, satisfied sigh. I was home and the thought of long, blissful days all on my own, where I would be the sole sovereign of my own castle, sent me into a delightful, heavenly slumber.

I awoke approximately ten hours later, fully refreshed and ready to reign; granted, without any subjects to rule over; but I did have the whole of my kingdom completely at my disposal and what delightful fun this was going to be!

Now, let me remind you folks that, up until now, I have rarely ventured past the servants' quarters, in other words, the kitchen due to Toni's strict set of rules and regulations. Henceforth, however, I could wander wherever I chose without my Toni giving me the disapproving eye. This was most certainly a time to snoop around; but, more importantly, a time in which to luxuriate; for, I know, without a single doubt, that such a pampering opportunity would not come my way again. But, first things first, my tummy was beginning to rumble making my eyes dart to my bowls, which were still full of doggie food and water. I sauntered over to them and ate and drank a little; for, things had to be rationed if I was to survive. Having eaten enough to satisfy my immediate hunger; but, not a morsel more, I sauntered off to explore, in detail, my kingdom.

Into the lounge I leisurely strolled, my eyes lazily gazing around the plush surroundings and remaining a while on the cream leather sofa, displaying a bountiful host of delightful cream cushions of very plush and soft textures. Slowly I wandered on taking everything in, reflecting on the luxuriously soft and thick cream carpet beneath my paws. This, I mused, would be a super-duper place to roll about in, have a little snooze or just sit and ponder about the meaning of life. My eyes lifted to the rocking chair, also in cream upholstery. What endless fun I could have on that contraption, I smiled my doggie smile, my eyes sparkling at the anticipation of the potential fun I could have, as I wandered into the cream coloured hallway and approached the stairs, where I sat and pondered for a little while. Toni's secret sanctuary was up there; a place I had never entered into. Sorry, I tell a lie; on one occasion, when my Toni was laboriously getting ready for one of her dates, I did get as far as sitting outside her bedroom door and having a ghastly brown skirt thrown carelessly my way which, to my utter disgust, landed on my head. Yuk! The memory still haunts me to this present day. Anyway, back to the present. There I sat at the base of the stairs wondering, should I? Shouldn't I? Should I? Shouldn't I? For five seconds I thought of the consequences then, without further ado, I pounded up the thick carpeted stairs at top speed and stealthily approached a partly opened door. For long, ponderous minutes I sat and stared at the white painted wood of the door. Would Toni mind so much if I just took a tiny peep inside? Yes, she most certainly would! Thundered a loud voice in my head. But, just a quick peep? Most certainly not. Just a miniscule peep? Don't you dare!! The annoying voice in my head reiterated. But… but… one peep? Not if you want to see your next birthday, came the ominous warning. But, before I knew it, my paw had moved the door further back and I sat, saucer-eyed, staring into Toni's sleeping quarters. And, let me tell you my dear friends, while I sat and stared at her sumptuous room, my love for my Toni crashed and burned; for, I was staring unblinkingly at a room full of luxuries while I, King Kamehameha; a king of very high esteem and honour, am banished into the servants' quarters. Granted, I have my plush, comfy Hawaiian duvet, and matching tropical cushions, but Toni's boudoir is fit for a queen. I continued to stare wide-eyed at her king size bed, with a luxurious cream coloured quilt and loads and loads of magnificent cushions, scattered at the head of the bed as delightful thoughts started to whirl about in my fun loving head. This bed of Toni's, I mused, would do very adequately as an excellent trampoline; nice and soft and, no doubt, nice and bouncy too. My friends; save that brilliant thought of mine.

My eyes moved on to a kind of table with a mirror, I think it's called a dressing table. On this dressing table were displayed small, delightful, colourful tubs and containers of all sizes, sprays, a rather elaborate silver brush, comb and mirror set and all sorts of other beauty paraphernalia. My inquisitive eyes flitted to the opposite side of the bed where… where… my good friends, there I was! I was, would you believe, staring at my grand 'old' self, through a wall-to-wall mirror, which seemed to be in three sections. My super intelligent brain cells told me they were, in fact, mirrored wardrobe doors. I stared and stared unblinkingly and came to the unarguable conclusion that I, indeed, looked a very fine specimen; a most beautiful, distinguished and elegant king. This place, I decided, would do perfectly well for future inspections, and detailed assessments, of my wonderful self. Still, there was more to explore. Reluctantly, I withdrew my lingering eyes from the wonderful vision in front of me and, begrudgingly, I sauntered out of this delightful oasis.

I ambled to the entrance of another bedroom. From what I could see, it didn't seem to resemble a proper bedroom at all; in fact, it seemed to be a kind of a study. I ventured in a little and saw, to my horror, stacks and stacks of books on ceiling-to-wall bookshelves; a formidable looking desk, a bit like the one in the police station, but this one was littered with stacks of papers, a lamp, a laptop and Toni's glasses and behind this desk stood a high-backed black leather swivel chair. I felt a doggie smile coming on. This stick of furniture promised a swinging time in the future. My inquisitive eyes drifted to the black leather sofa and I quickly started to assess its potential fun qualities. I shook my head despondently. Apart from the chair and the sofa, the room was far too stuffy for a fun loving guy like me.

I strolled along to the bathroom and my eyes immediately lit up. Now, here was lots of potential for experimental fun. My wide, inquisitive eyes flitted from tubs of something or other, to colourful bottles perched on the window sill, to a peculiar looking thing containing water; I think it's called a toilet. Yes, I concluded, there most certainly is lots of promise here. And, having finished my exploration of the upper quarters of my castle, I ambled happily down the stairs, ate a little more of my doggie food and lay down in my den; for, by now, I was well and truly ready for a nap. When I awoke there would be many plans to be made; delightful schemes to be created which would incorporate happy, solitary, unforgettable times in one's kingdom, without the inconvenience of being yelled at, frowned upon, punished; or, even banished. Yes, I mused, as I settled my chunky body into a comfortable position; this was going to be fun!

Re-energized, I opened my eyes wide and pondered. Where to start?

The bathroom, with its colourful bottles and squashy tubes and other interesting containers beckoned me. Up the stairs I scrambled, as fast as my chubby body and poorly bandaged leg would carry me, and into the bathroom I went. With my strong pearly whites, I grabbed the first bottle I saw. Luckily it was made from some kind of bendy plastic, which I was able to clutch between my strong teeth. I dropped it to the wooden floor and studied its contents for a good while, noticing that it was some kind of pink solution and as I tossed it this way and that, to get a better look, I noticed that some of the pink stuff was leaking out of the pink coloured top and the more I turned the bottle, the more of this pink substance was coming out, and not only was it coming out but it was also filling the bathroom with a sweet, rosy fragrance which immediately reminded me of my favourite flower, the rose. And with that came memories of happy, sunny days; bumble bees and my very special friends, the gorgeous butterflies. I needed to smell more of this delightful stuff; so, I turned the bottle this way and that; tossing and turning; pulling, pushing and rotating the bottle with my front paws and my teeth over and over again until… I don't exactly know what happened; but, I saw, and followed with my eyes, the pink top rolling across the bathroom floor and out of sight and all of this delightful, gooey, sweet smelling stuff deliciously escape out of its confined prison. Transfixed, I watched as the smooth, silky, pink stuff oozed out and along the floor like a long, pink snake. Cautiously I stuck my nose into the solution and inhaled deeply its intoxicating fragrance. Wonderful! Slowly I placed my healthy paw into the stuff, as I continued to inhale its heavenly perfume, and felt the smooth silkiness deciding, there and then, that I like the stuff; I liked it very much and, as my eyes swept across the window sill, I noticed there lots more bottles with colourful liquids and ornate glass containers containing colourful little balls, bigger colourful balls and funny shaped soaps. I noticed all sorts of jars of all sizes containing, I guessed, all sorts of lotions and potions, not that they did my Toni any good.

Toni! I'd completely forgotten about her in my exuberant excitement and now, I felt, her looking down on me, with such a treacherous look on her face, I'd rather not explain in great detail. Suffice it to say, she did not look a happy bunny. My eyes flitted back to the little, fascinating colourful balls; my busy mind thinking that they'd be great to have a little game with. Like an eager squirrel, gathering in its winter store, I stood on my hind legs and, with some intricate techniques, I managed to manoeuvre the jar, with the delightful looking balls, off the sill and on to the floor and, to my surprise, the glass top came off in the process. Carefully, taking some balls into my mouth, I sped out of the bathroom, scrambled down the stairs and entered the servants' quarters. By now, folks, I couldn't see where I was going that well; everything was becoming a massive blur, as the little balls were creating a weird, fuzzy sensation in my mouth. I plopped the balls into my water bowl and was in the process of swallowing as much water as I possibly could, in the shortest amount of time when, abruptly, I stopped. Astounded! Horrified!! Delighted!!! Frightened!!!!

Shaking like a big, wobbly, golden-white jelly, my eyes as huge as flying saucers, I stared at the amazing scene below me. The bowl; or rather the little colourful balls in my water bowl, were all erratically fizzing and fusing together. Fizz… fizz… fizz! They all went, giving off the most pleasurable perfume of summer flowers. I felt all my senses fizz and reel with a surge of flowery intoxication, as my eyes continued to stare at the balls, which were still delightfully fuzzing, fizzing and merging together until, sadly, one by one they disappeared, as did the fizz, and I stared down at the multi-coloured, somewhat misty, looking water in my bowl. What a show! I concluded. What a fantastic extravaganza!! Who needs the West End when I, King Kamehameha, can create this wonderful, unique display of showmanship in my own castle, without spending a penny? And, there were more of these little balls in the bathroom!

Up the stairs I proceeded to bound, wishing I was a few grams lighter; down the stairs I scrambled with my precious cargo, and into the bowl the balls went and the second act commenced. This went on for some time until, finally, all the balls, small and big, had performed; I had got my fun fix for the time being and decided that a good, old snooze was in order.

Desperately gasping for water, half sleepily, I sauntered to my water bowl, took a large swig and, my dear, dear friends, it's a wonder I didn't pop my clogs, there and then. What my discerning taste buds tasted was the 'driest', grittiest, powdery water they have ever had the misfortune to sample.

After a certain amount of spluttering, gasping, heaving and choking I managed to, somehow, narrowly escape death. I stood and glared disdainfully at my drinking bowl, as the sequence of events clearly passed through my mind: the little colourful balls; the fizzing and fusing, whooshing and hissing making all my drinkable water misty, colourful, magical and undrinkable and still I stared at the now stagnant liquid. The show had well and truly ended; the actors had left the stage and I was left with no drinking water and the more I thought about it, the more I craved water; the more I craved water, the more I reflected about the whole dastardly situation. Water… water… water… I stood, transfixed, and glared into the colourful, distasteful water and there I saw my dismal future which, my dear friends, was far too bleak for me to relate to you. Suffice it to say, it was not looking good.

What was I to do now? The answer came crashing into my skull sometime later. Without water, King Kamehameha, you shall expire, I told myself in no uncertain terms. Turning away from the repugnant water I sadly plodded into my den, buried my miserable head well into my paws and desperately begged my intelligent cells to come to my aid in my hour of need.

As always, my super intelligent grey cells obliged and by nightfall I had my solution and, it was only under the blanket of night, that, I knew, I could solve my life-threatening dilemma.

It was all to do with Mister Frobisher, my next door neighbour. Now, let me tell you about this dude. As I have mentioned, he lives next door; he is an elderly sort of chap who lives on his own; but, more importantly, he has a heart of gold; a bit like my Auntie Anusia's heart. Anyway, this guy has helped me on numerous occasions, when I've managed to get myself into a scrape, or three. Two spring readily into mind. One occasion occurred on Bonfire Night, when I was just a wee pup. I decided to have myself a little adventure and off I scarpered into the whizzing, fizzing, banging, whooshing colourful night only, by the end of it, I found myself hiding in the sanctuary of a friendly bush. It was Mister Frobisher who, eventually, found me, scooped me up and saved me from a dismal fate.

Another incident involved Mister Frobisher's washing pole and my Toni's oversized pants. That particular event is far too ghastly for me to relive in this life or the next. Anyway, I have more pressing things on my mind, like the real possibility of dying of dehydration, if I don't get a drop of decent water down my oesophagus in the very near future. My friend, Mister Frobisher didn't know it at the time; but he was going to be my saviour and, my dear subjects, at the time of going to press, I didn't know what a charming life-saver Mister Frobisher would turn out to be.

By now, I had already established how I was going to get out of my castle; the same way I got in; though, I must say, the mere thought of it all did not thrill me at all. If you remember, I almost became permanently stuck in my window and who's to say, I won't become an everlasting window fixture this time round? But, my friends, a faint heart never gets anything worthwhile getting and I needed water; so, I quickly psyched myself up for my gruelling ordeal and rose from my comfy duvet.

My dear, dear friends, I needn't have worried at all; remarkably I scrambled out, without getting any of my precious bits entangled in the process and off I went and, with a run and a jump, I was over the fence and standing, none the worse for wear, in Mister Frobisher's immaculate garden.

I knew exactly where I was going so, onwards and forwards, I boldly strolled until I got to the very edge. For a few brief seconds, I stood perfectly still and looked into the still, dark, glass-like surface. Bending my head, I stuck out my tongue and slurped the cool, refreshing water; silently thanking Mister Frobisher for having had the good sense to create a pond. To be honest, I swallowed a goldfish of his in the process which, I must say, was a delightful bonus as I was quite hungry by now.

Feeling much better, I turned and looked fleetingly at my neighbour's dark house then, hurriedly, scrambled back into my castle. Little did I know that a curtain had twitched and a pair of wise, old eyes had witnessed my thieving feat.

I lay down on my duvet, my Hawaiian cushions all around me, feeling mighty relieved and happy. I had an entire kingdom to myself and also a refreshing oasis next door. What more could a king want? I closed my eyes only to open them a second later. Food! An annoying voice crashed into my sleepy head. I'll cross that bridge when I need to, I decided, and, anyway, I still had a fair bit of food in my bowl. I closed my tired eyes once more.

Dawn brought with it a treacherous gnawing in my tummy. I rose and strolled over to my bowls. The coloured water was still there and, next to it, was an empty bowl and, suddenly, it all came back to me in a flash.

I'd had a particularly lively dream, in which I was being chased by a fierce looking, and very ravenous, grizzly. I escaped, you'll be pleased to know; but, only in the nick of time and the whole frightening affair made me mighty ravenous myself; hence, the now empty bowl, devoid of all rations and not even a single crumb in sight. The heavy sigh I heaved did nothing whatsoever to smooth my inner turmoil. Without food I would surely pop my clogs. I needed a refreshing slurp to get my scattered thoughts together. Up I climbed, out the window and down into... YUK... into... something soft and very mushy. I looked; or, rather, I gasped with saucer-like eyes. I must, I concluded, be in some kind of dream zone. Snapping my eyes shut, I squeezed them tightly, opened them and stared and... stared and... stared and... stared, not believing what I was actually staring at. There, below me, was a bowl, full to the brim, with delicious looking, and delicious smelling, doggie food generously laced with bits of chicken and steak, with my bandaged paw firmly planted in the mix. I looked sideways and there was a bowl of clean, refreshing water. I continued to stare thinking that this was all my wishful thinking; a mirage that would instantly disappear. But the bowls, with their contents, remained firmly fixed and my eyes remained firmly fixed on them. By now, all of my doggie senses, together with my highly intellectual grey cells, were furiously going round and round, weaving independently and interweaving with each other and coming up with no answer to this delightful mystery. What to do about this situation? What would any pooch, in his or her right mind, do? I devoured the entire delicious contents, licked my happy chops, silently thanked my generous benefactor and scrambled back into my castle restored, energized and ready to encounter my next slice of fun.

Where to begin the fun day? After some deep thinking, I decided the lounge was the place to start proceedings; after all, a king needed a little siesta after all that thinking. I ambled in and looked around. Yes, I assessed, everything certainly had a place, where my Toni was concerned, and she certainly put everything in its place, including dispatching me to the servants' quarters. Well, not today, I concluded. Today I was going to rule like a king!

I narrowed my eyes in thought and scrutinized the area carefully. The plush cream cushions on the sofa were far too tidy looking, I thought, and into them I scrambled pulling them off and throwing them randomly on to the floor. I kind of performed a merry little dance on them before, I decided, to test them out for their snoozing qualifications. Soft and squashy; not bad at all, I thought, as I trampled away before I, finally, settled my fluffy self on to them and what a delightful bed they made!

After a little nap, I ventured up the stairs and on to Toni's bed and there I settled; but, not for another snooze. Oh no… no… no; I had a much more important job to do. Reclining in a comfortable position, I admired myself in the large reflective glass and what I saw, I justifiably venerated. There was I, King Kamehameha, in my castle, in sumptuous surroundings, my belly full and satisfied, looking at my beautiful, elegant self. Yes, I was indeed an aesthetically pleasing specimen to the eye of the beholder. Yes, I know I am a bit on the podgy side; but who admires and looks up to a half-starved looking king? Yes, my golden-white fur coat was looking a bit ruffled; but that's the price I am prepared to pay for my independence; but, apart from all that, I was looking at a royal, proud, handsome, elegant monarch. I gazed and gazed at my wonderful self, until I felt myself drowning in my own spectacular reflection.

From the corner of my eye, I espied an interesting looking, circular container sitting on Toni's dressing table; it was interesting because it had a very shiny, sparkly bow on the top. This bow intrigued me very much and I set my little intelligent cells into wondering what could be inside this mysterious looking receptacle. Curiosity got the better of me. As quick as lightning, I jumped off the bed and approached the dressing table sniffing; but I could smell nothing. What on earth was inside? I decided to investigate further. Cautiously, I moved my healthy paw towards the box, furiously scrambled with the lid until it popped off and I peered inside. I peered more. Powder! I was staring at some sort of pink powder. I stuck my paw into the soft stuff and, instantly, created a lovely pink cloud; I stuck my bandaged paw into the luxurious softness and, somehow, I managed to dislodge the container from its resting place, forcing it to fall and, as it tumbled down, a bigger, lovelier cloud of pink floated above me showering the bed, the dressing table and Toni's cream coloured carpet with pink powder. I jumped back up on to my Toni's bed and took another good look at myself and, my friends; I had to look again; harder.

I kind of looked like a pink, cute looking ball and, boy, did I smell sweet! For a good while I admired myself. Not bad; I thought, if I was about to audition for a job in the travelling circus. But I firmly conceded, I am a king; a king of honour and splendour and not the local laughing stock. I had to, somehow, get back to my respectable looking self; but how? I stared and stared at the pink stuff clinging on to my fur coat and, as I stared and pondered, an idea popped into my head.

First, I had to shake the pink stuff off and the idea of Toni's bed to be used as a trampoline came into fruition. Up I rose and, without further ado, I started to jump up and down like a jumping bean and, immediately, I saw the powdery stuff fall away from me, allowing some of my gorgeous self to peep through. Up and down I jumped and, with each jump, my energy level rose, thus, propelling more vigorous and higher jumps. Wow! This was far more exciting than a mere common trampoline; for, I could see my good, beautiful, bouncy self in the mirror and the sight was one to behold!

My eyes spotted the cushions and their potential thrilled me so much, I thought I was going to burst. I grabbed a cushion with my pearly whites and threw it on to the floor; then another and… another. In the process of grabbing a fourth cushion I must have, somehow, tugged at it a little too hard; for, to my immense delight, a soft, white, little feather came floating out. I stopped bouncing immediately and stood staring, as if transfixed, at the floating feather. From where did this delightful little thing appear? I wondered. Tentatively I touched the cushion from whence the feather came. This was indeed a mystery.

I tugged at the cushion; then tugged a little harder and, to my surprise, another little white feather floated lightly upwards. Wow! This was magic!! I tugged and pulled harder and more feathers appeared and escaped; by now all of my senses, and little intelligent cells, were bulging and surging with wild and excitable curiosity. I tugged and pulled, my ears attune to the tearing sound and my eyes staring at a hole I seemed to have created in the cushion. And there inside the hole, my friends; nestled comfortably a host of these little white plumages. I placed my poorly bandaged paw into the midst of this fluffy white nest, watching some escape and float on to Toni's bed and down to the floor beneath. By now, an uncontrollable excitement was surging through every single vein in my body. In, both front paws went. Out, flew a multitude of feathers. I decided to do some more rummaging to add to the mix and what a good idea that was. As my paws went in and out, this way and that out flew the little white things. For a little while I sat and watched them float lazily hither and thither. Then, I checked myself firmly. This was no time to idly observe; this was a time to create more exhilarating fun. Grabbing another cushion with my pearly whites, I jumped up and down with it swinging it this way and that; swinging it more vigorously from side to side until, I almost knocked myself out in the process. I continued digging my teeth through the material and into the nest of feathers; flinging the cushion every which way I could. Result! The feathers flew out creating a wonderful feathery shower covering me, the dressing table; pot, tubs and everything else in sight. Another cushion; another shower; another cushion… You get the picture. When I, at last, paused for a rest I got the surprise of my life, when my incredulous eyes feasted on a white, fluffy wonderland. I took one look at the last lonely cushion left on the bed and had a little think. Better I leave it, I thought. Toni needs something on which to rest her weary head. Talking about weary heads, a sudden wave of exhaustion seemed to rapidly sweep over me. I plopped on to Toni's feather bed and embarked on some well-earned, blissful shut-eye.

Sometime later, wide and startled, my eyes stared unblinkingly at an image, which made my blood and my whole body freeze with it. Was I staring at an abominable snowdog? As I blinked it all, slowly, started coming back to me; Toni's cushions and the fun time I had with them, the white fluffy shower of feathers and so on. My eyes looked around at the mass of settled feathers wherever I looked. I closed my eyes. My Toni was not going to be pleased. Flashing thoughts of a permanent ban on doggie treats was the least of my worries; homelessness and starvation were more of an issue and, as for my royal status… It didn't bear thinking about. Once more I opened my eyes to my own feather-strewn image. Perhaps, I sadly thought, the travelling circus might not be such a bad idea; after all, at least I would have board and lodge.

Clambering down from Toni's feather bed, I walked towards the door and took one last backward glance and that was enough. I fled down the stairs and straight into my den and turned my head into the depths of my own Hawaiian cushions.

"Kamehameha!"

Was that Toni?

"Kamehameha!!"

My ears pricked. It was a voice I recognized a friendly, cheerful, welcoming voice. I rose and strode out of my sanctuary and dared to peep out of the window.

Mister Frobisher! My eyes widened and spread further, as they focussed on two bowls in my neighbour's elderly hands and I felt the saliva, uncontrollably, slither down my face. I looked up at my saviour and gave him one of my special doggie smiles and, let me tell you, I don't give them willingly to any old Tom, Dick or Harry.

So far, I concluded, thankfully, my life had been spared. Mister Frobisher, my good friend, had saved me from dying a gruesome death of starvation. My heart danced happily; but, not for long as uninvited thoughts of Toni crashed into my mind. She, my dear friends, was not going to stay away forever; well, not unless she happened to pop her clogs and, even then, I think she'd come back and haunt me in revenge. I closed my eyes, desperately willing the image of her feathered boudoir to go away; but, no matter how hard I tried, it kept seeping into my mind; the feather-strewn bed and carpet, the pink powder sprinkled here, there and everywhere, the torn and tattered cushions; I tried and tried but I couldn't obliterate the haunting image. And now, to add to my despair, Toni's thunderous face was forcing its way through too. Quickly I ducked underneath my plush Hawaiian duvet deeper; deeper and deeper I ducked and clearer and clearer became Toni's angry red face; her burning eyes and contorted mouth shouting untold revenge. Louder and clearer; clearer and louder they all became until I could stand it no more. There was only one thing left for me to do. I had no choice; but, to run for my life!

Tossing the cushions to one side I almost ran to the window and, just as I was about to climb up and ease myself out and run for my life, I stopped. If I was to abandon my castle; my beloved kingdom forever, then I had to abandon it in style. I might as well, I smiled, have one last, big adventure; or, a series of little ones, I haven't decided which yet. But, yes, that was definitely the way to go!

The bathroom came crashing sharply into my minds focus. There was lots of potential for fun there. So, to cut a long story short, let me tell you that I thoroughly enjoyed squeezing all the little tubes and watching all the creamy stuff come squirting and slithering out into the world, like long white, pink, green and blue snakes; I absolutely revelled putting my paws into the creamy stuff and making delightful paw marks as I strode along. What fun! And, when I glanced back, I noticed that my paw prints had actually created some very eye catching, intricate and very delightful designs and, so, I continued to carry this spectacular art work downstairs; scrambling up the stairs, a few minutes later, to replenish my cream supply and carry on with my wonderful paw print creations. After a substantial amount of unique handiwork; or, should I say, paw-work, I paused, examined the interweaving patterns on the carpet, the sofa, cushions and wooden floor of the servants' quarters; but I hasten to point out, not on my plush Hawaiian duvet and luxurious tropical cushions. I sat on my hind legs and smiled my biggest, proudest and most satisfied doggie smile ever.

I surveyed my living quarters with a critical eye, musing thoughtfully. My living space didn't quite match the rest of the castle and neither did that boring, stuffy place with the books. Quickly I jumped up and scrambled up the stairs, as fast as my tubby body would let me, and into the study room I ventured, stood and stared with a most disdainful eye. Who, in their right mind, would spend a split second in this morbid mausoleum? But then, it proved a point that my Toni was not quite in her right mind, bless her. I raised my eyes and surveyed the piles and piles and piles of books closely packed together, like sardines in a can; some thick; some thin; all looked excruciatingly boring. Right, I asked myself, where to start? I lowered my eyes to where I could easily see what was in front of me and, from that particular area, I commenced.

It was easy. I manoeuvred one thin book out with my paw; out it came and on to the carpet it fell; then another followed suit and another. Soon, I had little collections strewn all over the place. I gazed at one empty shelf and scanned the others; there was much work to be done. Like a super trouper, I dug in tugging and pulling at the books and watched them fly out and fall all around me. One unfriendly, heavy tome hit my head and, temporarily, made me see a multitude of stars; but that didn't deter me for long. On and on I ploughed, until the room was scattered with paperbacks and hardbacks containing love stories… YUK… thrillers, historical sagas, comedy, murders, the odd play, an anthology of various poems and all sorts of other boring stuff. I cast my eyes around the motley collection and heartily congratulated myself on my work; for I had, would you believe, created little, and not so little, book sculptures which were, I must say, quite aesthetically pleasing to the eye. However, I was not at peace; not yet, anyway. One thing bugged me; the books sitting on the upper shelves, which I could not reach. Surely, there was a way of getting them down and, my friends, no sooner had I set my little intelligent cells to work, I found the answer.

Scanning one very boring looking bookshelf, half full and half empty, I braced myself and, after a few seconds of deep thinking, I set my good, determined self to work. Carefully, I placed my pearly whites around the base of one empty horizontal shelf and started pulling. Nothing happened. I tugged and pulled a little harder. Still nothing happened. I tugged and pulled substantially harder and sharper and thought I felt something wobble. My eyes shot upwards and, sure enough, a couple of books swayed; I tugged harder and one tumbled down. I repeated the process with a bit more vigour and four more books came tumbling down and, so, I continued with my former resolve with a great deal more zest and vigour and everything went according to plan until…

My dear subjects, everything went black as the whole thing came down with a mighty CRASH! I just about managed to swerve and save my life by the skin of my teeth; a tenth of a centimetre this way or that way and I most surely would now be standing at the Pearly Gates, trying to explain my mischievous actions to a not too happy Saint Peter.

Everything went as still as the grave. I felt my heart had stopped ages ago; but miraculously, I still managed to keep breathing. My eyes were definitely alive and working to full capacity and I so fervently wished they weren't; for, what I saw before, around and beneath me was pure and utter chaos; books, as you can imagine, were scattered everywhere covering the carpet, resting randomly on the sofa, on Toni's desk where, even her laptop had to share its space with a heavy, thick tome; but, worst of all was the sight of the bookshelf which, incidentally, was no longer a bookshelf, as it had lost most of its shelves on its journey downwards. I closed my eyes. The time to abandon my kingdom was most definitely NOW!

I did not need to take one last look at the scene I was exiting; the devastating image will probably follow me into eternity.

I was on my way out, heading towards the kitchen window, when a thought struck me and my eyes darted to the kitchen cupboards. I had, my friends, always wondered what was inside their mysterious doors. It was now or never!

They were easy to open; one tug of the handle and job done. I sat on my hind legs and stared at the hundreds of tins, packets; small packages of something or other, containers, jars and all sorts of other things. It was, for some strange reason, that the paper bags, with whatever it was inside, intrigued me the most. Out one came; into the bag my gnashers dug making a little hole, and out my pearly whites exited covered with some kind of white, powdery stuff. Lowering my head down, I sniffed but could smell nothing. Grabbing one bag I ferociously tossed it from side to side and, to my delight, out sprinkled some white powdery stuff making me smile; it reminded me of my favourite time of the year when the snow fell. My eyes lingered on the bags still in the cupboard; there were bags and bags, all different sizes and stacked next to each other. In no time at all, the entire kitchen was covered with the white powdery stuff. How wonderful, I thought, as I gazed upon the white wonderland. But there was more work to be done.

With my strong teeth, I eased off a lid of one curious looking container and found, to my delight, that inside were lots of little red, sticky balls. Now, as you well know, I had a not too pleasant experience, when I popped a colourful ball into my mouth; so, I decided, not to taste these balls, no matter how alluring they were. Instead, I decided, to play ball with them and, although they were a little sticky, as far as my paws were concerned, they rolled about quite well. I quickly released them all from their prisons.

Next, tins; now, they were a little more tricky to handle. I eased one out of the cupboard with my paw, let it fall to the floor and allowed it to roll; my paws and my long, super intelligent nose, would you believe, were excellent tools for this rolling job. Last time I looked there were fifteen tins, like mini oil drums, scattered in different parts of the kitchen.

I dug my inquisitive nose in deeper and further into a cupboard and, with my eager paws, I drew out a small bag of something; swiftly I tore it open with my paws and pearly whites and proceeded to scatter the contents randomly about. Actually, I was quite taken with the contents and examined the little things in great detail; for, they were little brown grains, resembling small crystals; some kind of sugar, I think. I stuck my tongue into the granules to sample a few. Yum! I liked the taste. I took a generous mouthful, closed my eyes and savoured the sweet, melting sensation. This was Heaven. I closed my eyes and had a little, well-earned, snooze.

Time to go! But, as I stood up and walked on, I accidentally bumped into my water bowl, still full of the misty coloured water, and managed to overturn it. The last thing I saw, was the horrid, multi-coloured liquid seeping into the scattered brown sugar and white powdery flour. I fled. Out of the window and down the other side. There, I stood proudly and surveyed my kingdom one last time.

All kinds of scenarios, in no particular order, were racing through my mind: Toni's Hawaiian evenings; the day I saved our castle from flooding; the numerous guys Toni managed to, temporarily, harpoon; my very first day in my castle when I was placed in a doggie basket, big enough for three elephants; the time I brought my Toni back from the very brink of death; the day that obnoxious date of Toni's, the one with the ghastly socks, fell over, slid on Toni's home-made trifle and ended up in casualty and, now, it was time to say a heart breaking goodbye.

The loud, hearty laughter made me turn abruptly. My eyes widened like two enormous saucers. My saviour, Mister Frobisher! Unblinkingly, I stared at this wonderful fellow before me; for, he seemed to be in the grasp of some uncontrollable fit. By now, I noticed, he was doubled over and he wasn't a tall man to begin with. I think he was laughing; or, was he… popping his clogs? Anyway, I stood and stared at this unusual spectacle, waiting for him to plop down and be taken away, in a white van with flashing blue lights to join my Toni, wherever she may be; but, to be honest with you, the less I know about Toni's whereabouts, at this stage of the proceedings, the better.

I sat with my head held high, my royal torso nice and straight and my face serious, waiting patiently for what was to be, and I certainly wasn't expecting what, finally, came.

A second bout of uncontrollable laughter! Every time Mister Frobisher decided to look at me, he doubled over with this fierce attack of uncontrollable laughter, while I sat and wondered what kind of lunatic Mister Frobisher really was. Anyway, this went on for a good five minutes until, finally, laboriously, Mister Frobisher managed to come to his senses and regain some kind of hold of himself; but, even then, I noticed an amusing smirk on his lips, trying desperately to escape.

I was just about to say a big, THANK YOU, for saving my life with my extra special doggie smile; bid him a fond farewell and start my march into the big, wide world when I felt something silky going around my generous-sized neck and, when I looked up, I saw that my neighbour was minus his red, silky tie and I was sporting a nifty accessory.

"Come on, Kamehameha, you are coming with me." He said in a gentle voice, a chuckle escaping his mouth, as he led me out of the grounds of my kingdom and into the grounds of his kingdom.

Our first port of call, after Mister Frobisher had spread extensive covering inside his castle, was the full-length mirror in his hallway and, as we stood there gawping, my guardian broke out into another fit. I looked into the reflective glass and, immediately, a big doggie smile spread on my joyous face. There, in front of me, stood a multi-coloured abominable pooch. Imagine, a tubby little fellow, covered with white and pink powder; coated, in parts, with pink and green sticky solution on which, randomly, protruded small white fluffy feathers, laced with brown crystals and decorated with little sticky glacé cherries; a couple of sultanas, not to mention, the odd currant. My happy doggie smile died as I stared. Toni was not going to be amused. My happy doggie smile quickly reappeared. Toni was not here now and what she can't see… Firmly, I placed the potential of her future appearance on to the back burner of my mind and focussed on the present, namely, how to impress Mister Frobisher. I raised my eyes, and my bandaged paw, to my host and again, somehow, he had managed to control himself with just a smile; but, for how long? I wondered.

Mister Frobisher frogmarched me up the stairs, which wasn't a great experience for me as, annoyingly, I had torturing flashbacks of scrambling up and down the stairs of my castle, at top speed, and making as many delightful, intricate patterns, with a mixture of powders and solutions, as I could possibly manage. Oh, if only I could turn back the clock… Anyway, once I was ensconced in my neighbour's spick and span bathroom, I was placed into his bath and promptly, and vigorously, scrubbed and rubbed; blow dried, combed and brushed until I gleamed like a brand new penny. We strolled down the stairs to the hallway mirror where I stood, all high and mighty, and took a very good, long look at my beautiful, regal self. Yes, I am still the king, even though it's in a different castle. I wondered what kind of glorious, engaging adventures I would get up to in this particular kingdom…

I needn't have bothered wondering, my friends. My visit, though enjoyable and very pleasant, was very brief. Before I had time to lick my appreciative chops, after enjoying a most sumptuous meal, consisting of succulent pieces of roast chicken, sprinkled generously into my yummy doggie food, and a nice bit of chocolate cake for afters, my ears stood up on end to the sound of loud knocking on Mister Frobisher's door.

I lay my head on to my soft paws and started planning new adventures. The voice on the other side of the partly opened door, made me abruptly stop planning and my whole body freeze, like a solidified statue including, would you believe, my super intelligent brain cells. As I began to gradually thaw out, a huge doggie smile spread on to my façade. My Auntie Anusia! And then, I remembered, and my doggie smile which, incidentally, was getting rather fed up of appearing and disappearing, died once more; for, as you may well remember, folks, I left my Auntie Anusia's residence without even thinking of saying, goodbye. And, now, she was here; standing outside Mister Frobisher's door and taking in the latest news of my escapades. I took a deep breath and braced myself for the inevitable fallout.

"He's here! Kamehameha is here!!" She squealed with untold delight.

Now, you and I know for a fact, I have a most exceedingly terrific, intelligent brain; but I must admit, on this particular occasion, I was completely flummoxed; in other words, utterly puzzled. I could not tell, from Auntie Anusia's high-pitched voice whether she was excited, happy, utterly shocked; or, uncharacteristically furious and I couldn't see her, from my vantage point, to get a clearer picture of the whole scenario because, not only was she still standing outside; she was two metres away from the door.

Furiously, I tried to make sense of it all; but you know how it is my dear friends; sometimes, the more you think, the more confusing a situation becomes. Was my favourite auntie here to rescue me, not that I needed rescuing from kind-hearted Mister Frobisher; or, was she here to totally disown me for abandoning her in the way I did?

It all came to light in the next half hour, as I was sitting comfortably in the front of my Auntie Anusia's battered, old car and on my way to her castle, as she related to me the whole facts.

"And so you see, my dear Kamehameha, we have been searching for you high and low, hither and thither, and you had decided to escape and have a vacation with our lovely Mister Frobisher." I saw a smile creep on to her lips as

I gazed lovingly at her, listening to her comforting words. "I'll forgive you, Kami; thousands of others wouldn't."

One particular person, in that calculation of Auntie Anusia's, immediately sprang to mind and, immediately, I forced my Toni's thunderous face out of my mind.

As for my friend, neighbour and saviour, Mister Frobisher, I wasn't, at this juncture, sure how many of my misdemeanours he had related to my auntie and, to be honest with you, I didn't want to know.

On my arrival at my auntie and uncle's residence, it was clear that my infuriating cousin, Suzi, was not impressed with me at all; though, why, I could not tell; after all, I had left her in peace while I went off gallivanting. There she sat, all regal and queen-like, in the centre of the kitchen, observing me intently as I casually breezed in, stepped into the comfy den my Auntie Anusia had the good foresight to prepare and buried myself in deep thought; for, my friends, I had a lot to think about. My Toni's inevitable reappearance was right on top of my thinking list; for, I was informed of my mistress's impending arrival.

My little cells were all on full throttle as they spun; whirled and twirled with intricate plans, and in-depth schemes, of explaining away my, somewhat, exuberant behaviour while I was home alone. Some of my plans and schemes were of the highest calibre; some, downright ludicrous; but, each one needed and deserved my careful consideration for, believe it or not, sometimes in life it is the most ludicrous, wildest, nonsensical scheme that proves to be the most successful.

To begin with, I decided, that to play numb and dumb was the cool thing to do; after all, if I acted all innocent and ignorant, my Toni may well come to the conclusion that our castle was visited by some kind of excited robber with a penchant for cherries; after all, some of Toni's glacé cherries would be missing because, as you know, they ended up decorating my sticky, powdery coat.

Another plan would be to feign death once more. On second thoughts, that's not such a brilliant plan. What if it gives my mistress some outrageous ideas, like committing murder and we all know who the poor victim would be.

Then, there was the thought of leaving home once more. To be honest, though, I'm still recovering from the last experience.

So you see these, and many more schemes and ideas, weaved in and out of my mind until the door opened and in walked... Toni!

I gasped, gulped and wished fervently that I was a million light years away; or, at least, on that far-flung island called, Kauai; anywhere would do but not here; not two metres before my mistress.

I blinked several times but my fervent wishful thinking brought no fruitful results; she was still standing before me, as large as life, with a grin from one side of her chops to the other. This, indeed, was most perplexing. I continued to stare; not knowing whether I was staring at an excited, happy gal who hadn't seen her precious pooch for a good while; or, was, in fact, staring at one hundred per cent of undiluted anger and frustration, with a heavy mix of impending revenge, disguised as a grin? Whatever I was staring at, I couldn't deny the fact that my Toni was standing before me.

With a heart as heavy as stone, I sauntered to her side and pressed my worried head against her plump thigh, silently begging her to forgive me and all of my faults; although, as yet, I did not actually know what she knew.

Quickly I was gathered into my Auntie Anusia battered car and off we sped toward my dishevelled kingdom and, as we careered along the flat and fertile Lincolnshire countryside and Toni hummed happily away, I guessed, she didn't know anything and with every minute, as we drew nearer and nearer to our destination, my heart became heavier… heavier.

"Agh! Whap!! Whoosh!!! CRASH!!!!

Toni knew!!!!!

Silence

Silence and stillness, as heavy and grim as death itself, reigned inside my castle for long, torturous seconds. Had my Toni suffered a fatal heart attack? Slowly, I opened my tightly squeezed eyes and snapped them shut.

"Agh! Agh…"

I wondered. Do I run for my life; or, hide? I stood transfixed, my eyes now starkly opened wide and fixed down below on my mistress, who was sprawled out in a most unattractive way, while a tin of something or other rolled casually towards a cupboard door. Even before I closed my eyes, I started praying fervently for my life to be spared; for, I had seen Toni's incredulous eyes survey the spilt flour, the scattered sultanas, raisins, currants and glacé cherries before, finally, resting on the offending tin of her favourite vegetable soup, which had happened to trip her up.

Within minutes, Toni was once again hauled away in a white van with flashing blue lights, to that place from which she had just emerged from and I was tucked into the front seat of my Auntie Anusia's battered car; safe and sound and planning my next adventure.

Lockdown Escapade

Now, my dear friends and most loyal subjects, you may think that after my recent brush with, almost, being severely punished, disowned and banished forever from my kingdom, I would have learned my lesson and you wouldn't be wrong. I have learned a most invaluable lesson; never own up to anything. Now, this particular rule does NOT, of course, apply to you little people in this world. Oh no… no… no. You see, us pooches, and especially those of us who are royal pooches, have different rules to you human beings. You should, and MUST, most definitely own up to anything wrong that you have done it is, after all, the right thing to do. As you know, I am King Kamehameha and, as such, I am in a unique privileged position of making my own rules up as I go along. But I shall be honest with you folks; the chaos I created in my own castle, on reflection, did not make me feel good; but, still, it was a lot of fun!

Friends, King Kamehameha had to pay a heavy price for his fun. I am now locked up in lockdown with my cousin, Suzi, for company. Such is life!

To be honest with you, I thought I'd get some kind of ticking-off from my auntie; in fact, I was well psyched up for a stern lecture. It never came. However, what Toni will do if she ever, finally, returns home is another story, which I'd rather not contemplate at this moment in time.

I settled into my temporary lodgings once more; but I must confess, already I was itching for a new adventure. This lockdown business is all well and good for keeping our human pals safe and cosy in their homes; but, for us restless pooches, it is no picnic. I, for one, yearned to be out in the wide, open spaces and go wherever my heart, legs and intelligent nose, would take me and the more I yearned, the more penned up I felt and the more penned up I felt, the more I yearned until one day, I decided, I was well and truly ready for the outdoors and all that it promised.

On the stroke of midnight, I peered around. All was silent and still; all but Suzi, who seemed to be having somewhat of a restless time as she tossed and turned, then lay and stared wide-eyed at me. How utterly rude, I thought; to stare at a king so blatantly and unashamedly. My friend, Henry, would have had her scrawny neck on the block in a jiffy, for that kind of unacceptable, and most inappropriate, behaviour. I closed my eyes and feigned sleep; after all, it wouldn't do to arouse her suspicion.

After what seemed a reasonable amount of pretending time, I cautiously opened one wary eye. The little fiend was still staring at me, as if I was some despicable worm and I, a king! I snapped my eye shut in utter disgust and decided to make snoring noises. That should do the trick, I smiled deviously to myself. A dream, or two, passed by; but, as they are nothing juicy to write home about, I won't bother. Gingerly, sometime later, I opened both eyes and, abruptly, closed them. I got to thinking that my dastardly cousin was either plotting something very sinister against me; or, she was falling deeply in love with me. To be honest with you, I'd much prefer the first option. As I heard the clock chime twice, I opened my ever hopeful eyes, I needn't have bothered; you get the picture, my friends.

What was I to do; give up or rev up? Well, as you know, I never give up on something; so, I started to rev up all four of my cylinders and, simultaneously, prepared my mind, body and spirit for action and adventure and, if the little rascal wanted to follow me, so be it; after all, I have got worse punishments winging their way to me. I rose, stretched out my beautiful torso and approached the window. Easily, I clambered out the opened window; remember, my tubby body has had lots of practise in this sort of thing and, in no time at all, I was standing in the dark, silhouetted garden, casting my eyes this way and that and wondering which direction to take. In the end, I stuck an imaginary pin into my mind map and turned a sharp right.

And, so did Suzi! I was horrified at this turn of events. I turned around and there she was, my friends, as bold as brass. I sat down on my hind legs and carefully assessed her firm stance, her stubborn-set eyes and her determined face, telling me she meant business; in other words, this gal was not for turning; not without a fight, anyway. Quickly, I donned my diplomatic hat and, in the end, decided the gal could come along; after all, she did save my life once and, I guess, I owed her a favour. Begrudgingly, I granted her my permission to follow my lead; though, where we were going, I hadn't the slightest idea. All I knew was that it was very dark; the cold, sharp, north-east wind was doing untold things to my joints and it had also started to rain. I trotted and Suzi followed; onwards and forwards into the unknown.

I came to an abrupt stop and so did, Suzi, making me jump two metres in the air as she collided into me. I turned sharply, about to give her one of my stern looks, and a sterner lecture on the rules of social distancing; instead, I closed my mouth, my regal eyes looking down on a pooch, that wasn't worth wasting my breath on, let alone my energy. A flash of jagged lightning, followed seconds later by rumblings of thunder, forcing my wide eyes to stare into the ominous darkness and ask myself, what on earth had possessed me to embark on an adventure at the onset of, what promised to be, a violent thunderstorm? Sighing heavily, I walked boldly on. Where? I didn't have a clue.

At the crossroads I stood, thought reflectively for a few moments, and took a left turning as did my cousin, Suzi. The unfriendly rain was now lashing down in straight sheets, making my golden-white fur coat stick to me in a most uncomfortable way. To add to this misery, I was feeling cold and miserable and was experiencing nagging thoughts of turning back, scrambling through my Auntie Anusia's window and into my den and set my thoughts on the serious matter of drying out. To my surprise, while I was contemplating my next steps, my cousin took the initiative, leaving me to stare after her wide-eyed as the unrelenting, lashing rain partly obscured my vision. Onwards she went like a determined soldier while I stood firmly stuck on the cold, wet terra firma, wondering what on earth to do and there I stood dithering until Suzi became a blurred, rain lashed spot in the distance. Adventure or a cosy den; those were the two images fighting a mighty war in my intelligent head. Adventure meant fun; a cosy den meant comfort and relaxation. I made my move.

Onwards and forwards I ran through the rain lashed streets until I, finally, caught up with Suzi who, incidentally, I thought was looking none the worse for wear at this stage of the proceedings. Still, it was early days, I concluded. It was only a matter of time before she looked how I felt; bedraggled and fed up. I fell in step with her, with a firm resolve of overtaking her and establishing myself as the leader of our team, at the first given opportunity. For a time, though, I allowed her to walk side by side with royalty; though, where we were going, I still did not know; neither did I know what we were going to do, once we got to wherever we were going.

It was, I pondered, not a good night for setting off on an adventure, with a heavy blanket of ominous darkness above and around us; the houses and gardens looking miserable and unfriendly looking in the rain drenched night; the desolate roads and pavements devoid of all traffic and humans; for, who in their right mind would be out in such a horrible, cold, rainy night? Deep in thought of what I had left behind, namely a cosy bed and an overflowing bowl of sumptuous food, I plodded miserably on and decided to take a right turning which, subsequently, led me on to a narrow lane. Suzi followed me. But, to be honest with you, I wasn't all that bothered about who was the leader of our team anymore; all I could hear, and feel, were gnawing rumblings in my empty tummy. On and on we went under the wet, overhanging branches of aged trees, their glistening leaves showering us with drops of cold rain. By now, I must admit, I wasn't sure, and didn't care, where I was heading. The lane seemed to be getting narrower and narrower; it most certainly wasn't a place I recognized. On and on we relentlessly went until we came to an opening and there, before us, stretched black water on which rocked a small vessel of some sort and, for the first time since leaving the safe sanctuary of Auntie Anusia's castle, my heart leaped.

This was indeed a blessing. In no time at all, Suzi and I had jumped on board and tucked ourselves under a bench which, to our relief, was partly covered by some sort of dark tarpaulin. Under it we both scrambled and made ourselves as comfortable as we possibly could, under the dire circumstances we found ourselves in. It was not Buckingham Palace; but it was shelter and, in minutes, I was in the clasp of exhausted slumber.

When I opened my still sleepy eyes, the lashing rain had subsided into light drizzle. Suddenly! I was aware that something wet and clinging was sticking to me, like an obnoxious barnacle. A rat! I opened my mouth as wide as I possibly could, to give it a good old bite for daring to invade my territory, when a small whine made me freeze, my mouth still wide open and catching night flies; though what they were doing out in this atrocious weather, I couldn't fathom out. I gaped, my eyes matching my mouth and all as wide as saucers; for, there was my dastardly cousin, Suzi, clinging to me for dear life, her pleading eyes begging me to bestow on her some sort of genial mercy. What was a great and honourable king to do; abandon his subject in her hour of need? I thought deeply on this dilemma, as my wise eyes stared at this little despot; wondering whether to comfort or abandon this fiend when one of my ancestors, from ancient Hawaii, boomed in the sternest voice I ever heard, making me shiver all over. My friends, my heart softened; for, when I took a closer look, my pest of a cousin did, indeed, look a sorrowful sight. Begrudgingly, I placed my royal paw on to her wet torso which, immediately, seemed to give off some sort of signal and, before I knew what exactly was happening, she took it upon herself to move in closer and place one of her drenched, grateful paws on to my head. On to my head! And, seconds later, she fell into a contented snooze, while I lay and pondered on the twists and turns that life, haphazardly, throws upon us and then I closed my tired eyes.

When we both opened our eyes, we were refreshed and raring to continue with our adventure. Instead, we felt movement. Yes, we were most definitely moving, with the sound of lapping water beneath our moving vessel.

Very slowly I raised my confused head and, cautiously, peered out of a small gap of torn tarpaulin, my bemused eyes widening with incredulity as they rested on shadowed, silhouetted overhanging branches go by; the odd building scattered here and there and vast open spaces, fields of some sort. My eyes flitted to a bulky figure hunched up in front of me, rowing the vessel we were occupying to some mysterious destination. Where were we going and who was this ominous looking stranger before me? Surreptitiously, I stuck my head out further and peered into the gloom. It was still kind of night, I determined, though the unfriendly rain had stopped and the grey light of dawn was slowly beginning to filter through. I cast my eyes to Suzi. Would you believe, the gal was still snoozing her head off for England? What to do? That was the question. Do I make my royal presence known to this stranger; or, do I remain unobtrusive? After all, this sailor of ours could be a ruthless pirate; on the other hand, he could be an invaluable friend. Oh, if only, my dear and wise friend, King Solomon, was here; he would surely know how to solve this perplexing quandary. Quick… quick; I had to think; but, again, that infuriating thing happened when the more I frantically tried to think; the more I thought not at all, while all kinds of dark and weird scenarios flashed in and out of my buzzing head. And, as for my super intelligent brain cells; well, they had well and truly vacated the premises.

The water lapped gently against the boat and, by now, the rower had lit a cigarette and had proceeded to smoke and hum intermittently. I ducked back beneath the heavy, greasy sheet and listened to his humming and, I must confess, it was of a much higher calibre than my Toni's humming ever was. My grey cells, you'll be pleased to know, gradually returned and I got to thinking that, perhaps, this sailor chap was a friendly kind of fellow; after all, Toni hums when she's ecstatic; you know when she's just about to harpoon herself a guy. So, maybe, I should embark on making his acquaintance; on balance, thinking about it logically, what possible harm could it do? Without giving the matter anymore of my valuable thinking time, I stuck my damp head right out, took a deep doggie breath and crept out from beneath the grimy sheet, stealthily taking one cautious step before I sat down beside the sailor.

Big mistake! Big… BIG mistake!! Next thing I knew, the whole world was turning upside down. There was lots of splishing, splashing and most certainly spluttering; not to mention a good measure of shouting, gasping, sighing and even screaming and, then, I felt the cold water all around me and I was sinking… sinking; deeper and deeper into the depths of a watery grave, with only the sailor's moans and groans, and Suzi's whining, echoing in my ears as I… SANK!

Once more Suzi came to my rescue roughly tugging, and vigorously pulling, my fur coat as she desperately tried to save me from wandering up to the Pearly Gates. I ducked and dived several times and, when my head briefly surfaced on one occasion, I saw the upturned boat and our, not too jolly, sailor, hanging on to it for dear life.

It was a miracle that we all survived. After many heaves, sighs, groans and a certain amount of growling we, somehow, managed to turn the boat over and the three of us scrambled madly in. Drenched to the skin, and looking as miserable as sin, we made the most forlorn threesome the world has ever known. There we sat on the bench and there we reflected on what had happened. I cast one surreptitious eye on my sailor friend and surmised that he was trying to work out, how on earth he had managed to acquire such an unexpected precious cargo. Suzi, no doubt, was having regrets about saving my life and secretly revelling in the fact that I now owed her a most gigantic favour and I was asking my super intelligent head, what on earth had possessed me to venture out on this dastardly adventure, on such a perilous night.

After long minutes of intense thinking, where no answers were forthcoming, our sailor turned his full attention on me and, let me tell you, his unfriendly looking eyes were set too close together for my comfort, his tight-lipped mouth was also too stern looking and, I concluded, he did not look the picture of happiness.

"So," he said in a deep gruff voice, his dark beady eyes set firmly on me, "you are the culprit."

My dear friends, believe me when I tell you, that every single fibre in my body quivered uncontrollably under his no-nonsense glare; for, his eyes were not the eyes of a friendly giant. Oh no… no… no; his eyes were the eyes of an ogre seeking revenge and revenge was what he intended to get.

Our journey was shrouded with mystery and suspense. Apart from the lapping of the water against the oars and boat, we sat there in complete silence and, while our sailor contemplated our future, Suzi and I contemplated our fate and there was much to contemplate.

Finally, we reached the bank and disembarked. I was ready to make a run for it; but just as I was about to place one bold foot forward, I felt the grainy roughness of a rope around my neck. My eyes darted to Suzi and I saw that there was no hope for her either. We were firmly positioned on either side of the sailor; but, before we all marched off into the unknown, our sailor friend turned back to the boat, reached out for a large holdall, unzipped it, checked its contents and slew it on to his right shoulder, allowing it to dangle just above my head and then we proceeded to walk.

Now, at this stage of the proceedings, I am not quite sure whether I was in some sort of trance; in the middle of a delightful daydream; or, indeed, in the surge of wishful thinking; but I was sure I inhaled the delightful whiff of sausages. And, there it was again! If it was, indeed, a dream then I yearned to dream on as I marched on. And, as I dreamed, I inhaled deeply the wonderful raw, meaty smell; beef, I think it was. I raised my very intelligent, and very sensitive, nose upwards and yes… yes; there it was again; but now much stronger and much more real. There were sausages in that bag; but, how to get at this heavenly delight? That was the ultimate question. For the time being, I resigned myself to sniffing and dreaming and, resolutely, walked on. I cast a cursory glance at my cousin, Suzi's thunderous face and I could tell at once that she was not amused at this turn of events; still oblivious to the precious cargo our sailor was carrying. I smiled to myself; the happy doggie smile I reserve for very special people; or, events and this sausage event was one in the making. It was, I silently but firmly determined, just a matter of time and then… and then… The sheer anticipation of it all was too glorious for me to explain to you in words and, so, I marched on silently, apart from the rumblings in my tummy, and my vigilant eyes for opportunity.

And it came. Our sailor friend needed a rest; for, he was I could see, not the fittest of men. You know the type I mean; the type that detest the place called the gym and, by the look of his flabby face and body, the type that likes to indulge in one steak and kidney pie too many. And, by the sounds of his puffing and panting, you'd think he had ventured three-quarters of the way up the Himalayas. Anyway, spotting a flat topped boulder, he perched his bulky body down and, as he placed down his holdall, about to withdraw a large spotty handkerchief with which to wipe his sweaty brow, I seized my chance. While sailor boy was swiping the beads of sweat from his brow, I had my long nose in his bag and my pearly whites into his sausages. Out… out… out they came and off… off… off I ran as fast as my legs would carry me, with the long string of sausages trailing behind me like a wonderful, fat snake. A fleeting backward glance told me that Suzi had unleashed herself too and was hot on my paws and poor sailor boy was sat on his flat topped boulder, his podgy face beetroot red and contorted with all sorts of fierce looking twists; his chubby arms flying out wildly in all directions and his angry mouth spewing out words, a true gentleman would never use.

Off we ran; me, the long string of sausages and Suzi; well, the sausages didn't actually run but you know what I mean, folks. Away… away we went until our friend, the sailor, was a distant spot. We later learned that this guy was, in fact, supplying the residents, who lived on this side of the river, with lockdown provisions. But, my friends, after assessing our dastardly deed I, personally, did not feel guilty for too long; after all, my cousin Suzi and I, King Kamehameha, were both lockdown victims too.

We found ourselves in a vast, interesting looking place and having satisfied our empty tummies with delightful sausages, and saving a generous supply for future meals, we secured strings of sausages around our respective necks and set off to explore our surroundings and it wasn't long into our exploration, that I figured out we were in some kind of animal establishment; a zoo, I thought.

Like bezzy mates Suzi and I walked on side by side, admiring the different breeds from a safe distance. I didn't want to get too friendly with the penguins and ostriches, as we casually strolled by, as I wasn't intending on staying in this place for long; neither did I fancy sharing my sausage meal with them all; but, while we were on this wee visit, I yearned to visit one specific enclosure and that particular enclosure, my friends, belonged to the king of the jungle; the lion. You may well scratch your head and wonder why on earth I would like to, literally, walk into the lion's den. The answer; or, answers in this case, are straightforward. One; I wanted to ask this lion fellow, in no uncertain terms, what on earth he is thinking of calling himself a king, when we all know there is only room for one king in this universe and we all know who that is. Two; as you know my friends, the little folks who are lucky enough to reside near me, and pass me by on the pavements sometimes, often compare me to this imposter saying, as they point their chubby little fingers in my direction, "Mummy, Mummy, there's a lion across the road;" or, "Dad, I'm scared, there's a lion over there," before diving under their father's overcoat. The worst thing I have ever heard is, "That thing over there looks like a lion; but, isn't half as pretty." Well, I must admit, I was certainly not impressed with that last statement at all and I kept my doggie smile well and truly locked away from that particular fiend, as I walked off; my head held regally high and my sensitive ears attune to the rascal's giggles. Anyway, back to the zoo. My curiosity, as always, got the better of me and I simply had to see, with my own intelligent eyes, who it was I was so often compared to and whether this comparison was, indeed, justifiable; or, whether the little blighters concerned, could be put before a stern looking judge for deformation of my character.

I saw HIM from afar; or, rather I heard a mighty majestic, excruciatingly loud roar which, let me tell you, set all of my senses whirling erratically, all my pearly whites to chatter uncontrollably and all four legs to wobble like four sticks of jelly. Apart from my shaking pins, I stood frozen to the spot and stared wide-eyed at something I could not see because, my friends, everything had become a massive blur: the trees, zebras, cages, flowers, monkeys, pandas, bamboo branches and even Suzi who, incidentally, was frozen to the spot too. There we stood, transfixed by the terrifying roar that was emitted from the most cavernous and ravenous mouth, belonging to the king of the jungle. It was a roar informing the universe that the king wanted his breakfast and he didn't much care what, or who, was on the menu. As the roar subsided my paws began to thaw and my legs ceased their wobbling; but what increased by the second was my curiosity and my overwhelming yearning to acquire such a majestic roar, to compliment my royal status. After all, with such a roar in my armoury, I would like to see Toni quibble over who is the true sovereign in our castle. I was on a mission.

Before we set off towards the lion's den, I decided to sit down and have a little snack. Taking a generous bite of my sausage, I licked my chops and set off on my challenge; my disciple, Suzi, hot on my heels. I didn't object to her presence; after all, I concluded, I needed all the cavalry behind me I could muster. Onwards we marched and the nearer we got to the lion's enclosure, the more I thought of abruptly turning back and running for my life, before it was too late; but, like a true trouper, I placed one brave paw in front of the other and advanced; for, as you and I know, a brave king does not quit once he has set off on a challenge.

I sat on my hind legs, all mighty and proud, and stared and… stared and I would have stared until kingdom come at the majestic, powerful looking creature before me, if it wasn't for the fact that I noticed a suspicious glint in the eye of the beast, as he stood before me, as bold as brass, with just a cage and some kind of moat between us. With eyes of true admiration, I surveyed his beautiful golden coat, especially admiring his mane which surrounded his no-nonsense face which, let me tell you, assumed the air of ultimate authority and I seriously wondered whether to run, remain seated or bow down graciously before him. After much pondering, I decided to remain where I was and wait for him to take the initiative.

His orangey-brown eyes had now lowered and, I noticed, he was peering admirably at my unique sausage necklace and also, I noticed, he had opened his mouth and was licking his chops in a most keen manner. I set my intelligent little cells to work. Should I offer this important looking beast one of my precious sausages? I hummed and hawed; I hummed and hawed a little more and then my answer came. Yes, it was a matter of etiquette. After all, Suzi and I had invaded his territory; so, it was only right and proper for us to come bearing gifts, even though we were bearing them somewhat begrudgingly. I cast a hopeful look Suzi's way. My hope immediately dashed; there was no way the little blighter was going to surrender one of her sausages. My eyes flitted back to our lion friend; only now he was not looking very friendly; well, actually, he was not looking friendly at all. His eyes were now narrowed to mere slits; but, still, totally focussed on my sausages which, in turn, made me inwardly rebel. Why should I give him a taste of my treasured sausage, when he can't even be bothered to look gracious? No, I decided firmly; if he wants sausages, then he has jolly-well got to show some manners. There and then, I decided, to show this upstart who the real king was. Up I rose, away I turned and was about to walk away without a backward glance. Glued to the spot I remained, my ears subjected to the most treacherous roar it was my misfortune to experience; so loud and horrible it was I thought it would force the sky, and all the planets, to come crashing down on and around us. Fleetingly, very fleetingly, I turned my eyes back and I so wished I hadn't. The eyes of the monster I saw before me were wide, gleaming and threatening to not only devour all of my sausages; but, also, to devour me in one swift gulp. To say I trembled all over like an autumnal leaf would be a laugh. My whole body had turned to a quivering mush, including my super intelligent brain. I summoned all of my departed Hawaiian royal ancestors to come to my immediate aid and I ran, my sausages dangling precariously around my neck. I ran and ran and… ran not daring, for one split second, to glance back for fear of what I may witness. Eventually, when I could run no more, I stopped, for a mere second or two, gasped for much needed air and dared to glance back. The fierce looking lion, and his faithful followers, were heading my way. I blinked. They were still following me, advancing nearer and nearer with each pounding step. As for Suzi, she may well have been eaten by now; she was nowhere in sight. I ran faster. The lion and his devotees stepped up a gear too. The last time I looked he had recruited an ambush of tigers and, I think, I saw an eager looking zebra also. By now, I didn't know where on earth I was going and, just when you needed a human or two to intervene, there was none to be seen for love or money.

I sped past various compounds and out of the main gates, noticing that I was now followed by a motley troupe of animals: lions, tigers, the eager looking zebra, a pair of podgy grizzlies, some funny looking ostriches, two determined elephants and three waddling Emperor penguins, all with one thing on their minds; my sausages.

Down the deserted roads we pounded and by now, I must admit, I felt like slowing down somewhat; though one backward glance at the treacherous looking lion behind me, followed closely by a ravenous grizzly, gave me an immediate boost of energy.

The running went on for a considerable amount of time. Down wide roads and narrow lanes I went, through sparsely grown woods, on to a river bank and on to a boat. I ducked under the tarpaulin and, immediately, pretended I wasn't there. To my immense relief, a few seconds later, I felt the vessel move off. Very cautiously I peered from beneath the heavy, dirty sheet; hoping with all of my doggie might, that the sailor was not the dastardly lion. Well, my friends, my eyes stretched wide like two saucers with absolute incredulity. Astonishingly, I had jumped on to the same boat which had, earlier, brought Suzi and I across the river and the sailor was none other than our sausage man!

I decided to play it safe and hide under the tarpaulin and what a jolly good time I had. My beefy sausages were still, miraculously, intact and splayed decorously around my fluffy neck, without the lion and his mates getting their greedy paws on one single sausage. I stuck my pearly whites into one fat sausage and my senses immediately reeled delightfully in its raw, meaty texture as I wondered what on earth had happened to my cousin Suzi, the lion and his gang. As I heartily devoured my second sausage, I swept them all from my intellectual head and gave myself a mighty satisfied doggie smile; for, now we all know who the real king is; the one who ate the sausages!

Homecoming

Well, you may wonder, my dear subjects, what happened next. Allow me to go back a little to the Suzi situation. To be absolutely honest with you, I'd thought I'd seen the last of her and had already started composing the first few lines of her eulogy for her memorial service. I should have saved my precious energy and invaluable time. Would you believe, the spruced up scoundrel greeted me at Auntie Anusia's door as I stood there wet, bedraggled, exhausted and with hundreds of bits of twigs, dead leaves, bits of feathers and a host of other odds and ends, nestling comfortably in my scruffy looking coat. I stared wide-eyed at that smug face of hers, wondering how on earth she had managed to escape the lion's jaw; get herself home, bathed, shampooed, groomed and smelling of roses whilst I, King Kamehameha, had endured such a treacherous ordeal. In the midst of my gloomy pondering, my heavy heart lifted as I heard a most delightful greeting.

"Kamehameha… Oh, Kamehameha; you've come back!" And, despite the fact I looked like the king of scarecrows, my Auntie Anusia bent down and gave me the tightest and longest hug ever.

I'd come home; well, not quite home but as near to my own castle as I dared to venture. Remember, my friends, I had left my castle looking pretty much like a war zone and, dare I say, of my own vigorous making and my Toni had barely ventured into our war zone, when she slipped on one of her favourite cans of vegetable soup and swiftly ended up back from where she had just departed, the hospital. So, you can understand why I wasn't in such a hurry to be setting off back to my kingdom. No, I decided, I was quite happy to reside at my favourite auntie's castle; forever, if need be. As for encountering my Toni once more, the mere thought sends prickly shivers up and down my spine, not to mention my legs and everywhere else. Between you and me, I don't think Toni is having kind, soothing thoughts about me either, while she's laid up on her bed of pain, with a poorly back and her leg in plaster. So, no, I am in no hurry to; either go and visit the invalid; or, for the invalid to make a swift recovery.

Anyway, now that I am bathed, shampooed and smelling fragrantly sweet, I'll tell you how I managed to get here in one piece. As you know, I was ensconced back on board the boat with our friend, the sailor; you know, the one I'd stolen the nice, beefy sausages from. As we docked and I peeped out from beneath the dirty, greasy sheet and saw land, I tried to make a hasty run for it; but, not before the ghastly man had spotted me, identified me as the thief of his sausages and threatened to make two hundred and fifty-three hot dogs out of me, plus a nice winter coat for himself. I stood and listened to his despicable threats, my eyes darting this way and that; for, the dastardly fellow had blocked my escape route with his huge frame. While the boat rocked to the left and to the right, I made a frantic dash for freedom; well, actually, to be more precise, it was more of a pronounced leap and on to land I sprang with echoes of, "Help! Help!!" followed by a loud splash reverberating in my ears. Briefly I glanced back, my astute eyes lowering and there, in the murky waters below, the silly guy was splashing for Team England his threatening, spluttering words ringing loud and clear in my head. "I'll make a hot dog out of you yet!"

I thought it was two hundred and fifty-three hot dogs; still, this was no time to muse on calculations; or, to wait for him to get out his frying pan. I ran like the wind until I found myself, once more, in familiar surroundings.

Now came the hard part; the part where I had to start thinking clearly, and concisely, about my impending reunion with my Toni and I knew, for certain, I could not scramble out of this, sure-to-be, agonizing ordeal. I lay my weary body down, allowed my super intellectual head to recline on my golden-white, fluffy paws and set my clever cells to arduous work and, let me tell you, the more I thought, the more treacherous the looming ordeal was becoming in my head.

There were various options to consider; leaving home was not one of them, I'd decided, I'd had enough of this particular game.

Firmly denying all knowledge of what had happened inside our castle, and portraying a picture of innocence, was, I thought, a pretty reasonable road to take; but, was it an honourable route a great, upstanding king should consider? Well, we all know the answer to that one.

So, what else was there for me to do? I dug deep into my clever little brain cells and rummaged most fervently; but, rummage as I did, I could not come up with anything else and so I let fate take its inevitable course and waited; or, rather, dreaded the sentence that would surely follow.

Back to the present; as I was reflecting on my past and pondering on my future, the outside door opened and my heart stopped, as my eyes caught sight of the shiny black shoes I know so well. Toni had been released.

I did not rush to the door to warmly welcome the invalid inside; I did not stand loyally at her side and raise my loving eyes to her. I buried my head deep into the depths of my sumptuous bed cover and there it remained.

The determined click… click… click of her footsteps, told me she was coming nearer… nearer making my heart turn to a solid, heavy stone of guilt, shame and remorse for what I had done; for now, my dear friends, my part in Toni's downfall, excuse the pun, had become perfectly clear to me. I had ruined our castle and I had, inadvertently, sent my Toni back on to her bed of pain; all for the selfish pursuit of an adventure, or two. So, yes, at this moment in time, I was feeling mighty guilty and, if Toni's Father Macloud was out of quarantine, I would be heading straight towards the confessional box.

With bated breath I waited for the inevitable; but, my dear friends, the inevitable did not come. Instead, I felt a pair of chubby arms wrap themselves around my fluffy neck and, as I cautiously raised my bemused head, I looked into the most loving pair of eyes any pooch has ever looked into. I blinked. I blinked harder. My loyal subjects, I was not, as you may think, in some weird twilight zone. There was my Toni beaming down at me and, almost, hugging the very life out of me. I didn't understand. I was truly and utterly flummoxed! Had she, I wondered, lost the remaining few marbles she had in the fall? Did she remember anything of the fall and the devastating mess in her kitchen? Had she seen the state of her stuffy study; her boudoir or the bathroom where she spends many an hour, without any striking positive results to show for her efforts? Had she ventured into the lounge? What about Mister Frobisher's role in the proceedings? By now, all my intelligent cells were whirling and twisting erratically and coming up with not one single answer and Toni's gasps and sighs were only adding a great deal more confusion to the mix.

"Ah Kamehameha; my dear, dear Kamehameha; how wonderful it is to see you again." She murmured endearingly.

This, and other, enthusiastic comments confirmed to me that; either, Toni had, indeed, crossed over to the world of lunacy; or, the bang to her head had induced into her a most admirable sense of fun. Personally, I was all for the second option. Imagine if you will, folks, my future existence with Toni, filled to the brim, with nothing but fun! My heart soared as I imagined. Toni's next words made my joyful heart spiral rapidly downwards and sink. "We must go home, Kamehameha; the sooner, the better."

All kinds of scenarios floated in and out of my whirling head. What if Toni had a temporary bout of memory loss, we go back to our kingdom the very best of mates, we open the door of our castle and then… and then… It doesn't bear thinking about.

After a good, hearty meal of which, I must admit, I didn't taste much; endless cuddles from my Auntie Anusia and an overflowing bag of goodies, thrown into the car for my exclusive consumption, Toni and I were on our way. I took several deep breaths and prepared myself.

The door slowly opened. In we walked. I gasped; my eyes as wide as saucers. Were we standing in the right castle? Everything, my friends, was spick and span. No tins, currants, glacé cherries, sultanas, spilt flour or grains of brown sugar crystals were anywhere to be seen; my bowls were empty and sparkling clean and the floor highly polished and smelling of refreshing pine. I stood glued to the spot absorbed in a shroud of puzzlement. This was not how I had left my castle. The last time I looked there were raisins, currants and hundreds of other things littering the floor; my drinking bowl was empty and the surface beneath my paws was extremely gooey and sticky.

"Just as I left it." Toni smiled satisfactorily.

Either Toni was losing her mind; or, I was! Sadly, I miserably concluded, one of us was certainly not in their right mind and I was seriously beginning to think it was my head that needed testing. With bated breath, and a heavy amount of incredulity, I followed my Toni up the stairs and, folks; she didn't even bother to stop me!

This was the moment of truth. I opened my astounded eyes as wide as they would go and my heart fell. It was me that was going mad! Everything, my friends, was in its right place. The stuffy study looked perfectly boring; the bookshelves were standing upright with their heavy burden of literature; the polished mahogany desk was there with the lamp, laptop and other paraphernalia; the floor was devoid of all mess. The bathroom, too, was as tidy as a new pin. We sauntered back downstairs and, I noticed, the lounge was in perfect and neat order; cream cushions plumped and in their right place and no tell-tale marks of any past mischief anywhere. I was truly at a loss. This was not how I had left my kingdom and yet – what could I do but saunter into my luxurious den and ponder my dismal future; for, I knew without a doubt, that I was a perfect candidate for the loony bin.

I waited for the white van, with the flashing lights; but, this time, it was not going to take my Toni away. I waited and waited and, in the process, I had completely lost my appetite; lost the taste and joy in the bountiful treats Toni left by my side and, indeed, I had lost the will to live. Instead, I psyched myself up for the eventual arrival of the gentlemen and ladies in long, white coats and braced myself for the straightjacket and padded cell. Dusk fell and they still hadn't arrived on the scene. I didn't bother to contact my little intelligent cells for answers; they didn't work anymore. And so, I fell into a dreamless sleep.

The morning broke bright and cheerful, a complete contrast to my heavy burdened, sad heart. I would have been content enough to have wallowed in my misery; but my mistress was having none of it. After a certain amount of earnest and futile cajoling, trying to entice me into succumbing to food, she ushered me outside and proceeded to scrub her already scrupulously clean kitchen floor.

To be honest with you, I couldn't be bothered to happily stroll along the stepping stones, with my regal head held proudly high, this morning, when I'd got the world's problems on my shoulders. Instead, I planted myself down on a patch of cool grass, buried my royal head well into my paws and continued to wallow in peace.

Not for long, did I wallow.

"Good morning, Your Majesty," chirped a much too cheerful voice for my liking.

I raised one beady eye to Mister Frobisher and a little bit of my heart melted; for, how could I be glum and rude in the presence of my saviour? A sudden thought struck me. But, was he my saviour; if I am, indeed, going mad then Mister Frobisher…

"Have you recovered from your fun adventure, Your Majesty?" Mister Frobisher looked down on me with a mischievous glint in his eye, making me scrutinize him intently. Had this elderly chap gone mad too?

"You most certainly had fun with those little colourful balls and, as for the glacé cherries…" He did not finish his sentence, as a bout of uncontrollable laughter besieged him, making his shoulders heave up and down while I continued to, cautiously, assess his strange behaviour, with scattered thoughts crashing into my mind… the flour…the glacé cherries… Mister Frobisher's full-length mirror… the little colourful balls… It was all coming back to me with vivid clarity and here was Mister Frobisher confirming it all. I was not going mad, after all! I had not imagined things. I did have a whale of a time; but… but… the spotless castle… Toni's uncharacteristic forgiving nature… What on earth was happening?

It all became clear in the next few minutes when Mister Frobisher, finally, managed to take control of himself and throw much needed light on the whole situation as he said cheerily, giving me a few gentle pats on the head, "So you see, my dear Kamehameha; we saved the day and we have to thank the bump on your mistress's head, and her subsequent temporary loss of memory, and your Auntie Anusia, and her hubby, for restoring your castle to its former majestic glory."

I stared wide-eyed at one of my saviours. Wow; my auntie and uncle joining forces with my lovely, kind neighbour and all coming to my rescue in such a delightful way and my Toni, none the wiser! A happy doggie smile spread on to my chops; it was a smile, which bestowed on the kind-hearted Mister Frobisher a thousand *thank yous* for being such a splendid chap, neighbour, friend and saviour.

Suddenly, my tummy rumbled furiously and I sped through the door and on to my Toni's sparkling polished floor, leaving behind a host of cheery paw marks, as I headed straight for my bowl and demolished the delicious doggie food in minutes. As for the tell-tale paw prints, they were swiftly wiped away and on Toni's chops I saw a most delightful smile.

Her Kamehameha was back on true form and ready to resume his reign!

A Note from Toni, 'King' Kamehameha's Long-Suffering Servant

My dear friends,

Well, what can I say?

You've heard it all now and so have I.

It has certainly been a strange time, this lockdown business. Anyway, we seemed to have, somehow, survived; at least, for the time being.

I must admit, I had to sit down and gulp a very strong cup of tea, in the process of reading what my Kamehameha had to say for himself and, I must profess, I was not amused when I found out about all the things the rascal got up to behind my back; or, rather, when I was on my back, trying to recover from the effects of his ingenuous misdemeanours.

A number of ideas came into my mind, in the form of punishments. In the end, all were banished from my mind; for, between you and I, when I look down on the scoundrel, my heart melts. He has got this magical knack of twisting everything to his own advantage and, no matter what I do; he always manages to, somehow, win in the end. Apart from that, we have all lived through a gruelling time in the history of the world and, because of lockdown, I am going to forgive Kamehameha for ALL of his misdeeds; after all, without his company, no matter how infuriatingly mischievous he became, it would have been a very long and torturous lockdown without him; so, I kind of owe him one; but, for goodness' sake, don't tell him that. His head is too big as it is and if it gets any bigger, his majestic crown will topple off and what is a king without his crown?

Long may the king live!

Toni x

An Address from His Majesty, King Kamehameha

My dear, loyal subjects,

It is now time for the majority of us to, cautiously, step out of lockdown and I, for one, can't wait to be free again.

I agree with my Toni, it has been a most weird time in our lives and I, most certainly, would not relish the prospect of living through another one of these lockdowns, under any conditions; once was more than enough for me. However, I must admit; but, for goodness' sake, don't tell Toni, I felt my mistress was the best person with whom to share lockdown, when she was not incarcerated in the hospital, of course.

But, you know, in spite of lockdowns gloom and doom, I remember fondly the spontaneous fun times and the few very strange times, when neither Toni, nor I, knew whether we were coming or going. One such episode which readily springs to mind, is my sleepover at the local police station; though, I must admit, I am eagerly looking forward to my next overnight stay in that particular hotel.

Mister Frobisher, I have decided, is one of my top favourite people in the universe; together, of course, with my Auntie Anusia. Above all, they stood by me and saved me from what could, potentially, have been a quick and untimely exit out of this world.

I must admit, that no matter where I ended up during the course of lockdown, my castle is my castle and there is no place like home and no gal like my Toni.

I am going to grant her my royal permission to stay in my kingdom and long may I, King Kamehameha, happily reign as her sovereign.

Keep well my lovely friends. Don't forget to let me know about all of your lockdown adventures and, above all, I command you, to have plenty of fun!

Love,
King Kamehameha x

Ingram Content Group UK Ltd.
Milton Keynes UK
UKHW021827260423
420831UK00003B/16